HOW TO ~~LOVE~~ LOSE A BEST FRIEND

by JORDAN K. CASOMAR

Entertainment
BOOKS

NEW YORK   LONDON   TORONTO   SYDNEY   NEW DELHI

This book is a work of fiction. Any references to historical events, real people, or real places are used fictitiously. Other names, characters, places, and events are products of the author's imagination, and any resemblance to actual events or places or persons, living or dead, is entirely coincidental.

MTV

Entertainment
B O O K S

An imprint of Simon & Schuster Children's Publishing Division
1230 Avenue of the Americas, New York, New York 10020
First MTV Books hardcover edition September 2024

Jacket photo-illustration and hand-lettering by Jenna Stempel-Lobell
Jacket photographs by Sweenshots & Shaymone/Stocksy (couple),
Javier Díez/Stocksy (portrait), and katyalitvin/Shutterstock (texture)

Simon & Schuster: Celebrating 100 Years of Publishing in 2024
For information about special discounts for bulk purchases, please contact Simon & Schuster Special Sales at 1-866-506-1949 or business@simonandschuster.com.
The Simon & Schuster Speakers Bureau can bring authors to your live event. For more information or to book an event contact the Simon & Schuster Speakers Bureau at 1-866-248-3049 or visit our website at www.simonspeakers.com.
Jacket designed by Heather Palisi
Interior designed by Ginny Chu
The text of this book was set in Alda OT CEV.
Manufactured in the United States of America
2 4 6 8 10 9 7 5 3 1
Library of Congress Cataloging-in-Publication Data
Names: Casomar, Jordan K., author.
Title: How to lose a best friend : a novel / by Jordan K. Casomar.
Description: First MTV Books hardcover edition. |
New York : MTV Books, 2024. | Audience: Ages 14 and Up. |
Summary: When sixteen-year-old Zeke expresses romantic interest in his best friend, Imogen, her unexpected reaction sends their relationship into a tailspin.
Identifiers: LCCN 2023056245 (print) | LCCN 2023056246 (ebook) |
ISBN 9781665932097 (hardcover) | ISBN 9781665932110 (ebook)
Subjects: CYAC: Best friends—Fiction. | Friendship—Fiction. | Dating—Fiction. |
High schools—Fiction. | Schools—Fiction. | African Americans—Fiction. |
BISAC: YOUNG ADULT FICTION / Social Themes / Dating & Sex |
YOUNG ADULT FICTION / People & Places / United States / African American & Black
Classification: LCC PZ7.1.C4394 Ho 2024 (print) | LCC PZ7.1.C4394 (ebook)
| DDC [Fic]—dc23
LC record available at https://lccn.loc.gov/2023056245
LC ebook record available at https://lccn.loc.gov/2023056246

for doreen, ruth, and lawrence

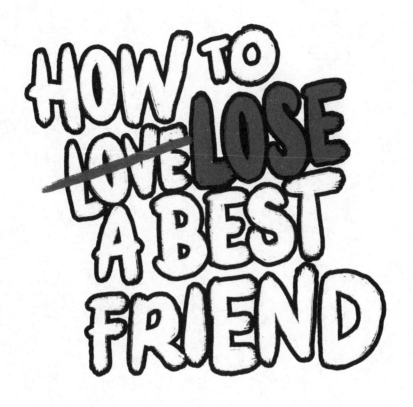

chapter one
ZEKE

Of all the possible places someone can celebrate their birthday, a hospital's gotta be one of the worst.

Between the harsh fluorescent lights overhead and the sterile, antiseptic smell, there's nothing joyful about the place. All the balloons in the world couldn't make Ida B. Wells Memorial Hospital anything but what it was, though that didn't stop my mom from trying. Didn't stop her from filling Pops's room up with two dozen big balloons shaped like baseballs, baseball bats, baseball gloves, all of them bouncing along the ceiling, riding the faint breeze from the hallway as I opened the door to his room.

"Well, well, Zeke Ladoja, the birthday boy himself," Pops said, his voice hoarse. "Sixteen years old, Nessa. Can you believe it?"

"I'm the one who pushed his big ol' head out, course I can," my mom said.

"Gross," I said.

"Baby boy, you don't know gross until you've had a tube going down your throat and up your behind at the same time," Pops said. "Ever seen a handful of anal polyps get pulled out your—"

"Samson, the only thing Zeke wants to hear about less than what came outta me is what came outta you," my mom said.

That got us all laughing and for a moment, it was like we were back home, before we found out a bunch of polyps wasn't the only thing growing in Pops's guts. And then Pops clutched his belly and winced in pain, and that brought us all back to reality, back to the oncology ward, back to a small hospital room with powder-blue walls and a drafty window overlooking the parking lot, back to where my dad was sick. Real sick.

"Hey, Pops." I hustled to the side of his bed. "You okay? Need the nurse?"

After a few long, deep breaths, he shook his head. "Just . . . stings when I laugh. I'm fine. I'll . . . be fine."

"Here, drink," my mom said, holding a cup of water to his lips. "How'd drills go this morning, Zeke?"

"I mean, you *know* I'm ready," I said, eager to change the subject. "So's Braejon. No way we're getting knocked out right at the finish line this year, no way. Coach's been working with Axel and Yovani—"

"Them bad Perez boys with the filthy mouths?" my mom interrupted.

"Ma, they're not bad."

"They sure ain't *good*. Good boys don't track wet mud through my house without cleaning it up."

"Ma, that was, like, three years ago!"

She sucked her teeth loud. "And?"

"As I was saying, Coach's been working special with them. Axel's got a hell of an arm on him when he really tries. And Yovani's got quick feet now. Pops, this season, we're gonna be untouchable."

"Can't wait." Pops gave me a weak smile, his energy just about spent. "I'm fading, Nessa, so let's give it to him before I fall asleep."

My mom nodded, reached into the depths of her purse, and pulled out a small package about the size of a textbook, wrapped in gold paper and tied with thin black ribbon.

"It's not much, but . . . ," Pops said.

I opened it slow. Inside was an article from last week's newspaper, matted on a black background and set in a silver frame.

LADOJA, PANTHERS IN IT TO WIN IT

Last year, the Fred Hampton College Prep High School—more commonly known as Hampton High—Panthers made it to the Super-Sectionals for the first time in over twenty years, in large part due to the pitching prodigy that is Zeke Ladoja.

"Zeke's one of those rare talents in that he's as skilled off the field as he is on it. He makes the whole team better," Coach Edgar Quintero said in an interview with the *Tribune* after a close loss ended the Panthers' near-unstoppable march to the state finals last year. This year, Coach thinks things are going to be different.

"When I came aboard two years ago, we weren't winning games and we weren't playing well, but what we *did* have was a wealth of raw talent. Between "Big Swings" Braejon [Biggs] and the Perez twins on first and second base, we had something really special, but it took Zeke to bring it all together. He was the glue we needed."

More like *superglue*. We asked Ladoja how he felt about his coach's praise, and he had this to say:

"I don't really know what I'm doing for the team, besides throwing a ball pretty good, but I appreciate Coach's kind words," Zeke said. "I just love the game, love the team, and want everyone to succeed. My pops, he always says it's important to act in service of others. So I'm just here for Coach and Braejon and everyone else, to do what I can do to make everyone happy."

And if last year was anything to go by, what Ladoja can do is a lot. When the season begins next month, we'll get to see just how much.

"I'm so proud of you, baby boy," Pops said, a smile on his face. "So, what do you think? Great present, huh?"

I smiled and nodded. Pops didn't know I already had a clipping of it in the box under my bed, where I kept all my important possessions. A framed one was nice, sure, but—I felt something on the back of the picture, something hard and plastic, with indentations on its surface—pressable buttons, I realized, on a car key. When I pushed one, I heard the unmistakable sound of my dad's 1987 Mercedes-Benz 300E from outside the window. It was more than twice my age, without any bells or whistles save the keyless entry he'd installed a few years back, but none of that mattered because it was a car. A *car*.

I looked up at my dad, who had a satisfied smirk on his face.

"Come on, you didn't really think that was it, did you?" Ma said. "For our baby's sixteenth?"

"Thank-you-thank-you-thank-you," I said as I rushed over to hug my parents. I was so excited, I forgot to go easy on my dad, and he let out a small hiss of pain after I squeezed him a little too tight.

"Aw, shit, sorry," I said.

"Beg your pardon? What was that?" Ma said.

"Oh, uhh—I meant 'aw, shoot,'" I stammered. "That's what I said, Ma."

"Mm-hmm. I want you to go straight to the DMV, and you should hurry, because they close early on Saturdays. Since we're not able to take you, they're going to need this consent form," she said, and handed me an envelope. "They won't give you your license without it. And you've got your permit with you?"

I nodded and patted my wallet in my back pocket. "Always. I keep that thang on me," I said, and grinned.

"Good," Ma said. "Now, we've got a few rules. First, we'll cover your insurance, but you have to pay for your own gas. Second, no driving after midnight. You can be out past midnight, within reason, but we don't want you on the road. Too many drunks, too many people driving high, too many chances for something to go real wrong. This is your one and only warning. Third, absolutely no drinking and driving. I know you and Manny like to dip into Jojo's stash when you're over there—"

"We do not," I scoffed. "We've never—"

"Boy, it hurts to laugh, so don't make me," Pops said. "Jojo marks the levels of his bottles. He knows, we know, you're not in trouble."

"Not with us, anyway. Jojo might feel otherwise, seeing as you've been stealing sips of his nice-nice tequila," Ma said. "Azure Reposado or something like that?"

"Azul," I said before I could stop myself. "Shi—shoot." I've always been a terrible liar.

"Good catch," she said. "Anyway, that's rule number three."

"Is that it?" I took my eyes off my parents and turned to look out the window, down at my birthday present. Bright and black against the snow-covered ground.

"Just one more," Pops said. "We don't want any funny business going on in this car."

I turned to look at him. "Funny business?"

"Especially between you and a certain *some*body," he said.

I felt my face grow hot. "There's not gonna be any 'funny business,' because me and Imogen are just friends. That's all. That's it. She can't date till she's sixteen anyway, so, it's—we're not—I'm gonna go to the DMV now," I said in a huff.

My parents gave each other a knowing glance. "Hey, you're the one who brought up Imogen, but whatever you say, kiddo," my mom said. "Go on, enjoy your birthday."

"And drive safe," Pops said. "I may be giving him to you, but I reserve the right to take him back. You better take good care of him. No scratches, dings, dents. Or else."

"Pfft, don't even worry, Pops. I'ma treat this thing like it's my own baby. Ain't nothing gonna happen, I swear," I said.

"Yeah, yeah, go enjoy your birthday, baby boy. Proud of you, always," he said.

I kissed Ma on the cheek, Pops on the forehead, and took off down the hallway, moving a little too fast. A few nurses glared me down from a near run to a brisk walk as I passed their station. I drummed on my thighs as what had to be the slowest elevator in all of Chicago made its descent from the third floor. It felt like half a day passed before the doors opened.

Outside, the cold February air came at me quick. I had been outside for all of two seconds when I started shivering and my teeth got to chattering. I hurried over to the car, opened up the door, and slid inside onto the cold, black leather seat. I put *my* key in the ignition and started *my* car.

It wasn't my first time driving the Benz. My parents had let me take the wheel a couple times. Mostly, I learned on our old minivan, so busted up that I could run into poles or hit curbs and no one'd ever know the difference. Not that I ever did.

I already had a mental wish list of everything I wanted to do to the car. First up, a new sound system. It needed a good wash and wax, some fresh rims. I didn't have money for any of it, not yet. But I could at least clean the inside. If there was time after I got home from the DMV, I was going to go to town on the seats and the floor mats until the car looked and smelled fresh.

And then I could pick Imogen up and take her on long, romantic drives, and once it warmed up a little, we could go to a drive-in, 'cause she liked cute stuff like that. Just a few more weeks until her sixteenth, when everything was going to be different.

It took longer to drive to the DMV than it did to get my license. I had just started to get comfortable in my chair when my number flashed up on the screen. I leapt to my feet and hurried over to the counter.

"How're you doing today, ma'am?" I said to the woman behind the glass. She looked at me with empty eyes and ignored my question.

"The forms," she said, chewing her gum with impatience.

"Sure thing, got 'em right here," I said. I put them through the slot in the glass. "It's my birthday. Just turned sixteen."

"Where's the proof you completed driver's education? You got it or not, kid?"

Excuse you, I wanted to say. From my wallet, I pulled out the signed and notarized certificate of completion from ChicaGO Driver Education Services. She snatched the paper and started typing so hard I was afraid she'd break the keyboard. She didn't say a word and, a few moments later, shooed me away from the counter to get my photo taken. Like most driver's license photos, mine came out bad—black and white and overexposed like a murderer's mug shot—but, hey, a license was a license. Well, a temporary paper one, anyway, until the real one came in the mail.

I took a picture of the paper and sent it to the group chat. Notifications from my best friends Manny, Cara, and Imogen started rolling in, everyone excited about meeting at Cara's later. Then I got into the driver's seat and drove home, no parent in the passenger seat, street legal for the very first time. I was methodical about it, learning the car's ins and outs, and after pulling into our alleyway garage, I sat in the car a little while and flipped through the car manual to make sure I hadn't missed anything. Once I was finished, I headed inside to grab the vacuum to start cleaning out the Benz. I had several hours before the party at Cara's—plenty of time.

I was thinking about what I was going to wear—with Imogen's

birthday around the corner, it was time to step up my game—and was so up in my head that I didn't notice anything unusual when I walked into my house. Like how the back door was unlocked. Like the sound of Imogen and Cara snickering, or the sight of Manny's foot sticking out from behind the couch, and when they jumped out from their hiding spots and yelled, "*SURPRISE!*," I damn near pissed myself.

chapter two
ZEKE

Manny and Cara sang as Imogen lit the candles on the cake. In booger-green icing, the cake read SNOT EVERY DAY YOU TURN 16! I could just make out the photo on the cake in the candlelight as they set it down on the kitchen island.

"You just *had* to pull this one back up, huh," I said, looking right at Imogen.

Her face broke into a broad grin, her eyes sparkling. "Uh, obviously. Your mom gave me her photo album and I just couldn't resist."

I was seven years old in a broccoli suit during a play about the food pyramid and I sneezed. *Hard.* Snot was on my hands, my face, everywhere. And my mom, who I'm *supposed* to love and trust, took a picture!

"Bro," Manny cut in. "You look like you just got slimed by an alien or some shit. Nasty."

"I was right next to him when it happened," Cara said, pointing to a banana just out of frame. "I saw the windup, then the pitch, and then that nigga was *covered*. Like a car crash in slow motion."

"Thanks for reminding me, everyone. What a great memory to relive on my birthday," I said, rolling my eyes.

"Oh, you love it," Cara said as she punched me in the arm.

"Damn, girl, you punch like a mouse," I laughed.

"You know damn well I can knock you out. Did it when we were kids, I can still do it now. Unless you think you a prodigy at not getting your ass beat too?" Cara said. They'd all been clowning me, calling me "prodigy" ever since that article came out.

"Look, I came over here to eat cake and watch *X-Files*. Now, correct me if I'm wrong," Manny said, "but we don't seem to be doing either of those things."

"Hear, hear," Imogen said. "I've been waiting all damn day for Mulder and this cake and I'm not trying to eat wax, so quit messing around."

"Okay, okay," I said, turning to Imogen. In the firelight, her brown eyes glowed like polished wood, framed by the parted curtain of her braids, lit glossy-black by the flames. The dancing shadows accentuated her full, dark lips, parted to reveal a mouth of perfect teeth. She had never looked more beautiful to me, and I couldn't keep myself from staring.

Manny nudged me with his elbow. "You gonna blow them candles out or what, homie?"

I shook my head, as if I was waking from a dream. "Sorry, I was trying to decide on my wish," I lied. "But I got it now." I took a deep breath, taking in the smell of the melting wax, the sugary cake, the tangerine of Imogen's shampoo, and exhaled.

Jordan K. Casomar

As soon as the flame was out, the guilt crept in—I hadn't wished for more money so that my mom wasn't stressed and didn't have to work all the time. I hadn't even wished for my dad to be okay and for the cancer to magically leave his body and never return. All I'd wished for was Imogen.

Manny turned the lights back on, then pulled a small, square package from behind his back. Technically, it was wrapped, but the paper was thick in some places, thin and torn in others, and covered in bits of tape.

"A dog get to this or something? Goddamn," Cara laughed.

"Yeah, yeah, I can't wrap for shit, what the fuck ever. It's what's inside that counts," Manny said.

"With your Hallmark-greeting-card ass," Cara said.

"Z, open that thing up before I bust my cousin upside her head," Manny said.

"I'd like to see you try," Cara said.

"Same," Imogen and I said at the same time.

"Man, just open the damn thing," Manny said.

"Homie, I'm tryin," I said, picking at the tape and the tattered paper until I saw what was inside. "Yo, is this . . ."

Manny grinned. "Bet."

Inside the horrific packaging was a true treasure: a baseball memorialized in a glass cube, and not just *any* baseball, but one signed by Roberto Clemente on December 28, 1972, a few days before his fatal plane crash.

"It's from my dad's collection. One of the balls from Clemente's very last game. Wasn't a home run or anything, just a foul ball that popped my old man's way, but still, he held on to it. Couple months

12

later, they were both back in Puerto Rico for Christmas, and my old man got it signed. Then Clemente took off to go help with the earthquake in Nicaragua, and well, you know the rest."

"He said I could have it? Isn't this, I dunno, worth something? Don't he got some sentimentals about it?"

"It's a decent chunk of change, but nothing wild. The old man, he's good with it. Was his idea, even. Thought it might cheer you up, seeing as you ain't had many reasons to be cheered up lately."

"Damn, I don't know what to say. Thanks, Manny. And tell Jojo—"

Manny waved his hand, cutting me off. "You know I will."

"That makes my present look like chump change," Cara groaned. She set a large, gold-wrapped package on the kitchen table. It was the exact opposite of Manny's—well-wrapped, like a professional had done the job.

"See, Manny? This is how it's supposed to look," I said.

Manny gave me the finger and laughed.

"I hope you like it," Cara said. I swear I saw her blush, just for a second.

The paper unfurled with something close to elegance, like the little origami figures that Cara made when she was bored in class, and revealed a box about as long as my forearm.

"Is this . . . ," I started to say.

"All of the *X-Files* is in that box. Every season *and* the movies. With commentary. Deleted scenes. Gag reels. Bloopers. It's got everything, so now we don't gotta keep checkin the DVDs out from the library or watch it all stutter-step on your busted Wi-Fi."

"Cara, this is amazing," I said. I wrapped my arms around her in a big hug. "This must've been expensive."

"Don't be pocket-watchin now," Cara said.

"Yeah, so, mine's not . . . it's personal," Imogen said, her voice all quiet. "You guys mind?" She looked over at Cara and Manny.

"Girl, why you being so shady? Since when we keep secrets?" Cara frowned, rooted to the floor.

"It's not a secret, it's just—"

"Cara, come help me get the TV set up. Z, we're gonna open this box set up, you good with that?" Manny said, a lifesaver.

I nodded. "Go on ahead."

Manny grabbed the box off the table and left the room, but Cara lingered, casting glances at me and Imogen.

"Cara! I don't know this Blu-ray shit!" Manny shouted.

Cara groaned. "Ugh, fine, have your secret little talk. But you *best* come out with cake for me and Manny," she said as she exited the room, leaving me and Imogen alone in the kitchen.

"So, what'd you wish for?" Imogen asked. "Your dad?"

"Uh, yeah," I lied. "It's silly."

She shook her head. "It's what I wished for too. I know it doesn't work that way, since I'm not the one blowing it out, but, hey, you never know," Imogen said. She reached into a tote bag and pulled out a small package wrapped in shiny copper gift wrap.

"It's not expensive or fancy or whatever. It's . . . I know it's been a rough year and I thought maybe it'd be nice to have a reminder of the good times," she said.

My heart hurled itself against my ribs as I opened the present. Inside was a slender photo album. The first picture was of me and my dad in Imogen's backyard when I was six. A blurry child's body took up most of the photo, but in the background, caught in focus just beneath the mystery child's armpit, were me and my dad, both unaware of the camera. I was bawling, tears streaming down my cheeks. He was kneeling down, his forehead to mine, his eyes closed, mid-speech, trying to comfort me.

"Where did you—I've never seen this before," I said, my voice tight from the knot in my throat.

"After I found the snot picture, I went looking through all ours, too. Mom's kept, like, every photo she's ever taken. Even the bad ones, the ones focused all wrong or overexposed or whatever. She's got them all in boxes and boxes in the basement, so I went looking and found a whole bunch of you and your dad at our house."

I was clenching every muscle in my body, trying my hardest not to cry as Imogen turned the page to a photo of me and her in a tree house, with Pops and her dad, Brian, standing at the base of the tree. Our dads were clearly visible in the photo, but our faces were gone, washed out by too much light. All you could see were the faint edges of our grinning faces and matching overalls because Ma and Jean, Imogen's mom, thought it was cute, dressing us alike, even though we were eight years old, well past the age for that kind of thing. People used to ask if we were twins.

"You remember when they built this? It only lasted a week, because my dad didn't listen to your pops. He thought he knew what he was doing," Imogen said with a snort as she cut into the cake.

"It wasn't even that windy!" I laughed.

"Right?!" Imogen said. "But we found pieces of that tree house everywhere, everything except the foundation, which was right where it was supposed to be."

"'Cause that's the part Pops did," I said, laughing extra hard to give myself some space to let a few tears go. "Thank you. Gen, I love y—this. I love *this* so much." If she noticed my slipup, she didn't react any.

"It's a little corny, but I thought it might be nice. You're my best friend, you know? And things are rough right now, but we're going to get through this. And I do mean *we*. I got you, Z. We all got you."

We were alone in the kitchen. No eyes on us. I heard Manny and Cara fussing over how to get the TV set up right, loud enough that they wouldn't hear a kiss, and I was so close to her, intoxicatingly close. I smelled her perfume, her cocoa butter lotion, the tangerine of her hair. I wanted to lean in and kiss her. I wanted—

The *X-Files* theme blasted out of the speakers in the living room, so loud it shook the house, rattling the picture frames on the walls. Imogen and I clapped our hands over our ears, and just like that, the moment passed.

"Shit, sorry!" Manny shouted.

"Manito, you dumbass," Cara said once the volume was down to a tolerable level. "You two better get out here, 'cause this train ain't waitin for nobody. Even you, birthday boy!"

"They *best* not start without us," Imogen said.

"You know with your whole heart that's exactly what they're gonna do. Let's go," I said as we placed four big slices of cake on the plates Cara had set up and hustled into the living room.

"What took so long?" Manny asked. "Were y'all, y'know . . ." He waggled both his eyebrows.

"Emmanuel Léon, if you don't shut the hell up," Cara said.

She hurled a pillow at Manny, hitting him in the chest. I was glad for the dark—I wasn't part of the high-yellow crew, but I was still light-skinned enough it wasn't hard to tell when I was blushing.

"She was just showing me her present," I said. Manny snorted, then yelped in pain as he took a pillow to the face. "It's a photo album of pictures of me and Pops, stuff she and her folks had, so we were looking at it."

"Well, shit, now I feel like an asshole," Manny muttered.

"Cuzzo, that's because you *are* an asshole," Cara said.

"Guess that puts you on the spot, Z," Manny said, ignoring Cara. "Gen's birthday's, what, a month away? She just set a high-ass bar. You gotta get her a pony or something now."

"Ew, a pony? Gross," Imogen said. "I'm not a big presents person, besides."

"Well, now that we're on the subject, what *do* you want?" I asked.

"A dope party," she said without a moment's hesitation. "Like the kind of party you see on TV shows. Dancing. Drinks. A DJ. A blowout."

"Oh, hell yeah, girl, that's what I'm talking about," Cara said. "Let's get *grimy*."

"Then . . . what if I plan the party? That'll be my gift. What you think?" I asked.

"What about your dad? Won't you be busy?" Imogen said.

"Nah, it'd be nice to have something to do instead of sitting around at the hospital stressing about how he's doing. C'mon, don't worry about me. It's your birthday. Your party. Trust me, I'll make this look straight off Netflix. Promise. What do you say?"

A slow smile broke out across Imogen's face. She threw her arms around me and hugged me tight. "You're the best friend I could ask for. Yeah, I'm in. Let's do it."

If I had died right then and there, I would've died happy.

"*Okay*, people. We can talk parties later," Cara said, her voice rippling with irritation and impatience. "Mulder and Scully *been* waiting. So sit your asses down and shut your mouths and let's get this show on the road."

chapter three
ZEKE

"Zeke, shh, you have to be quiet or we're gonna get caught," Imogen said.

"It's cool, Gen, no one's home. Dad's at the hospital, and Mom's working a late shift. We don't have to be quiet," I said, placing my hand on the small of her back. I traced a single finger up the length of her spine, a wave of goose bumps following in its wake, until I reached the clasp of her bra.

"Nuh-uh." Imogen grinned. "Not yet." She pushed me down onto my bed, her beautiful darkness illuminated by the moonlight coming through my bedroom window. She was down to her underwear—a lacy tangerine bra and a pair of black boy shorts that made her booty look even more heavenly than usual.

"I shouldn't be the only one in my underwear. I don't see how that's fair," Imogen said. She bent forward and crawled on top of me, back arched. My breath quickened as I felt her fingers undo the button of my jeans, and I got goose bumps of my own at the sound of my zipper coming undone.

"Your shirt. Off. Now," she ordered.

I obeyed.

"God, I want you so bad," Imogen said. "It took everything I had not to rip your clothes off, when we were alone in the kitchen."

She tugged my pants all the way off, then straddled me. I felt something happening between my legs as she reached up behind her back to unclasp her bra. I heard a soft *click* and watched the straps loosen on her shoulders. She let them down slow, teasing me, drawing it out, until—

I woke up to a pair of wet boxers. I closed my eyes and tried to ignore the feeling, eager to slip back into the dream, but I couldn't. The dream was gone. The warmth and weight of her body on mine, gone. Her booty and her breasts, gone. The smell of her from the party earlier still lingered, but nothing else.

"Damn it, Zeke, you couldn't have lasted another minute?" I muttered as I slid out of bed. It was 3:21 a.m., and I knew I had to be extra quiet. The last thing I wanted was to wake my mom up and have her start asking questions. I just needed to clean myself off, change my underwear, and hop back into bed with no one the wiser. I threw the soiled boxers into my dirty clothes basket—ever since my dad got sick and my mom started working doubles, I'd been in charge of laundry, so no one was going to touch them except me—and grabbed a clean pair from my dresser.

I opened my bedroom door with a practiced quiet, crept into the bathroom across the hallway, and cleaned myself off. As I eased the bathroom door open again and tiptoed out into the hall, I heard the rustle of paper from downstairs and, beneath it, my mom's quiet sobs.

I froze mid-step, my heart running out of control. Her crying could mean anything, but my mind jumped to one thing and one thing only—something had happened to Pops. Maybe there were complications from his surgery or maybe the cancer had spread to his lymph nodes. Maybe he was already dead and I'd grow up knowing my dad died while I was having a wet dream. Maybe maybe maybe.

I had to know what was going on. I crept down the hallway, tip-toed down the steps, peeked around the corner, and saw my mom sitting at the kitchen table, backlit by the stove light, still in her nurse's scrubs. Her face was buried in her hands and her shoulders shook as she cried over the papers covering the kitchen table.

"Uh, Ma, what's up?" I said. I wasn't loud, but she jumped hard at the sound, like she'd heard a gunshot or a car backfire.

"Why aren't you in bed? What are you doing up?" she said, almost shouting, as she frantically gathered up the papers on the table. With her hands away from her face, I could see the exhaustion, the puffy redness around her eyes, the dried salt trails on her cheeks.

"What's going on? Why're you crying?" I stepped toward her, and she threw her arms over the table to hide the documents. "Did something happen to Pops?"

"It's nothing, just—it's been a long day. You better get your butt back in bed, Zeke," she said.

"Did something happen? Just tell me," I said, moving closer to the table.

"*Bed. Now.*"

But there was no way I was going to go back to bed, not until I got my questions answered. I darted forward and snatched at the papers on the table and started reading. I didn't see much before she ripped the papers out of my hand, but I saw enough. I saw the logo for Ida B. Wells Memorial Hospital. I saw BALANCE OWED and the five digits that followed, *before* the cents. I saw the words "delinquent" and "past due" and "collections." I saw enough.

"Ma, what the fuck? What is this?" I knew she was tired down deep in her bones when she didn't say anything about me dropping an f-bomb right in front of her. She just sighed and slumped back down in her chair.

"It's nothing to worry about, Zeke. I just gotta talk to the insurance people, and I haven't had time is all. Everything's fine," she said as she rubbed her temples, exhausted. "You don't need to worry."

"Then why are you crying? Doesn't sound like everything's fine," I said as I took a seat across from her.

"It's *going* to be fine. I just need to work it out with the insurance. I was just . . . stressed, looking at all the paperwork. But I'm fine and it's going to be fine."

"But Ma, if we need money, I can take a break from the team and—"

"*Trust me*, Zeke. What I need is for you to focus on school and baseball and being a kid, okay? What I need is for you to go back to bed and not to worry. What I need is for you to be my happy, strong, good young man. If you want to help, if you want me to feel better, *that's* what I need you to do. Okay?"

"But—"

"I said, *okay*?"

"Yeah. Okay. I can do that, Ma," I said.

"Good. Now give me a hug and get to sleep."

I did as I was told. I got up from the table, walked around, and wrapped my arms around my mom. Her body was stiff, her muscles tensed.

"Don't stay up too late, okay?" I said.

"You telling me not to stay up too late? How the tables have turned," she laughed. "Night, baby."

"Night, Ma. Love you." I went back to my room and got under the covers and slept none, worrying myself awake for so long, I heard the morning birds start singing their songs.

"Why don't we just do a GoFundMe?" Imogen said.

The four of us were at our usual table in the lunchroom discussing what I'd seen the night before, all of us leaning in and talking low like a bunch of thieves planning a heist. It was nug and tendies Monday, the only good day when it came to the food at Hampton High. Too bad I didn't have much of an appetite.

"Bro, if you're not gonna eat those . . . ," Manny said.

"For fuck's sake, we're talking serious here, Manny," Cara said, then turned to Imogen. "I don't know, Samson's not big on charity. I think he'd be pissed if we did that, right, Zeke?"

Cara and my dad were tight. Her own father, Maurice, was nowhere to be found. I didn't know the whole story—if he was alive or dead, if he had abandoned them, if they had abandoned him—and neither did Cara. All she knew about him—that he was Black as night and that he had a wide smile and mischievous eyes, both of which Cara had inherited—came from a couple photos hidden away in her mom's closet. When Cara pressed her mom, Lisette, for more details, Lisette simply said that he wasn't in their lives anymore, and she refused to elaborate. In Maurice's absence, my dad had become something of a father figure to Cara. She kept him company during his chemo sessions as much as I did. More than a few times, I walked in to find the two of them laughing and cursing each other out, deep in a game of chess. Sometimes it seemed like she knew him better than I did, and when it came to his feelings about charity, she was dead-on.

"Yeah, no. If he found out we were collecting money from people around town or from strangers on the internet, he'd blow his top," I said as I let out a massive yawn.

"'Never take a handout. Earn your way. Don't let anyone see you begging. Ever,'" Cara said, imitating my dad's gruff voice. "Says it all the time."

"But this is different," Imogen scoffed. "Besides, technically we'd be raising money for Vanessa, not Samson."

"It'd all be the same to him," I said. "It's not gonna happen, Gen. Other ideas?"

"You can sell that baseball Manny gave—"

"Uh, no, he cannot," Manny said.

"Uh, no, I cannot," I said at the same time.

"Jinx, vending machine, after lunch, orange Fanta," Manny said.

"Cuz, we are talking about how Zeke *needs money*," Cara said.

"Hey, a jinx is a jinx, and if a jinx don't mean anything anymore, what kind of world are we living in?" Manny said.

"For real," I said, and dapped Manny up. "Look, I don't want you to treat me different. I can afford a damn soda."

"You boys and your dumb pride," Imogen said. "So, if you're not going to go the crowdfunding route, what are you going to do?"

I yawned again, exhausted. "I don't know, I'm thinking."

"Well, while you think, I'm gonna go sweet-talk Lunch Lady Lorinne into giving me an ice cream sandwich," Manny said as he stood up and left the table.

"So, why can't you sell the baseball?" Imogen asked once Manny was out of earshot. "Isn't it worth a lot? It's just a baseball. I don't see why it's a big deal."

Cara rolled her eyes. "What if someone gave you a signed first edition or whatever of, like, those weird *Outlander* books you read? Would you sell it?"

"Well, that's different," Imogen shot back. "I can actually *use* those. I can read them. That baseball's just sitting in a glass box, doing nothing. And *Outlander* isn't weird. It's *romantic*."

"There's nothing romantic about being back in the 1800s."

"First of all, it's the eighteenth *century*, so the 1700s. And second—"

"Look, Gen, I get it," I interrupted. "And I thought about it too, believe me. But Clemente wasn't *just* a ballplayer. He was a hero of Puerto Rico. An American hero."

"Damn right," Cara said. "PR pride."

"And, plus, it was a gift from Jojo. That right there's a big deal, considering Jojo grew up down the street from him. Can you imagine if Jojo found out? I'd never be allowed back into Fro-Yo Jojo—" I stopped as a light bulb lit up in my head. "That's it! Cara, how much does Jojo pay you?"

Cara's eyes lit up at my question. "More than he'd like. It's fourteen an hour now."

"So, let's say I worked every day after school from, like, five to close, and then two full shifts on the weekends. That's almost full-time, right? Jojo's closes at nine, so . . ." I started counting on my fingers.

"Thirty-six hours at fourteen dollars an hour makes five hundred and four dollars a week, before taxes," Cara said. Math was a breeze for her. "With taxes, you're looking at around eight hundred dollars every two weeks."

"That's sixteen hundred a month! That's huge! It's February now, so I could make almost ten thousand dollars by the end of summer."

"Yo, yo, did I hear someone say dollars?" Manny said as he returned to the table holding a stack of four ice cream sandwiches. "Lorinne, she loves me, you guys. She says I look like a young Benicio Del Toro. Are my cheeks red? She kept pinching them."

He passed one ice cream sandwich to me, another to Cara. "Gen? You want one? You got your Lactaid on you?" Imogen shook her head. "Double-fisting for me, then. So, someone said something about money. Catch me up."

"Manny, you think you could get me a job at the shop?" I asked.

"Bro, you wanna work? For real? Are you crazy?"

"Believe it or not, cuzzo, some people don't like being lazy good-for-nothings," Cara said.

"Lazy? Give me that ice cream sandwich back, then, and you go up there and get your cheeks bruised up by an old lady's fingers, you think it's so easy," Manny said.

"Manny, can you get me the job or not?" I said.

"Yeah, I can get you the job. We could definitely use some help on the weekends. Another part-timer'd go a long way," Manny said as he chomped down on his ice cream sandwiches, bouncing from one to the other.

"Not part-time," I said. "Full-time. Every day, after school."

"So, uhh . . . ," Imogen said after a beat. "What about the team? There's no way you're going to be able to work full-time and still play."

My face froze. *Oh shit.*

"Like, I get that you're worried for your mom, but baseball is your *life*," she said. "Don't you think she'd be upset if she found out you stopped playing for her sake? What would your dad say?"

"If he knew how hard things were for my mom, he'd tell me to take care of my mom because he can't, not right now," I said. "You didn't see what I saw. I've never seen my mom like that. Just . . . *tired*. I close my eyes and I see her face, tears in her eyes, her forehead all scrunched up like a fucking Shar-Pei. I hated it, Gen. I *hate* it. Seeing her like that.

"Besides, the team isn't going anywhere. If I have to quit this year, I can just join back up next year. Sophomore year, that's the year that matters the least."

Imogen looked skeptical but shrugged. "You know I'll support you no matter what," she said. "If you need help figuring out how to tell Coach, we can talk about it. You know I've always got your back."

Cara and Manny nodded in agreement.

"I'll take the front," Cara said, her mouth full of ice cream sandwich.

"Gimme them sides!" Manny said. "And them nuggies!"

I grinned and slid my tray over to Manny. "Thanks, you guys. I mean it."

chapter four
IMOGEN

It was the ugly time of year in Chicago. The mounds of snow were no longer fluffy, brilliant white piles. Instead, they were a disgusting gray slush, and it was almost impossible to imagine they had ever been beautiful. I hated it. I hated the dirty city streets, the nasty slush, the fetid meltwater collecting on the side of the road. Every time I saw a car coming my way, my heart began to race as I prepared to leap away from a wave of grimy water.

Oh, how I longed to be in the countryside instead of trudging through the muck on my way home after school. I dreamt of looking out over rolling hills blanketed in blinding white that stretched on and on to infinity, of hiking through the Scottish Highlands like Claire Randall, my footsteps muffled by the snowpack underfoot, and walking the ramparts of Castle Leoch and watching the flakes fall to the ground.

"Hello, anybody there? Earth to Imogen Parker!" Zeke said.

"Oh! Um," I said, startled, so lost in my thoughts I'd forgotten about Zeke. We lived a ten-minute walk from each other and we often walked home together, except during baseball season, when Zeke had practice every day. "Sorry, what did you say?"

"You were in Scotland again, weren't you?"

"No way, I was thinking about your question."

"Which was?"

"It was . . . you wanted to know . . ."

"Called it. You had your space face on, a million miles from here."

"Not a million—3,600 miles, give or take a hundred. Which is around 5,800 kilometers, just so you know."

"I'm trying to talk to you about important stuff and you're over here thinking about *kilometers*, aka fake miles."

"Tell that to the rest of the world," I said, laughing. "But, yeah, sorry, I zoned out. What'd you ask me?"

"What should I say to Coach? I've been thinkin about it since lunch and I got a few ideas. I wanna talk to him tomorrow and—"

"Don't you think that's a little premature?" I asked.

"Hah, premature," Zeke snorted.

"Gross," I said, rolling my eyes. "Seriously. You don't even know if you've got the job yet. And what if Jojo can't afford to give you the hours you want?"

"Then I'll look somewhere else. Worst case, Coach'll take me back, right? He's not gonna say no, he'd probably just jump for joy, don't you think?"

Zeke wasn't wrong—the way Zeke played, no chance Coach would turn him away. "If you know it's going to be like that, why worry about what you're gonna say? Just be straight up with him, tell it like it is. But you're, like, really, really, *really* sure about this? You're already under so much stress, and baseball's always been how you let off steam. What if, right now, you need it more than ever?"

"For the last time, I'm *sure*. With Pops sick, I have to be the man of the house, take responsibility. Part of that means doing the hard thing, making the tough choice. Ma's relying on me. Pops is relying on me. If I don't do this, I'll regret it. So, are you gonna help me on this? 'Cause I really need you," Zeke said.

"You know I got you. Always," I said as I grabbed Zeke and gave him a hug. His arms encircled me and pulled me in tight enough that I felt his heart pounding in his chest, even through our puffy jackets. He held me there for a moment, and had I not started to pull away, I'm not sure he would've ever let go.

"So, Coach first, let's figure out what you're going to say," I said as I resumed walking. Zeke fell in alongside me, our feet smushing through the slush. I knew that it didn't matter what Zeke said, not really. Coach was going to be cool with it because Zeke was Zeke. He was the star player, a pitching prodigy; of course he'd go along with it.

"Like I said, just be straightforward. Everyone trusts you to do what's right. You're a little hardheaded, yeah. Little stubborn. Little bit of a dummy, too, now that I think about it," I said.

"Damn, is it Cut a Brother Down Day and no one told me?"

"*But*," I continued, "you're no fool. And when you decide to do something, you do it right and you do it well. Except, you know, in English class."

Zeke clutched his heart and acted like he'd just been shot. "The pain . . . it's too much," he said as he staggered around on the sidewalk.

"You're so corny," I laughed.

"*I'm* corny? Coming from the girl obsessed with books about White folks in Ireland way back when Christopher Columbus was sailin the ocean blue and shit," Zeke said.

"Boy, there's *so* many things wrong with that sentence, I don't even know where to start. *Outlander's* in Scotland, which is *completely* different. Second, it's set over three hundred years after Christopher Columbus and his bullshit. Third—" I glanced over at Zeke, who had a real shit-eating grin on his face. "You're just messing with me, aren't you?"

"What can I say? It's cute when you get all worked up."

"Oh, you think so? You think *this* is cute too?" I said as I shoved him hard. He fell into the snow and I broke out in laughter. Zeke scrambled to his feet, his clothes coated in wet slush. I didn't see the snow in his hand until it was too late. He brought his hand down on my head and frigid water streamed down my face.

"You . . . *you* . . ." I bent down and scooped up a handful of my own and hurled it right at Zeke's head. He reacted quick, tilting his head, and the slushball sailed right past him.

"Trying to outpitch a pitcher? Nah, girl," he said. "But if you want some pointers . . ." He flashed me a grin.

I shook my head. "*Anyway.* New subject—are you gonna tell me anything about the party you're planning?"

"Hell no! It's gonna be a surprise. You'll find out in a few weeks. Just be patient."

"You know I hate surprises," I said.

"You'll be a fan of this one, I promise. Who knows you better? Who knows what you like more than me? Nobody, that's who. I'm gonna throw you the party of your damn dreams, girl. It's gonna be one to remember, believe me."

He was right; there wasn't anyone in the world who knew me the way Zeke did. Even if he didn't understand why I liked some of the things I did, like why *Outlander*'s Jamie Fraser could *absolutely* get it or why I'd rather read *The X-Files* than watch it, he understood just about everything else. Always had, ever since we were kids, which was why everyone thought we were either together, going to be together, or should be together.

Maybe they were right. I mean, here he was, talking about putting together the party to end all parties—for *me*. His dad was sick, his mom was exhausted, he was putting baseball aside to help them, and he *still* wanted to make sure my birthday was something special, something to remember. In a lot of ways, he *was* Jamie Fraser. Devoted to his family and his loved ones. Loyal, almost to a fault. When he made a decision, he stuck to it. When he took on new responsibilities, he did so with 100 percent of his effort and his heart, which was perhaps his most endearing—and annoying—quality.

I watched his mouth move and thought about kissing him, not for the first time. Wouldn't that tell me everything I needed to know? That was how it worked in stories, right? The kiss unlocked all the feeling that was hiding or trapped somewhere. We had kissed once before, when we were kids playing pretend. I remembered nothing save that it happened, so it must not've been a big deal, but—

"Uhh, hello? Don't tell me you zoned out *again*," Zeke said as he waved a hand in front of my face. "We're at your house, Gen. Have you just been on autopilot this whole time?"

I was standing on the first step of my stoop, still too short to look Zeke in the eye, staring forward.

"Um, I guess. Sorry. I was just—do you remember that one day when we were real little and playing pretend?" I said.

"Wh-which day?" he stammered. "You were always tryna play doctor or whatever, you're gonna have to be more specific than that."

"Oh, that's right, it was doctor! It was when we were nine, I think. We were in my basement, our moms were upstairs drinking wine and gossiping about everything under the sun. I had some silly name, like Yvette or—"

"Odette," Zeke said, then backtracked. "I mean, maybe it was Odette? That sounds sorta familiar."

"Odette! Odette Billings." I smiled. "And you were my patient, Mr. Greenley or Greenman. Greenwood? I think it was Greenwood! You were having heart problems. Your heart was broken and the only way to fix a broken heart was with a kiss. We were so weird. Wild, that was almost seven years ago."

"Yeah, pretty weird," Zeke said as he fiddled with the zipper on his coat, shifting from one foot to the other.

"I know it barely counts, but you're still the only person I've kissed. Did you know that?"

Zeke choked on his spit and started coughing. "Uh, what?" he said once he could talk again.

"You know how my parents are. 'No dating till you're sixteen, no ifs, ands, or buts. We catch you breaking the rules, there'll be hell to pay.' And my dad's *really* serious about it, such a stupid rule. So, it's just been you."

Zeke grinned. "Well, I don't blame you. When you've had the best, why mess with the rest?"

I rolled my eyes so hard I swear the earth shook beneath my feet. "Please. You were nine years old. You could hardly tie your shoes, so there's no way you knew how to kiss well."

"First of all, that's where you're wrong," Zeke said. "I was a pro even then. And I'm even better now, seeing as, unlike *you*, I've had myself a little practice." I saw something flash across his face as he hesitated a moment. "I'll prove it. Kiss me right here, right now."

"Ew, gross," I said, relieved he'd brought it up. I didn't want to be the one to initiate this experiment.

"What, you scared? Scared you're gonna fall hopelessly, desperately in love with me? Yeah, I'd be scared of that too, if I were you. I mean, I'm fly, I'm fine, and I'm in high demand. I'm not surprised you find it and *me* intimidating."

"Oh yeah?" I said. I knew Zeke felt some kind of way about me, and now I needed to know if I felt some kind of way back. I needed to know once and for all if everyone was right, if we really *were* meant to be. So I leaned toward Zeke, placed a hand on his cheek, pressed my lips against his, and felt . . .

Nothing. No desire, no spark, no hunger for more.

I pulled away. "See? Only thing I'm scared of is your stanky breath. And if you ever say anything to anybody, it's your ass," I said, laughing, and headed up the stoop to my front door. I expected a response, but all I got was silence. I turned to look and saw Zeke's eyes glazed over, his body so still he could've passed for one of those wax figures. I could practically see the hearts in his eyes.

Imogen, you idiot, I thought as I scooped up a handful of snow and hurled it at him. "Now who's got their space face on?" I said as he shook himself back to life.

"I—I, um, I gotta go," he said, his words quick and clipped. "To the . . . the hospital? For my dad. Yeah. Uhh. I'll s-see you later? Okay. Bye."

I had never seen Zeke move as fast as he did right then unless he was on the field. He all but ran down the sidewalk, almost slipping on the ice as he sped off.

"It's going to be fine," I said aloud, but I could clearly hear my uncertainty. A quiet panic started to rise in my throat, and I felt like I was about to start choking.

"Imogen, how could you be so stupid?" I said to myself and rushed inside.

My throat was growing tighter. My breaths were quick and shallow. Dots of color danced across my eyes. I took off my backpack and held it upside down. Two novels fell out of the bag, then my writing journal, my notebooks, my pencil case, my school ID, my pocket dictionary for the rare occasions when I read a word I didn't know, and finally, my emergency inhaler. I grabbed it, shook it up like it was a can of soda I was giving to someone I hated, held it between my lips—which had just kissed Zeke—pressed down on the cartridge, and inhaled. A rush of coolness hit the back of my throat, and after another puff, my breathing began to return to normal. I could breathe again. I could see. I realized that my teeth were chattering, that my whole body was trembling. I was sitting on the floor, the hardwood ice-cold even through my winter layers.

I took slow, deep breaths, imagining the air I inhaled as blue and the air I exhaled as red, the way my therapist taught me. I inhaled a deep and dark and endless blue the color of the ocean, my breath calm as the waves washing against the shore. I exhaled the bad, a color somewhere between wine and blood that I knew was the color of shame. I don't know how long I sat there, breathing in the sea and breathing out my guilt, but once I had my lungs under control, my heart beating again at a normal pace, my hands steady, I grabbed my black writing journal off the ground, opened to the page where I'd left off, and disappeared into another world, one that was entirely under my control.

Valerie was sitting on the edge of the pier, watching the sun set, when she heard footsteps behind her. She smelled him on the air—pine, tobacco, oranges—overpowering the scent of the sea. Joshua.

Joshua didn't say anything as he sat down next to her. Valerie didn't either, until a gust of wind kicked up one of his locs and placed it on her shoulder so that the hair tickled her neck. She wondered if he could hear her heart pounding in her chest over the sound of the waves lapping at the shore. She was certain her rib cage would crack open, and she felt a squirming, tight warmth radiating from between her legs.

"Sorry about that," Joshua purred as he

reached over and pulled his thick length of hair from her neck. His fingernails brushed against Valerie's skin, and she had to struggle to contain the sigh of desire pressing against her lips.

"Why are you here?"

"I just had to see you one last time."

"But I told you I didn't want to see you. I wanted you to leave and never come back. To go back to—"

Valerie couldn't say it. To your wife. Your kids. The people you love, since you certainly don't love me.

"I never meant to hurt you, Val. I never meant to fall for you either. But I can't think of anything else except you. When I close my eyes, I see your face. When I touch my lips, I think of yours. I woke up today and smelled you and my heart ached," Joshua said as he placed a hand against the small of her back. A strong, warm hand.

Valerie remembered the first time he'd touched her. She was in the midst of a bad morning, and on her way out of a Starbucks, he moved unexpectedly, bumped into her, and spilled her coffee.

"Excuse you," she said as she whirled on him to make her displeasure known. But then they locked eyes, and Valerie melted. He smiled at her, a broad, brilliant smile, and his dark eyes seemed to stretch back forever, twin caves she wanted to explore and lose herself in. He grabbed a handful of napkins and bent down to clean up the mess.

"Real sorry, miss," he said. "Let me buy you a new one."

"Th-thank you," Valerie whispered. Something about him ensnared her in that moment. She couldn't quite pin down what it was. When he handed her the replacement coffee, their hands touched, and after that day, she couldn't stop thinking about how those hands might feel on the rest of her.

By the time I was done, I had almost forgotten about the kiss with Zeke. Almost.

chapter five
ZEKE

Manny punched me hard in my arm.

"The hell'd you do that for?"

"Tell me what I was just saying."

"What?"

"Tell. Me. What. I. Was. Just. Saying."

"Uhh, well, I, uhh," I stammered.

"Shit, you just as bad as Gen. So you wasn't even listening. Why?"

"Umm, not used to being up this early outside of baseball season, I guess?" I lied.

The world was just starting to get light as we made our way to school Tuesday morning. We were only fifteen minutes from Hampton High, but we wanted to slide by Pappy's and get the good donuts before they ran out, and that meant twenty minutes in line on a good day.

"You gotta be one of the worst liars I've ever met. That don't even make sense. You get up earlier than this for workouts."

"Fine, you know so much, you tell me why—"

"Bro, you were all up in Imogen-land, don't even play. I know your Imogen face better'n you know your Lil Zeke," Manny said. "And I *know* you know your thingy well, 'cause baseball's the only game you got."

For a second, I thought about telling Manny about the kiss, but I knew he'd go in on me for it, and it was way too early for all of that. "First of all, I don't wanna hear you say 'your Lil Zeke' ever again. Nasty. Second, tell me what you said. I'll listen this time, def."

Manny made a big show of clearing his throat before he started up. "*As I was saying*, this ol' paper-pale face came in the shop yesterday, talkin all this mess about how we'd charged her too much and how it was my fault. Shit, Z, I was ready to go off and start cursin her ass out."

"Watch out," I said, pulling him aside just before he set his foot down on a lump of freshly squeezed dog doo-doo. At least, I hoped it was from a dog.

"Thanks, homie. Anyway, so, this blanca, she starts comin at me full-force Karen with that 'Where's your manager?' shit. So I told her I *was* the manager. So then she asks me how old I am and you know what I told her? I told her I was twenty-one. And she *believed* me, bro. Imagine that shit. Imagine it! These White folks, I swear. If it ain't another mayo-face, they don't have a goddamn clue how old somebody is. Wild."

"I can't believe anyone'd think you were a day over sixteen," I said, laughing.

"That's what I'm saying!" Manny said, shaking his head. "Like, if it'd been you, that woulda been different. You got all that height and all that thicc. But me? Come on, now. I got this acne. I got this bottom retainer in my mouth. My arms are hairless, smooth as a freshly Zambonied ice rink. So, like, what?"

"For real, one look at that depressing attempt at facial hair on your face would tell me all I needed to know," I said. "Between your upper lip and your chin, you got, like, ten hairs total."

"Pfft, rude," Manny said. "You know I'm a grower, not a shower."

"Bro, don't put that image in my head," I said as Manny doubled over in laughter.

"So, what about Imogen was you thinkin about?" Manny asked a moment later. "You in your feelings about her birthday party? Sweet sixteen!"

"Uhh, well, sorta," I said. "I think . . . I think I'm finally gonna ask her out at the party."

Manny groaned, clutched his stomach, and fell into the slush.

"C'mon, Manny. Be serious."

"Zeke, my guy, you're killin me. Like, really. Look at me, I'm dying."

"*You* asked *me*. I'm just answering your damn question," I said as I put a hand out to help Manny up.

"Look, you know you're my day one. Ever since we got them Legos taken away after I put all them pieces up my nose and you made me laugh so hard they went flyin every which way, you've been my boy. You know that, right?"

I knew where the conversation was going. Whenever we got on the subject of Imogen, the conversation only ever went one way.

"I'm tellin you, as your ride-or-die homie: You gotta give it up, Z. If it hasn't happened by now, it's not gonna happen."

"Yeah, yeah, yeah, you think Imogen's got me in the friend zone, what else is new," I muttered.

Manny slapped his forehead. "Man, there's no damn such thing as the friend zone. Someone's either feelin you or they ain't. Either you're a friend or you're not, and that's all there is to it. It's not a 'zone,' someplace to escape. It's just how it is."

"So, how come she hasn't tried to get with anyone else? How come I'm the only one she tells all her secrets to and feels all her feelings around?"

"Bro, you tell me all your secrets. I'm the only one who knows about that one folder on your laptop. Or that you've been crushing on Ms. Devries since day one of freshman year, that you said you could 'watch her solve for *x* all. Damn. Day.' So, that means you and me oughta be fuckin, is that what you're saying?" Manny asked.

"Okay, genius, then why'd she kiss me?"

Manny groaned again, even louder, and stomped his feet as he walked, almost slipping on a patch of black ice. "Y'all were *nine years old*. I kissed my cousin Marisol when we was eight and playin make believe, but you don't see us out here gettin on each other."

"That's not the kiss I'm talkin about," I said, grinning wide.

Manny cocked his head and looked at me, confused. "What kiss you talkin about then?"

"Yesterday. I walked her home. When we got to her house, she brought up the kiss *you're* thinking of. And then, right after that, she kissed me, and not on the cheek. Right on the lips."

"Tongue?" Manny asked, his eyes wide.

"Nah, no tongue."

"So, then what? What'd she say after that? What was the vibe? She laugh, play it off like a joke?"

"Nah, man," I lied. So what, she laughed. That didn't mean anything. Didn't mean anything that she hadn't texted, either. Bottom line, she kissed me, and that was all that mattered. "Why you always trying to poke holes? Can't you just accept she's feeling me and have my back?"

Manny, for once in his life, had nothing to say. An awkward silence settled between us. Thankfully, it didn't last long as we rounded the corner and saw Pappy's Donuts a block away, busy as usual. A quick-moving line snaked out the front doors of the small bakery, and we fell in behind an older Black man in a tracksuit, talking loud into a Bluetooth earpiece.

"Look at this unc-ass nigga," I whispered, breaking the silence.

"Even got the big-ass phone holster on his belt," Manny said. He laughed, then his voice got low and serious. "Look, you're my boy and because you're my boy, I gotta let you know, I think this is a bad idea. But that don't mean I ain't got your back. L&L Boys, in it to win it, bro." He dapped me up.

I nodded. "Appreciate it, fam."

"In other news, yo, you see Ray? Bad day, looks like," Manny said.

I looked at Ray through the window. His brow and bald head were shiny with sweat, and his face was twisted up with hurt he was trying to hide. Ray winced with every step he took, and although he was only in his late thirties, the pain made him look much older. He'd had a promising football career playing for Rice, but he blew out his knee his junior year and never fully recovered. He came back to Chicago years later, hooked on painkillers until his folks, Pappy and Deedee, helped him straighten himself out and put him to work.

I couldn't help but think about Pops in the months before his diagnosis. He had that same slickness on his face from straining in the bathroom, from the pain he felt in his guts as he tried to go about his day. He had the same weariness from sleep disrupted by frequent trips to the toilet and the feeling of nausea that just never went away. As quiet as he was—and as his weight plummeted, he became ever quieter—I still heard the creak of his feet on the floorboards, his soft grunts and sighs.

I'd thought those days were the worst of it. Now I missed them, because my dad didn't move much at all lately.

"Hey, Léon and Ladoja," Ray said, his deep voice snapping me out of my thoughts. I hadn't realized we'd reached the register. "What y'all need?"

"Two sausage kolaches and a vanilla cake with them sprinks," Manny said.

"Same," I said. "Knee's bad today, huh? You okay?"

"Yeah, little brother, I'm aight. It's this damn cold more than anything. When the wind hits, everything hurts ten times worse. Almost makes a nigga wanna . . ." Ray trailed off, then shook his head. "Old days. Old me. Never going back. I got responsibilities now," he said, more to himself than to us. "Anyway, y'all know the price."

I was reaching for my wallet when Manny stepped between me and the register and slapped a twenty down. "I got it," he said.

"I can get it, Manny," I said.

"Nah, man, I got it, it's cool," Manny said as Ray counted the change out to him.

"Stay well, y'all," Ray said, waving as we slid out the store.

"I thought a jinx was a jinx," I said a few moments later.

"What?" Manny said, his mouth full of donut.

"You don't gotta pay for me."

Manny shrugged. "Just get me back next time."

"Come on, man, I'm not some kinda charity case now."

Manny sighed. "I'm only gonna say this once, bro. My ma's got herself a good city job. My old man's got the store. They own their house, 'cause they been here since forever. They paid off their car years ago and refuse to buy another one until the one they got explodes. What I'm saying is, we got money. We ain't rich or nothin like Imogen's folks, but it doesn't mean a damn thing if I buy us breakfast. My pops ain't sick. My moms ain't workin doubles. You get me?"

"It's just . . . it's embarrassing, man," I said after a while, my voice quiet.

"What's *embarrassing* is having a best friend you've known since you was still wetting the bed, and thinking that the reason he wants to help you out is out of charity and pity instead of out of love. What's *embarrassing* is being that stupid."

Sometimes, Manny really had a way with words.

chapter six
ZEKE

"What's got you all perked up?" Braejon asked.

"Yeah man, you've had . . . a smile on your face since you got here," Rinky-Dink panted.

We were on lap five of twelve, our shoes slapping and squeaking against the gym's rubbery floor. We were the only ones running. The rest of the class was walking slow, gossiping, playing on their phones. Coach had long since given up trying to make everyone run. His only rule was you had to stay on your feet and in motion. If you didn't, you got marked absent for the day, and it didn't take too many of those to fail gym. And there was nothing more embarrassing than having to repeat *gym* just to graduate. Which was exactly why Braejon was running next to us instead of enjoying a free period like the rest of the seniors.

"Me? I'm regular-degular, but I still can't believe you failed gym. *Gym*, Braejon?"

"Nigga, don't be out here trying to change the subject," Braejon said. "You ain't never said 'regular-degular' in your whole human life. *And* you're runnin light, like you got wings on your feet or something. Don't he, Dink? I'm not just seeing shit, right?"

"Yeah, something's . . . up for sure," Rinky-Dink said.

"Dink, the way you breathing, you better get in shape and stop worrying about me," I said.

"That's called . . . deflecting," he said. "That's what . . . our family therapist . . . says my dad does . . . same thing."

"Damn, they still fighting and everything, huh," Braejon said.

Rinky-Dink nodded.

"Sorry, man. Shit sucks," I said. "You good? Anything we can—"

"Now I know it's up, this brother trying to change the subject *again*," Braejon said. "Something musta happened with Imogen."

I stumbled at the mention of her name but regained my footing before I tripped and slammed into the ground.

"Looks like . . . a yes," Rinky-Dink said.

Braejon put an arm out, slowing us down to a fast walk. "Dink, slow up, we gotta get to the bottom of this."

"Man, let me go, there's nothin to talk about," I said, but I couldn't keep from grinning wide, ear to ear.

"Nothin my ass! Spill it, homie. Now," Braejon said.

I looked at Braejon and Dink. They weren't going to let up. And besides, I was glad they'd noticed. I wanted to break the news to someone who wasn't Manny It's-a-Bad-Idea Léon.

"Don't go runnin your mouths, got it?"

Braejon and Rinky-Dink nodded in unison.

"Lock and key, my nigga," Braejon said.

"Same," Rinky-Dink said.

"All right, I was walking her home yesterday. We was talking about all kinds of stuff when, outta nowhere, she brings up the first time we kissed, back when we were kids. So she's talking about that, so I was like," I said, lowering my voice, "'I dare you to do it again. Kiss me now, unless you're scared.' Finally made a move, right? And she *did*."

"Shiiiiit, attaboy," Braejon said.

"Damn it," Rinky-Dink muttered. "I'll pay up after lunch, Braejon."

"Pay up?" I asked.

"We had a bet running. Rinky-Dink thought it'd never happen. But I had faith in you, fam, and now he owes me twenty."

"Yeah, yeah, you'll get it," Rinky-Dink said. "Congratulations, Zeke. You been waiting since forever. I'm happy for you. Happy for me, too, 'cause once you're locked down, all the girls pining for you'll give the rest of us a chance."

"Don't put your lack of game on me, Dink," I said. Although he wasn't wrong. I glanced around the room and caught a couple girls staring at me. They switched up soon as I looked their way, talking to their friends in a flurry of whispers.

"Bruh, you know I ain't lying even a little. You got all the girls after you. They'd get with you at the drop of a hat while the rest of us out here scrounging," Rinky-Dink said.

"Speak for yourself," Braejon laughed. "Braejon Biggs does *plenty* well for himself, lemme tell you. So, Z, worth the wait?"

"Oh yeah. I knew it would be but, yo, when we kissed, it just felt *right*, you know? Felt good," I said.

"Homie, don't go bustin out your shorts on us. I don't wanna see that shit," Braejon said. "So, what, you two a thing now?"

"Well, uhh . . ." I rubbed the back of my neck and took a second to get my story straight. "Nothing *official* yet but pretty much, yeah. We're gonna talk about it today, figure out what we are."

"You better lock it up quick," Braejon said. "For every girl that wants to get with you, there's a nigga who's been wanting to run game on Gen. Me and the team, we got your back, we make sure that shit don't happen. Plus, folks like you. Star of the school, good son, smart enough—you got no enemies. But everyone knows she can't date till she turns sixteen, and I'll just say, you're not the only nigga round here excited for her birthday."

I stopped in my tracks. "Who? Who else?" I shouted at Braejon and Rinky-Dink.

"Keep it movin, Ladoja!" Coach bellowed, filling the gym up with his voice.

"Yes, Coach!" I hollered back, got my feet moving again, and caught up to my two friends. "For real, Braejon. Who?"

Braejon shrugged. "I'm no snitch, not now, not ever. I'm just tellin you what I heard."

I looked at Rinky-Dink. "And what've you heard? You waiting to get with Gen too?"

"Of course not, man. I'd never do that to you. I know the two of you got something special. But, uh, I *have* heard similar things."

"So it's good you aboutta get this locked down then," Braejon said, slapping me on the back.

"Yeah. Good thing," I mumbled.

"You got your girl, we got this season. Gonna be a good year! Gonna send me off right!" Braejon said.

In my excitement about the kiss, I hadn't given a single thought to how I was going to tell Braejon, Dink, or the rest of the team that I was gonna be out for the season, and I still didn't because, instead, my mind was full up with worry over all the boys waiting in the wings to move in on *my* Imogen. I sped up from a quick walk to an all-out sprint, leaving Braejon and Rinky-Dink behind, pumping my legs harder and harder until I couldn't think about anything except my breath, the heat in my muscles, the sweat running down my face. I kept running, around and around and around, until my legs gave out and my thoughts with them.

chapter seven
IMOGEN

"Word on the street is, we got a new kid coming," Cara said.

"So what? There's new kids all the time. Someone's always getting kicked out of somewhere and ending up here," I said as I opened my locker. I was still a little on edge from my kiss with Zeke the day before.

"Nah, Gen, he's not from around here—he's from *Houston.*"

"Where'd you hear this from? Mrs. Dionne from the front office?"

"No way, that old bag hates me."

"Probably because you keep calling her an old bag."

"Is she or is she not an old bag?"

"Don't be rude," I said.

"Uh, have you met me? Anyway, no, I didn't get it from her. I got it from Ray."

"Pappy's Ray?"

"The one and only," Cara said, a hint of irritation in her voice. "He's been around a lot lately. I think he's into my mom."

"*Into* her, huh." I grinned as I switched out my textbooks.

"Yuck, Gen."

"Sorry, I couldn't help myself. So, you heard it from Ray? How come he knows?"

"Get this," Cara said, whispering for no apparent reason. "He's *Ray's* kid."

"*Excuse* me? Since when does Ray have a kid?" I asked.

"The kid's our age, and I'm guessing Ray must've knocked someone up during college? Ray wouldn't tell me why he's moving to Chicago all of a sudden, but he's gonna be here any day now. Changing schools in the middle of second semester, that's gotta suck ass. I think Ray's all kinds of shook. He didn't even know about this kid, and he's been acting like a baby-ass bitch ever since."

"Wow. Cara Ramirez, your capacity for empathy is truly beyond compare."

"I get to call any nigga that's tryin to get twixt my mama's legs whatever the fuck I want."

I let out a loud bark of laughter. "Fair enough, girl," I said as I shook my head, still giggling, and closed my locker. "He show you a picture? 'Cause Ray's kiiinda fine. Bet his kid is too."

"Girl, gross. And, besides, you got a man," she said with a hint of irritation.

"I *don't*. Just a bunch of crushes. On Curtis, Marvin, Jeremiah—"

"Oh yeah? Does Zeke know that?" Cara interrupted. "Anyway, I gotta get. Can't be late, else Ms. Devries is gonna have my ass. I don't get it—I'm, like, her best student! No one does this math shit like ya girl, but every time I do a little something—"

"It's *because* you're so smart that she's hard on you. She wants you to do well!"

"That's the stupidest shit in the world. Okay, peace, girl," Cara said as she darted up the main hallway.

Passing period was almost over—if I didn't hurry, I was going to be late too. I hurried through the hallway, past the wispy clouds of vape smoke drifting out the bathrooms, past a teacher trying to interrupt two kids making out something fierce, past the comments of a couple guys leaning up against their lockers—

Love seeing you walk, girl!

Damn, she thicc with it!

C'mon, girl, just give me a chance.

I'll treat you better'n Zeke ever could, no cap.

—and was so focused I ran right into Braejon's back, solid as a brick wall, bounced back, and fell to the ground.

"Who the—" Braejon said, confused. "Speak of the devil! Z, it's your girl, man."

Zeke turned around and looked down on me with a smile, that infectious grin that always made me feel better. At least, before the kiss. "Hey, you good?" he asked, extending his hand to help me up.

"We was just talkin about you! Heard the two of you had fun yesterday," Braejon said as Zeke helped me up.

"You mean, on Saturday?" I asked, confused. "For Zeke's birthday? It was nice, yeah. I really gotta get to class though, so—"

"Yeah, *same*," Zeke said, glaring at Braejon.

"Nah, girl, after that. You know what I'm talkin about,"

Braejon said. He made a kissy face at me and laughed. I must've given him a look because he didn't laugh long.

"I'll, uh, catch you guys later. Zeke, don't forget we got a team meeting after school," Braejon said as he took off down the hall, leaving the two of us standing in the intersection.

I whirled around to face Zeke. "What the *hell* was that?" I asked.

"What the hell was what?" he said, his hands up, defensive.

"Zeke, don't."

"I . . . the guys always do that when you're around. They *been*—"

"You're lying," I cut him off. "You told him."

The bell signaling the end of passing period started to chime, its loud electronic siren echoing through the emptying hallways.

"We should, umm, we should get to class probably," he said.

"Oh no, you don't. You're not skipping out on this conversation, no way," I said, the heat rising in my voice. "Who else knows? Who else did you tell?"

"Gen, I didn't—"

"You *did*," I interrupted, moving closer to Zeke as the halls grew quiet. "Did you tell Manny?"

"I, uhh, I told Manny before school. Braejon was during gym. Rinky-Dink was there too," Zeke mumbled.

"That's it? You swear?"

"I swear."

I glared at Zeke. "I'm so mad at you right now. I asked you to do *one* thing, to just keep it quiet. You couldn't even make it a day!"

"Damn, Gen, I'm sorry, jeez. If I knew it was gonna be this big a deal—I mean, people been thinking we're together since forever. What's it matter that people know now?"

"Know what?" I asked, hands on my hips.

Zeke tilted his head and looked at me, confused. "Know about, y'know, *us*?"

I wanted to say, *There is no "us," Zeke. Not the way you think. Not the way you want.*

But I didn't say any of that. He looked like he felt bad enough already, and I hated seeing Zeke upset. Plus, I didn't want him thinking I only said that because I was angry or that I didn't mean it. I needed Zeke to know, in no uncertain terms, *Yes, I mean it.*

Instead, I took a deep breath and said, "My parents are so strict about dating. You know that. And you know how Manny can get, he just talks and talks, and what do you think they'd do if they found out? Grounded the rest of the year, for sure. No party, either—just me, alone and sad in my room on my birthday," I said. I was a much better liar than Zeke, having learned from my father, and he bought it without question.

"Shit, sorry, Gen. I didn't even think about that."

"So you can't just . . . *tell* people, okay? Especially when *we* haven't even talked about it."

Confusion flickered across Zeke's face again. "What do you mean? What's there to talk about?"

"That was your only takeaway from what I said?" I shouted, angrier than I intended. I caught a flicker of movement out of the corner of my eye and turned to see a half-dozen folks crowded around the narrow window of a classroom door nearby, eyes wide, watching and listening to our every word.

"Look, Gen, I'm really, really sorry. I mean it, I messed up, I know. I won't say nothin about nothin, promise."

"Better not," I said, eager to be away from all the peering, leering eyes.

"I'm gonna make it up to you with the party. It's gonna be wild, Gen. I got lights, a dance floor, speakers, and Manny's gonna DJ. Cara says Ray'll slide us donuts and shit on the sly," Zeke said, a grin on his face.

"I mean, that does sound pretty good," I said, relieved we were getting away from the subject of "us," and smiled at Zeke.

"Just you wait. I got an extra-special surprise that'll make your night. It's gonna be perfect!" Zeke called out as he walked off toward his class, waving as he turned the corner.

The smile dropped off my face as soon as he was out of sight. The party *had* sounded good, but the mention of an "extra-special surprise" gave me a nervous, nauseous feeling I couldn't shake.

It was still there, heavy like a rock, when I got home from school that afternoon. I walked into the house, sat on the bench by the front door to remove my shoes, and took a long, deep breath, then another, until I felt the knot in my chest start to unravel.

"Genny-Gen, is that you? Come, I need your eyes," my mom shouted from upstairs.

I got to my feet and trudged up the stairs, my legs weighty with anxiety. I heard soft music as I climbed—some smooth jazz, the kind that put me right to sleep—which blared loud as I opened the door to her home studio.

A canvas eight feet square hung on the wall opposite the window, facing the setting sun. The canvas was a single color, a deep red. At least, it looked that way at first. But as I got closer, I started to see figures in the paint. I found the bodies first, then the faces, and then their empty, hollow eyes, almost imperceptible.

"What do you think? Is it too . . ."

"I love it," I breathed. I got closer and closer to the wall of red until it was all I saw, until it felt like I was tumbling into it.

"I don't know why. It just . . . ," I said, my voice little more than a whisper. "It's anger and passion and hate and love, all at once. Like, all these empty people, they're lost in it. *I* get lost in it. I just want to keep looking, until it almost feels like it's got me trapped. I see a face and I start to think that if I'm not careful, I'll end up just like that, and I know I should just look away, but I can't, or I won't, and now I'm stuck. Cornered," I said. It wasn't until I felt my mom's hand on my shoulder that I realized I was crying.

"Imogen?" she said as she turned me toward her. "What's going on? Did something happen at school?"

"No . . . well, yeah, kinda." I paused. I had a question on the tip of my tongue that I wasn't sure I wanted to ask. "Why's it so hard to be honest about your feelings with the people you care about the most?"

"Oh, is that what this is about?" she said, smiling, wiping her hands on her smock. "First and foremost, yes, you're excited, but don't think for a second you can jump the gun because your birthday's almost here. The day you turn sixteen—and not a day before—is when you're allowed to date. Are we clear?"

I rolled my eyes. "Like I need reminding," I grumbled.

"To answer your question, I know first love can be stressful and confusing and you start second-guessing yourself, but I know what a boy in love looks like and believe me, you don't need to worry, Imogen. That boy's all for you," my mom said.

"Ugh," I groaned, regretting my decision to bring it up. "It's *not* like that! How many times—"

"I was the same with your father," my mom interrupted. "My best friend, your auntie Myra, I kept telling her, 'Girl, I dunno about this Brian guy,' but she knew I *definitely* knew how I felt. I just didn't wanna admit it. You and Zeke, it's the same way."

"Mom, oh my god, will you *stop*?" I said, raising my voice. I shouldn't have been surprised—every time the subject of dating came up, my parents started talking about Zeke.

"He's a catch, Genny-Gen!" my mom said, confusing my anger for embarrassment. "It's a little intimidating, finding your person, but he's so kind, caring, responsible. Loves his family, his friends, his passion. The two of you've got a bright future ahead."

"*I. DON'T. LIKE. ZEKE!*" I shouted, right in her face, louder than I thought my voice could go. My mom's eyes went wide, her eyebrows stretching toward the ceiling, as I charged past her and out the room, slamming the door behind me. I heard some of her paints and brushes clatter to the ground. I felt bad, but only a little, because I was so sick of everyone assuming Zeke was the one for me. He *wasn't*.

I stormed into my bedroom, kicked the door shut, and went straight to my closet. I moved a stack of shoeboxes aside. Behind the wall of shoes was a well-hidden seam in the drywall a foot square. I pushed on the top of the square and the panel opened like a mail slot. I pulled the piece of wall out and set it down on the ground. The hole had always been there, some sort of access panel left by the builders that my parents either forgot or never knew about, behind which, as fate would have it, was a plank of wood the exact dimensions of a composition notebook.

I looked at my secret notebooks, stacked tidy in the compartment. There were dozens, each one labeled and dated along the spine, split into two stacks—I journaled in the red ones; I wrote in the black. Some were thick with sticky notes, others with index cards paper-clipped to the pages, all of them badly worn and bent from use and love. My parents didn't know I liked to write, and I had no interest in telling them. My mom, she'd take it as a sign that I was like her, an *artist,* and would take it upon herself to be my creative mentor and guide. My dad, in the rare event he was home and not out in Vancouver or Los Angeles shooting something, would want to read my stuff and offer "an actor's perspective." Yuck. Because my dad wasn't above checking my computer and my phone, I'd decided it was safer to hide my heart in the walls.

I grabbed the most recent red notebook. It was still fresh, the spine unworn, unbent, and the only entry thus far was about Zeke's birthday.

Zeke really liked his present. I'm so glad!
He's had such a hard year. It sucks to see him
so stressed out. I wish I could help him more,
but . . . I dunno. The way he was looking at me in
the kitchen, for a second there I thought he was
going to . . . eh, never mind. Not worth talking
about. Anyway, my birthday's coming up! Zeke's
going to throw me a party and I'm excited. Mom
and Dad are taking a vacation to some island
somewhere for a few days. They asked if I wanted
to go. I told them I'd rather stay here for my

birthday. I didn't think they'd let me, especially
Dad, but Mom talked him into it 'cause they
haven't been on a vacation together in, like,
FOREVER. So I'll be fending for myself! Meaning,
I'll have to order a lot of food, hahaha. I won't
be cooking, that's for sure. Cooking just isn't
for me. Not my thing, just so much busywork.
Anyway, that's all I got for today. See you later,
notebook.

I jumped down a few lines and let it all out. After that stupid
talk, after storming out of Mom's studio, even after tearing myself
away from that painting, I was still seeing red.

I swear, if one more person says something about
me and Zeke, I'm going to explode. No one ever
listens to me. Mom and Dad sure don't. I've told
them a thousand times, for years, that it's not
like that with Zeke, but they're so effing fixed
on him because they like him. And, I mean, I
like Zeke a lot, as my friend. I guess, on paper, I
should like him. We should be a perfect match or
whatever. Like I can't say he's not good-looking
or whatever. He's tall, confident, sweet, and
he's in great shape, I guess. But, like, it was so
obvious when I kissed him the other day. It just
felt . . . weird. I'm still an idiot for doing it.
Like, what the hell were you thinking, Gen? But

I needed to know. I wish I could talk to someone about it. But I can't talk to Zeke, for obvious reasons. Manny can't keep a secret to save his life. And Cara, well . . . I don't know if she's the most objective on this subject. So I guess all I can do is talk to myself. I'm here for you, Imogen. Aww, thanks, Imogen, I'm here for you, too. It's just . . . what if they're right and I'm wrong? What if Zeke is the one? What if I mess this up and never find my person? What if, what if, what if—so many what-ifs. But this can't be what love is, can it?

I set my pen down and took a breath—blue in, red out—then carefully placed the notebook back on the pile. I pushed the drywall back into place and stacked the shoeboxes back in front of the opening, and even though it was just a little past six, I changed into my pajamas and sprawled out across my bed with *Outlander*.

My mom, for all her faults, respected my space. At dinnertime, she knocked on my door and let me know she was leaving a bowl of food for me. I cracked the door open, grabbed the bowl—she had made chicken fried rice, her specialty—and wolfed it down. I set the dish outside my door, texted thnx ma to her, and lost myself in time with Claire and Jamie and Diana Gabaldon until I drifted off to sleep.

That night, I dreamt I was a baseball in the palm of Zeke's hand. He threw me, a fastball, and I rocketed toward a batter who, I realized as I got close, was *also* Zeke. I flew up into the air, spinning myself nauseous, until I was caught by the center fielder, also Zeke. Everywhere I looked, I saw Zeke, and there was no escaping him. When I woke up the next morning, I heard my words repeating in my head—*This can't be what love is, can it?*

chapter eight
ZEKE

The situation between me and Imogen had been a hot topic of conversation since middle school, and the rumors about our tense moment the day before spread like stink on the wind. Someone had filmed our conversation through the window in the classroom door. There was no audio, but you could see our mouths moving, our hands gesturing, and that was enough to send the haters and the fans alike into a frenzy. Imogen was going to be pissed, but I couldn't help but smile at the fact that most of the comments were rooting for us.

> finallyyyyyyyyyy we *been* shippin
>
> ppl sayin she n Zeke been gettin it in!!
>
> them two is fine-ass #couplegoals
>
> smdh all u bettin against #blacklove
>
> #zekogen

I was distracted all morning and got to school just before the bell rang. I kept my head down and my eyes on my phone as I entered Hampton High and was about to rush down the hall to class when—

"Ezekiel! Zeke Ladoja! Come on in here," Mrs. Dionne called out. She was one of the front office ladies, a tiny raisin of a woman who, if I had to guess, was around 163 years old. Her wrinkles had wrinkles, more texture than a Sally Beauty Supply. She had been at Hampton longer than anyone except Janitor Randall, and as far as I could tell, the two of them were the sole reason the school functioned correctly.

"Boy, you just get bigger and bigger every day," she said, waving from the front office doorway as the bell rang to start first period. "Bet you could just spin me up over your head like I was nothing."

"I bet I could, but I wouldn't wanna hurt you, Mrs. Dionne."

"Hah," she laughed. "You couldn't hurt me in a million years. When I was a little girl, this cracker—"

"Virginia! Language!" a second woman's voice shouted from inside the office. That was Ms. Limm. She was much younger, much newer, and much stricter than Mrs. Dionne. No one dispensed more in-school discipline than Tina Limm. When it came to detentions and suspensions, she was putting up LeBron numbers.

Mrs. Dionne looked at me and rolled her eyes. "Oh, stuff it, you old coot," she said. She turned and entered the office, gesturing for me to follow.

"Old coot? Me?" Ms. Limm said.

"Yes, you! I'm trying to talk to Ezekiel! Why don't you go swipe for a man or whatever it is I see you doing when you think I'm not looking?" she said, 'cause Mrs. D a straight *savage*. "Principal's got a special task for you, Zeke. Just stay right here, baby."

Mrs. Dionne returned a few moments later escorted by a tall dark-skinned boy with a tight fade and Malcolm X glasses. I knew, just by looking at his build and the way he moved, that he played ball and played it well. "This young man's name is Trevor Cook," Mrs. Dionne said, patting the boy on the arm. "He's a new student, a sophomore like you, just transferred up here from . . ."

"Houston, Texas, ma'am," Trevor said.

"That's right, Houston. He'll be joining us, and the principal wants you to help him find his first class, show him the ropes, all of that. Trevor, Zeke's one of our best. Honest, hardworking, a good kid. He'll set you right."

"I really appreciate y'all's help and everything, Mrs. Dionne, Ms. Limm. I'm very grateful," Trevor said.

"Such a sweet boy. Now, go on, you two get going," Mrs. Dionne said.

I put my hand out and Trevor shook it. He had the rough, calloused palm of a batter.

"Good to meet you," he said.

The moment we stepped into the hallway, I came right out and asked him.

"How long you been hitting?"

Trevor laughed. It was deep, bass-heavy, from his belly, the kind of laugh that gets folks laughing along, which I did. "Boutta ask you the same thing. Since the first day I could catch and swing. You?"

"Hell, I came out the womb knowing how to throw good," I said.

Trevor laughed. "Nah, for real though, I sorta know who you are. My . . . Ray told me about you."

"Ray?" I asked. "The only Ray I know is Ray over at Pappy's."

"That's the one," Trevor said.

"What, you like a cousin or a nephew or something? I didn't know Dee and Pappy had any other family, thought it was always just the three of them," I asked.

Trevor closed his eyes and pressed his fingers to the bridge of his nose. He rubbed the spots where his glasses rested against his skin as his whole demeanor changed, like he had deflated all of a sudden.

"Sorry, I say something?"

"Nah, it's not that. Truth is, Ray's my dad. He found out a couple months ago. I found out after my ma died early last year. Ray didn't want me to go around tellin, but I'm not aboutta start lyin to folks my first day here."

I froze up, mind and body both. "Man . . . ," I said, searching for the words. "I'm . . . I'm sorry."

Trevor shook his head. "It's—she was . . . she wasn't great. I was with my grandparents mostly, but they're getting old, and my grandpa's mind's starting to go. When my mom overdosed, they found some stuff about Ray. Made it pretty clear he was the guy. Ma always told me my dad was some dude who bounced right after she told him she was pregnant, but it turns out, she just kept me a secret, and only she knew why and now she's gone," Trevor said with a dry laugh. "Sorry, I just dumped a lot of shit on you, man. You don't even know me like that, I should've—"

I held my hand up to cut him off. "First of all, we both play ball, so I *do* know you like that. Second, my dad's got cancer. It's been bad. We don't know how it's gonna go. He had a big surgery last week to take out some of his colon. They might still have to remove the rest later, but we won't know that until after his next round of chemo. The only good news is that he's finally leaving the hospital tomorrow, except I also just found out we're broke and behind on our bills and my mom's tryna hide it.

"So, now we know each other like that," I said.

Trevor chuckled. "Shit, well, I guess we do. Sorry, fam, about everything. That's tough. If there's ever anything you need—"

"I appreciate it, but . . ." I trailed off as an idea occurred to me. "Actually, now that I think about it, you being here makes what I gotta do a *whole* lot easier."

"Which is what?" Trevor asked, confused.

I paused to take a breath. "I'm taking the season off."

Trevor's eyes went wide. "The way Ray was talking, he made it sound like you're a goddamn legend. Calls you Goldenarm."

"No shit?" I said, laughing. "That name's terrible."

"That's what I keep saying," Trevor said. "So, why?"

"It's the money thing. Mom's working doubles more days than not, and it still ain't enough. I gotta do something to help. I can always pick baseball back up once my family's okay."

"Here I was, ready to argue, but I can't argue with that. That's real nigga shit right there," Trevor said, dapping me up.

"I was nervous for the team, leaving and all, but now—"

"Hold up. You don't even know how good I am."

I stepped back and looked him over. "Nah, I think I do. I think you got it."

"At a glance?"

"Am I wrong?"

"I guess we'll find out," Trevor said.

We grinned at each other.

"Aight, let me show you where your classes are at. Give me your schedule," I said. We walked and talked while I pointed out the doors to his classrooms. I showed him where the library was, which bathrooms to avoid, and by the time the tour was done, it was almost second period.

"You know where to go then, right?" I asked.

Trevor nodded. "Bet, appreciate it, boss."

"Any questions before we split?"

"Just one, but you can't laugh," Trevor said.

"Why would I laugh?"

"Do y'all have any sci-fi/fantasy or Dungeons & Dragons clubs here?"

I laughed. Pretty loud, too.

"Man, I told you not to laugh," Trevor said, and play-shoved me.

"Couldn't help myself," I said, still chuckling. "Nah, we don't, but I know a guy. You'll meet him soon enough."

"One of your homies?"

"Eh, sorta. He's on the team, but we're not tight like that. The real homies, you'll meet all them at lunch. Well, probably. Manny might be in detention. On any given day, it's like a one-in-three chance. Homie's allergic to shutting up. One of those who makes the teachers mad as much as he makes them laugh. And then there's Cara, she's cooler than all of us. Dope as fuck, the boricua queen up in here."

"The what?" Trevor asked.

"Boricua," I repeated, but Trevor still looked confused. "What, you ain't got Puerto Ricans down in Texas? Just Mexicans?"

"Nah, not just Mexicans. Guatemalans, Nicaraguans, Colombians, Hondurans. But I could count the number of Puerto Ricans I've met on one hand, if that. What's it mean?"

"What, boricua? Best I can tell, it's Puerto Rican for 'baddie,' at least the way she uses it," I said. "She's fierce and mad fine, but don't tell her I said so. She'd kick my ass for talking about her like that."

"Like what? It's forgotten." Trevor smiled. "So, she your girl or something?"

"Cara? Nah. I mean, I wouldn't say no, but nah, my girl's someone else. Not official yet, but soon. It's complicated, but I'm not supposed to say nothing to no one yet."

"Oh yeah? What's up with it?"

"Her parents got rules. We've known each other since we were little, and I think she's afraid to admit she's feelin me, honest," I said.

"You sure she just ain't feelin you like that at all? 'Cause, man, there was this girl Cassandra I was tight with since jump and I thought we was meant to be, but we weren't. I guess that's an upside to living here now, never have to have another uncomfortable conversation with her." Trevor laughed until he saw that I wasn't.

"Yeah, I'm sure," I said in a voice with more heat than I expected. My body was tense and I realized my fists were clenched at my side.

The moment might've become awkward, but we were interrupted by the bell for passing period. I let my anger go as a deafening mass of students flooded the hallways.

"I'm on the other side of the school, gotta jet. Find you before lunch?" I called out over the noise.

"No doubt," he said as I dapped him up and took off.

chapter nine
IMOGEN

"You don't know how ready I am to turn the *fuck* up at your party," Cara told me on our way to the cafeteria. "It's been a hot minute since I got to just go all out and throw this ass back and get wild."

"You are so extra," I laughed. "You know any new details?"

Cara shook her head. "Your guess is as good as mine."

I sighed. "I hate surprises. He should know that by now."

We had just reached the cafeteria entrance when Cara stopped dead in her tracks.

"Fucking fuck me," she said.

"Uh, what?"

"I fucking forgot Mrs. Young wanted me to come talk to her about the solo."

"It's hard to believe that you can sing so beautifully with such a filthy mouth," I said.

"Har har. Look, I'll be back in, like, ten minutes, okay? Wait for me?"

"And delay my consumption of Fred Hampton High's award-winning options in the cafeteria? Oh, if I must."

"You're so weird. You know that, right?"

I nodded. "Go on and hurry up. I'll just chill here. We should probably wait for Zeke and Manny anyway, assuming Manny's not in detention already."

"Bet," Cara said as she raced off down the hallway and almost slammed into Mr. Randall, the head custodian, along the way.

"Ramirez! No runnin in the hall!" Mr. Randall shouted, though he might as well've been talking to himself.

He was an older man who didn't look old. Beneath the hard years and hard work that hunched his back and slowed his gait, he was still handsome. The garbage smell that accompanied him made it easy—and common—for everyone to dismiss or ignore him. It never sat right with me, because he was very kind and extremely well-read, and I liked him a lot.

"If it ain't Miss Parker," he said, his voice like sand slathered with honey, as he passed me. "What you been readin, girl?"

"Hey, Mr. Randall!" I said, breathing through my mouth. "I picked up that book you recommended, *The Mothers*. It's next on my list! Sounds really good. But the next *Outlander* book's coming out soon, so I'm rereading from the start."

"You still on that? Makes sense, you got love on the brain, I hear. Good for you and that Zeke boy. Saw it coming since y'all got here last year. Reminded me of my wife. We met in high school too, except we didn't get together till long, long after, nearly twenty years after. Thirty-two great years together, then she passed."

I sighed. "It's really, *really* not like that, Mr. Randall. Zeke and I are not together," I said.

"Huh. That's not what every bathroom schoolwide's sayin. I've been seeing 'Zeke + Imogen' and 'Z + I' and 'Ladoja Parker' and 'Zekogen.' It's everywhere, girl. You and him ain't—"

"Nope, we're not. And we're not going to be either." There must've been some stank on my words, because he stopped smiling.

"Hmm." Mr. Randall stood there, thinking. "I'll get right on cleaning up all them graffitis everywhere then."

"What?" I was caught off guard.

"I can paint over 'em, no trouble. Nothin worse'n people spreading news that ain't news and telling stories on you that ain't true. Especially when they're about your virtue."

I gagged a little at the word "virtue," but I was touched. Mr. Randall was the only person who believed me when I said I didn't like Zeke. And not only was he on my side, but he was willing to make extra work for himself, just to help me out. Garbage smell or not, I needed to hug him. I needed him to hug *me*.

"Thank you for believing me," I said, sniffling as I threw myself at him.

"Hey now, it's gonna be fine," Mr. Randall said in a soft voice. "Don't ever let anyone pressure you into loving who you don't love, Miss Parker. I'll take care of all them writings. And *you* take care of *you*, okay?"

I felt tears pushing their way out of my eyes, felt their warm heat as they dripped off my jawline. I didn't understand why it was so hard for everyone else to do what Mr. Randall did so easily. "Th-thank you, Mr. Randall," I said, and took a seat on a nearby bench.

The moment was interrupted by the loud patter of sprinting feet slapping against linoleum floor. Mr. Randall spun around and saw Cara skid to a stop.

"Ramirez, I just told you! No running!" Mr. Randall shouted.

"Man, come on, walkin's too damn slow," Cara said.

"As slow as sitting still in detention? Now, *walk*."

"Yeah, whatever," she said as she stomped toward me. *"No running!"* Cara said in a mocking tone. "Old stanky-ass."

"Don't be rude. He's very nice," I said.

"Ow, fuck!" Cara screamed so loud and sudden I jumped up from my seat.

"What! What is it?"

"This damn *knife* in my back," Cara said, grinning.

"Oh, screw you, Cara."

"Look, you know I'm bi, and I'm flattered, but I just have to say no. For the friendship."

"Cara! I'm being serious. Don't mess with Mr. Randall. He's . . . he's doing me a very big and very kind favor, and I won't let anyone bad-mouth him," I said, and sat back down.

"Yeesh, okay, sorry!" Cara threw her hands up. "What's the favor?"

"He's gonna paint over all the graffiti about me and Zeke in the bathrooms, 'cause I told him we're not together."

Cara was ready with a smart remark but caught herself. She looked down the hall in the direction of Mr. Randall's office. "For real? Just like that?"

I nodded.

"Then from this day on, anyone who tries it with that nigga's gonna answer to me and mine," Cara said. "I can promise you that. Mr. Randall's a real one."

"Told you. Why were you running, anyway?"

"Oh!" Cara jumped up from the bench we were on. "I got big news!"

I sat up, excited. "You found out about the surprise?"

"What? No. No, I saw the new kid," Cara said.

"Oh." I couldn't have been more disappointed. "Okay, so what?"

"Gen. He's, like, *really* cute."

I rolled my eyes. "You don't have the most discerning taste. You think most people are really cute."

"Except White dudes."

"Obviously. Anyway, is that all?"

"*Is that all?*" Cara mocked me. "Look, don't take my word for it. Here they come." She pointed down the hallway.

Zeke was walking backward, talking and laughing with the boy opposite him. I couldn't make out any details with Zeke in the way, except that he laughed with his whole belly and I liked the way it sounded.

"Zeke!" Cara shouted. "Bring him over here!"

Zeke spun around at Cara's voice, saw us, and made a beeline for our bench. And as he did, two things happened.

The first was that I learned, without a shred of doubt, that I wasn't in love with Zeke. I wasn't even in *like* with Zeke. There was nothing there but the warm feeling I had for my best friend.

And I knew that because of the *second* thing that happened: when I saw the new kid and he saw me, I got goose bumps, and when we smiled at each other, I felt weightless. He was a little shorter than Zeke, dark-skinned like me, with perfect teeth and the most kissable lips I'd ever seen. He had on a pair of glasses with clear frames and gold edges that gave him a real serious, passionate, confident Malcolm X vibe that had me thinking *thoughts*. They lent a kind of emotional weight to his face that made him look older than the other boys in our class, and behind the lenses were these brown eyes I wanted to stare into forev—

"Gen!" Zeke said, clapping his hands. "She's like this, always spacing out, daydreaming and whatnot. She reads all these weird books about time travelers in Scotland and—"

"Oh, you into *Outlander*?" the new kid said as he turned toward me. "That's dope. I read the first two, I love stories with time travel—"

"Yeah, Trevor here's a huge nerd, just like you," Zeke cut in.

"A lot of sci-fi and fantasy, yeah. What can I say, the real world's just a little too *normal* for my taste. But, uhh, yeah, I'm Trevor. Trevor Cook," he said, extending his hand.

"Oh, uh, um. Hi. I'm I'mogen. Err, I mean, Imogen. Imogen Parker. Welcome to the Hamptons," I said as I placed my hand in his. I wondered if he could feel my pulse. If he could tell my heart was racing. If he knew how hard I was kicking myself for that stupid Hamptons joke. His hand was warm and strong, and though the moment only lasted a second, it felt to me like an entire universe had been born between our kissing palms.

"So, yeah, that's Imogen, and this is Cara, who I told you about. Since Manny ain't here, it looks like he got detention, so you'll meet him a little later. But right now, I gotta go face Coach," Zeke said with a heavy sigh.

"Appreciate you giving me the lay of the land," Trevor said. "Just remind him, he got the H-Town Hitter to help out now too. Tell him I'll hold down the fort till you get back."

"Bet, homie. So good to have another brother around who really knows how to play ball," Zeke said before turning to me and Cara. "So, can you guys walk him through how lunch works and everything? I don't know how long I'ma be gone for."

"Wait, wait, are you quitting? Is it official?" Cara asked. "Tío's giving you the job?"

Zeke gave a slow, sad nod. "Not quitting, just taking the season off. And yeah, me and Manny popped by the shop this morning. Jojo pulled me inside, and we did a quick interview. So, yeah, it's official. I guess we're about to be coworkers, eh?"

"Fuck yeah," Cara said, thrumming with excitement. "Don't worry about Country Boy here. We got him, right, Gen?"

"What? Oh. Yeah. Yep," I stammered. I gave Zeke a quick hug. "Good luck! It's going to go fine, I know it."

"Yeah, well, we'll see. I'll let you know how it went on the walk home," Zeke said as he hugged me back, then trudged toward the gym, his steps heavy and purposeful.

Cara grinned from ear to ear as she watched Zeke leave, then whirled around and marched her way into the cafeteria with me and Trevor in tow. Trevor and I—I liked the sound of that *so* much: Trevor and I—followed behind her. We tried to step through the doorway at the same time, bumping into each other.

"Ha ha, sorry," he said.

"I didn't mind," I murmured, too low for Trevor to hear, or so I thought.

"All you need to know about the cafeteria," Cara said, shouting over the noise of the lunchroom, "is that the food is shit, the lunch staff's dope, the ice cream sandwiches are legit, and Mondays are when we get chicken nuggets, aka the only food here worth eating."

Trevor leaned over to me as we walked behind Cara, still giving her tour, and said, "I didn't mind either."

I looked at Trevor, my mouth wide with surprise. He looked right back at me. And then he winked and the entire world tilted on its axis, just for me, as I fell and fell *hard*.

chapter ten
ZEKE

Coach was sitting at his desk, drinking coffee out of a metal thermos bigger than my head. He was leaning back in his chair, feet propped up on his desk, watching videos from last year's finals on a small TV mounted on the wall.

The door was open, but I knocked anyway. "Hey, uh, Coach? Got a second?" I said.

"We were *so* close," Coach said, and waved me in. He pointed at the screen. "Who'da thought that string-bean White boy could hit like that?" We watched, again, for the umpteenth time, a ruddy-faced North Sider with scrawny noodle arms connect on my fastball. It still hurt to watch. "But, hey, this year, we got 'em, right?"

My mouth went dry as Coach paused the video and turned to face me. Coach was a good guy, and I knew he'd understand my decision, but still, my pulse quickened.

"Uhh, so, about that . . ." I cleared my throat. *Just be straight-forward, like Gen said,* I thought. "Well, Coach, the thing is, I need . . . to take the season off."

"Yeah," Coach said with a sigh. "Had a feeling."

"You . . . had a feeling?" I asked. "You're not mad?"

"Of course not, Zeke."

"But you don't even know why I'm taking the season off."

"Because you need to help your family. My guess, Vanessa needs more help around the house with Samson but she's already stretched thin, so you've decided to step up and get a job to help pay the bills, probably at Jojo's spot. Am I right?"

I stared at him, mouth open. "You must be some kind of mind reader."

"Kid, you're about as subtle as a mariachi band. I know you. I know your family. I saw Samson the other day, saw how he was doing. He's having a tough time. So's Vanessa. I figured this might happen, sometime, because you're that kind of kid.

"So, if you need to quit to make sure your folks are okay, I'm not gonna stop you. You're our best player, but you won't be play-ing your best if you're in your head about your family. Besides, the team's not going anywhere, and who knows, maybe something'll change before the season ends and you'll be able to come back and finish it out. I always got a spot for you. Hey now, Zeke, don't cry. It's okay," Coach said.

I hadn't realized I was crying. I put my hands to my face and they came back wet and tear-warm.

"Come here, kiddo," Coach said as he got up from his desk and opened his arms to me. I moved, almost on instinct, into his hug.

It reminded me of the hugs my dad gave, before the cancer left him weak and bony and insubstantial. "I'm proud of you, Zeke. Takes a real man to do what you're doing. To be there for family, to set aside the game for the things that are really, really important."

"Thanks, Coach," I mumbled as I cried into his shirt. "Sorry about . . . all this," I said as I pulled away from him. "And . . . can you not tell anyone? I wanna break the news to people myself."

"I won't say a word until you give me the go-ahead. And don't worry about us, okay? Focus on you and your family," Coach said.

I nodded, drying my eyes with my sleeves. "So, you hear there's a new kid? Trevor Cook? I was showing him around. Back home they called him the H-Town Hitter. I don't know if Houston-good is the same as Chicago-good, but dude can play, I can tell."

"Hell, if that's the case, we won't even need you," Coach said with a smirk on his face. "You got somewhere to be? You need to eat?"

I shook my head. It wasn't chicken nuggets day, so it didn't matter none to me.

"Good, then let's me and you talk shop a minute. This new kid, he says he can hit, but can he throw?"

I shrugged and took a seat across from Coach. "He's got the build for it. He's not gonna be as good as me, of course, but I think he'll be better than anyone else we got."

We spent the rest of lunch theorizing on how to fill the gaps I was going to leave in the team's offense, right up until the lunch bell rang.

"Aight, Coach, I gotta get to math," I said as I got up from the chair. "Thanks for being cool about all this. You don't know how much it means to me. And, uh, can you not say anything to my folks? My mom, she was against me getting a job, but this is something I feel I gotta do. I'll tell them myself, when the time's right."

"Anytime, Z, anytime. Hey, one more question for you before you go: What's this I hear about you and a certain someone?" Coach asked with a sly grin.

I smiled. "Sorry, I don't kiss and tell."

Coach punched my shoulder. "Might not be scoring on the field, but off the field? Attaboy! About damn time, you ask me. Don't know what took her so long."

I didn't tell Coach about my argument with Imogen. I had been trying my best not to think about the argument at all, in fact. "Yeah, well, she's worth it. I'm putting together a huge party for her birthday coming up, and I'm gonna ask her out and we're going to make it official," I said.

"Well, you know I'm rooting for you, Zeke. Always have, always will. Go get her, son."

"Thanks, Coach, for everything," I said, then dashed out of the office and toward Ms. Devries's classroom, slipping in just before the bell stopped ringing.

After last period let out, I made for the front doors to find Imogen. We almost always walked home together. We used to walk to school together too, but she preferred to be alone in the mornings, said she liked starting the day off quiet. I stood around for a few minutes, waiting for her to show, and texted her when she didn't. A couple minutes later, I heard Manny and Cara approaching, talking loud as hell.

"Man, detention is so damn boring," Manny said.

"Then stop saying stupid shit and getting in trouble," Cara said.

"I didn't even say anything this time!"

"The day Manny stops saying stupid shit is the day I become a Cubs fan," I said as they came into view.

"Et tu, Ladoja?" Manny said as he dapped me up.

"How was the clink?" I asked.

"Same ol', same ol'. Bet Axel ten dollars in rock-paper-scissors."

"And?"

Manny held up a twenty and grinned. "His dumb ass went double or nothin on me."

"Hell yeah, my man," I said, and gave him a high five.

"So, how was Trevor? He get adjusted okay?" I asked Cara.

"Who's Trevor? That's a nerd's name. He a nerd?" Manny asked.

Cara snickered. "Yeah, it was good. He's cool. And yes, Manny, he is a nerd, and he's still a million times cooler than you."

"Hey, I never said nerds can't be cool. Don't go putting words in my mouth."

"Yeah, the last thing you need is more words in your mouth," I said, laughing as Cara giggled and Manny frowned. "You seen Gen?"

Cara shook her head. "Nope," she said. "Want to walk with us?"

"Yo, count me out, cuzzo," Manny said. "I'm picking some gear up for the party. Axel and Yovani's older brother Miguel's coming with the sound equipment I'm after."

"Then come with me to the shop?" Cara said. "You need to pick up your uniform anyway."

I looked around to make sure I hadn't missed Imogen in some dark corner, then sighed. "Yeah, I guess."

"Aww, come on, don't be so glum. I know Manny's your everything, but I think I'm pretty damn good company," Cara said.

"Who the fuck says 'glum'?" Manny snorted.

I checked my texts to see if Imogen had responded, but nothing. That was unlike her.

"You coming?" Cara asked as she held open the front doors.

"Yeah, I'm right behind you," I said. We talked as we walked, but I didn't hear a word she said because my mind was elsewhere, puzzling over Imogen's absence and her silence.

chapter eleven
IMOGEN

Trevor and I ended up in the same class for final period: honors English. It was, of course, my favorite class, taught by my favorite teacher, Ms. Granson. But not even she and the nightmarish but beautifully rendered details of Bigger Thomas's life in *Native Son* could draw my attention away from the exquisite sculpture that was Trevor Cook's face. I think that, somehow, Ms. Granson knew what she was doing, seating Trevor next to me. I'd need to thank—

"Well, Ms. Parker? We're waiting," Ms. Granson said.

I felt my cheeks go hot with embarrassment. "Sorry, I—what'd you say?"

Ms. Granson shook her head. "Do you think he's guilty of murder?"

"Well, he killed her, didn't he?" Dink shouted from the back.

"Yeah, but—" Trevor started to say, then stopped himself and raised his hand.

Ms. Granson smiled at him. "You can just talk, Mr. Cook. What's on your mind? You know the book?"

Trevor nodded. "Yes, ma'am. I read it last year. And *American Hunger*, too," he said, then swiveled in his seat so he could look at Dink on his left, Ms. Granson on his right, and me in front of him. Every time his eyes swept across me, I shivered.

"Like, the whole thing's about Bigger never even having a choice. From the minute he took that job and set foot in that house, the only result there was ever going to be was conflict, and because of the racial power structure in this country, that conflict was only ever going to end one way."

Ms. Granson's face lit up. "*Excellent* understanding of the book, Trevor. Anyone have comments on what Trevor just said?"

I could've kept staring at Trevor, but something didn't sit right with me about what he had said. "So you're saying he had no free will, no agency? That he *had* to do these things? Did he *have* to murder Bessie, too?

"Like, I get it, he was in a constant state of volatile, destructive fury because of racism and prejudice. But ask any woman in this room if she's ever had to face down the volatile, destructive fury of a man catcalling her on the street or threatening her space or just giving messed-up looks and gestures, and you'll get only yeses." Heads nodded, including Ms. Granson's. "But you don't see us out here murkin men left and right, saying we *had* to because of the way the world's set up. That's a cop-out."

Some of the girls cheered and Ms. Granson even gave me a bit of applause, but it was Trevor's response I was most interested in. In the moment between when I stopped speaking and when he and I made eye contact, I saw my life flash before my eyes, a life in which Trevor hated me for showing him up on his first day. And then our eyes met, and in his all I saw was curiosity, awe, and respect.

He opened his mouth to say something else, but the bell cut him off.

"All right, everyone! You're reading James Baldwin's critique of the book for Friday, got it? Don't come unprepared!" Ms. Granson called out as the class emptied of students.

"So, you're, like, mad smart," Trevor said as we packed up and walked out of the classroom. "I'd never thought of that, but you're completely right. Here I was thinking you only cared about *Outlander*."

I laughed. "I'm a well-read young woman, I'll have you know. Just because I *also* read historical romance fantasy doesn't mean I'm uncultured," I said with sarcastic pomp as I headed for my locker.

"Ah, excuse me, mademoiselle." Trevor gave me a bow.

"They make 'em weird down in Texas, huh," I said.

"Nah, I'm weird everywhere I go. Not a lot of places a brother playin Dungeons & Dragons ain't a little weird," he said.

"Oh *wow*, you play Dungeons & Dragons? Should I even be seen with you?" I joked, grabbing my coat out of my locker.

"Don't knock it till you try it," Trevor said as he led us out the nearest door, one of the school's side entrances.

I laughed as we stepped outside. "Oh, which way are you going?"

Trevor looked around, then pulled out his phone. "Uhh . . . ," he mumbled as he searched for something. "Sorry, still don't—the address . . ." The screen on his phone suddenly went dark. "Great. And now it's dead."

I laughed. "Boy, you gotta get it together. C'mon, I know the way to Ray's."

"You sure?"

"Yeah, I walk the same way to get home sometimes," I lied. "It's cool."

"Bet, I appreciate it, miss lady." Trevor gave me a nod, then followed after me. "Dungeons & Dragons is really just cooperative storytelling. You and a bunch of friends, bouncing off each other, writing a story together. I could run a game for everyone, just to give it a shot. I bet you'd love it."

"Storytelling, huh . . . ," I said, trailing off. I was quiet for a couple seconds, lost in thought. Then I decided to take a risk.

"If I tell you something," I said, "you gotta keep it a secret, okay?"

"Whatever it is, it's safe with me. I swear it," he said. He stopped walking and held out his pinky finger, a gesture that seemed so silly coming from him that I started giggling. "What! A pinky promise is the realest promise there is," Trevor insisted.

I was still laughing too hard to say anything, but I put my pinky finger out too. Our fingers touched, intertwined. It was below freezing outside, but in that moment, I was red-hot. A rush of electric heat started at my fingertips and spread in every direction, to the crown of my head and the soles of my feet. I wasn't laughing anymore. I was just standing, tingling.

"So, uhh . . . the secret?" Trevor asked after a beat.

"Oh! So, you were talking about storytelling. And . . . I write stories. I write a lot, actually. It's the thing I do the most. I've got, like, twenty notebooks of stories and a completed novel that's terrible. Writing's my favorite thing. The only time I really ever feel entirely myself is when I'm lost in the pages, seeing where the characters take me," I said.

The words tumbled out of my mouth, and I felt like I was rambling, like I should stop, but Trevor was looking at me like I was the most interesting person in the world.

"I've never . . . no one knows about them. Except you now," I said, breaking eye contact.

"Hey," Trevor said. "Thank you for telling me about something you love so much. Can I ask why've you kept it a secret? I think it's cool as hell that you're a writer."

"A writer, hah," I said. "I'm not—"

"You filled up twenty notebooks—you're a writer!"

"I have to publish something first," I said. "I keep it a secret because, I don't know. It feels super personal, like, that's *me* right there—the realest me there is. Everyone's got these expectations. My mom's an artist, and I know if I say anything about it to her, she's going to flip from being my mom to being my editor, and I don't want that. And my dad, he's an actor. I've heard how harsh he can be on the scripts he's reading. I think he'd tear me apart.

"It's just like . . . they want me to act like *this*, accomplish *that*, get *this* award, be with *that* person. And, I don't know, maybe it feels like, if they never know who I really am, they can't hurt the real me with all their pressure. And what's in my stories . . . a lot of them are . . ." I paused. I didn't want to tell him. I was afraid he'd laugh at me.

"They're what?" Trevor asked. He looked so interested, so earnest, and I knew I wanted to tell him everything . . . so I did.

"They're love stories," I said, shy. "There's some weird stuff too, like space travel and aliens, but mostly, they're about people falling in love."

"Why would I laugh? That's dope as hell," Trevor said. "So, your folks, I get. But why don't you want anyone else knowing? Not even your squad?"

"I just know Manny and his big mouth would probably spread it around. Cara thinks romance is stupid and she'd make fun of me. And Zeke . . . it's—"

"What's up with the two of you, anyway? People today, they talk about you and him like you're joined at the hip," Trevor said.

"Me and Zeke? We—oh shit!"

"What's wrong?"

"We were gonna walk home together." I pulled out my phone and saw he'd texted half an hour ago. I tapped out a quick reply and told him my mom had dragged me off to some art gallery and I completely forgot. It wasn't my best lie, but it'd have to do. "Ugh, I hope he's not mad."

"I don't get how anyone could be mad at you," Trevor said.

I felt that roller-coaster feeling in my belly, and my face went hot. "Yeah, well, you've only known me one day."

"And it's been a great day!" Trevor grinned. "So, you were saying? About Zeke? When he was showing me around, he was talking about someone he'd had his eye on a long time. Said it was complicated. Said they were afraid to admit their feelings for him. So . . . that you?"

"Ugh," I groaned. "This is all my fault, I'm such an idiot."

"Hey, hey now," Trevor said, his voice soft. "Don't be so—"

"I never should have kissed him," I blurted out. "It was a couple days ago. I just wanted to see if there was something there or not, once and for all. And just like I thought, I felt nothing. Absolutely nothing."

Trevor was quiet. The silence was heavy, crushing. I couldn't believe I had just told Trevor *everything* about me, all at once. He was going to think I was a complete psycho. I mean, I just talked about kissing a different guy a few days ago right to his face! Our very first walk after school was also going to be our last, because of me.

"So . . . ," Trevor said. I braced for the rest of his sentence, for the excuse that he needed to be somewhere else because he'd realized I was a lunatic. "You doing okay? Y'all talk about it?"

Trevor stopped walking and gazed at me with soft eyes. There was nothing there but kindness and care. I couldn't help but keep talking.

"No," I said as I kicked a clump of slush up into the air. "He's already dealing with so much. His dad's sick. His mom's exhausted. They're struggling to pay for things. It just . . . it just feels like it'd be too much to put on him. Just another thing to make him sad, and he's already . . . I just want him to feel okay, you know? He's my best friend.

"Like, I used to get these really, really bad panic attacks before I started taking medicine. Every time I did, if Zeke was around, he'd talk me through it. He'd bore me out of anxiety by going on and on and on about baseball. Or he'd breathe with me. If he wasn't around, I'd call him instead. Even if it was the middle of the night, he always answered."

"Yeah, but I asked if *you're* doing okay," Trevor said, and my heart fluttered.

"I just don't know what to do. I don't want to hurt him," I said, tears in my eyes.

I felt my chest tightening up, my breath quickening, my throat closing. Before I could go for my inhaler, Trevor stepped up close to me and pulled me into a hug. I felt our heartbeats—mine jackhammer-fast, his calm and steady—and we stood together like that until my heart and his beat the same rhythm together and—

"Get a room!" someone shouted out of the window of a car that looked familiar, though I couldn't place it, and sliced right through the mood. We broke apart, suddenly shy, which we hid under our laughter.

"I guess we have been here a while, huh," Trevor said, a nervous smile on his face. "Sorry, I hope that was okay. I used to get panic attacks too. After my . . ." He trailed off, then shook his head. "Never mind—you okay?"

His voice was so tender, so soothing. "Yeah. Yeah, I'm okay." I was so much better than okay—I was falling in love. With the way his arms felt around me, the way he smelled when we were pressed up close, the way we fit together—I was falling for all of it. All of him.

"Guess we should get going," Trevor said, and we continued walking in a comfortable silence for a couple minutes before he spoke again. "For whatever it's worth, I think you should tell him. Before things get any worse, you know?"

"Yeah, I know, you're right. I think . . . after my birthday party, I'm going to talk to him. I don't want to make everything awkward right before that."

"Hold up, when's your birthday party?"

"It's next Saturday. It's going to be a huge party. Put your number in my phone, I'll text you the details."

"Dope, a proper northern party. Let's see how y'all do it up here," Trevor laughed, then got serious. "Hey, next time you have a panic attack, you can call me, too. Anytime, okay? And whenever you feel up for it, I'd love to read your writing. But no pressure. Just know that I'm here, yeah?"

I nodded, and for the first time ever, the thought of sharing my stories didn't terrify me. For the first time ever, I felt like I had found someone I could share *anything* with. I didn't know why. I couldn't explain in a million years how I felt so safe with Trevor so quickly. I just did.

chapter twelve
IMOGEN

"Hey, girl, what's crackalackin?" Cara said when she answered her phone that night. "Where you been at? You wasn't around at the end of school. Did you get the picture I sent of Zeke in his Jojo's uniform? I gave him so much shit and he couldn't say nothin back 'cause, technically, I'm his supervisor. *I have the power!* Like He-Man, you remember?"

I was nervous, chewing my lip, quiet on the other end. I was the one who'd called her, but my words were stuck and I didn't know what to say.

"Um, hello? Gen? You butt-dial me with that big ol' booty?" Cara joked, before her voice turned serious. "Hey, Gen, for real, you okay?"

"Sorry, I'm . . . I'm okay," I said with a heavy breath.

"You don't *sound* okay."

"Yeah, I'm just . . . I have a lot on my mind."

"You think too much, you know that? You always got *somethin* on your mind, buggin you so bad you can't think right. You need to relax. I can get you some gummies if you want. Braejon's got the hookup, just say the word!"

I let out a little laugh. "No thanks. Look, can you keep a secret?"

"Of course. Cara 'Tight Lips' Ramirez at your service," she said.

"Uhh, might wanna rethink that one, C."

"I *said* what I *said*," she laughed, an infectious giggle that got me going too. "So, what's up?"

"So . . . I think I'm falling for Trevor," I said. "Hell, girl, I already done fell."

I held the phone away from my ear as Cara squealed in delight. "Gen! Tell. Me. *Everything.*"

"Well, you didn't see me at the end of school 'cause his phone died and he didn't know how to get to Ray's, so I walked him there and then I went home. I swear, Cara, I've *never* felt like this with anyone. Like, I just told him everything. I felt so comfortable with him. It wasn't awkward, I didn't feel self-conscious, I didn't wanna hide when he gave me sexy eyes—"

"He gave you sexy eyes?" Cara asked.

"I mean, I don't know if he knew they were sexy eyes but, girl, they were. We talked about books and life and he makes me feel like . . . I don't even know," I said with a blissful sigh.

"Damn, that was *quick*," she said. "I mean, I could smell vibes the second y'all started talkin bout your nerdy little books."

"Like you aren't out here reading Scully/Mulder fanfics like it's your damn job."

"Excuse me, but that's *high art*," she said.

"Oh, high art? What was that one you showed me? 'I Want

to Believe (in Us),' I think it was? I remember one sentence, and I quote, '"The truth is down here," Scully said, pushing Mulder down between her legs.'"

"And? It was hot as hell! Clappin cheeks every two pages. Anyway, what's the problem? Nice country boy like him, fine as hell, go on, get it, Gen."

"Come on, you *know* what the problem is," I said, annoyed.

"Huh, so now that Trev's here, all of a sudden you and Zeke's a problem?" Cara said.

"Hey now."

"Sorry," Cara apologized. "I don't know where that—"

"Girl, I'm out here confessing, just come out with it. You're down bad for Zeke."

Cara yelped in surprise. "Shit, is it obvious? Fuck me."

I could almost feel her blushing over the phone, and I broke out in a fit of laughter. "It's not obvious to everyone—not Zeke, that's for sure—but I've kinda suspected since the start of the year. You're always looking at him when his back's turned. You show up to every game when no one else, not me, not Manny, not even his dad—before he got sick, anyway—has perfect attendance. And that *X-Files* box set? Zeke's the only person I've ever seen you spend real money on. So, yeah, I noticed."

"And you never said anything?"

"I guess . . . I figured if you wanted to talk to me about it, you would. And I thought you might've secretly hated me because, well, y'know."

"I did a little, for a while. Honestly, sometimes I still do, and it comes out weird. Sorry for what I said. When I heard about the kiss, I either wanted to curl up into a ball and disappear or punch you in the face," Cara said.

I groaned. "Ugh, who told you? I'm sorry you didn't find out from me first, I just—"

"Girl, don't even, I get it. I learned from Manny, but he didn't tell me. He was just acting weird and I pried it out of him. Don't worry, though, he hasn't told anyone else, and you know I won't either." She paused. "This . . . this isn't weird, is it? Me talking about Zeke?"

I had never heard her sound so serious, so raw and open. "Of course not!" I said, though there was a small part of me, a little voice, that disagreed. Images flashed before my eyes of Cara and Zeke walking arm in arm, making out in the school hallways, lying in bed together. I didn't want him for myself. I didn't want her, my best girlfriend, for myself either. But it *was* odd to picture. My whole life, people put a future on me where Zeke and I were together. My mom talked about how beautiful our wedding would be. Samson made jokes whenever I came over to study—well, when I came over to help Zeke study—that we had to keep the door open, just in case.

Zeke's feelings for me wouldn't just disappear overnight, and I wasn't sure if Cara really had a chance, but I didn't want to stop her from trying in case she did. And, selfishly, I couldn't help but think how much easier things would be for me if they got together.

"So, it won't be weird if I try and go for him?" Cara asked.

"Heck no! We could go on double dates!"

She paused again. "Gen, are you *sure*? 'Cause if you are, I'm gonna make moves, no doubt."

"I'm sure," I said. "Vaya con dios, you have my blessing."

"No gods for me, thanks," Cara replied. "They can keep all that

Jesus shit 'cause, best believe—I get my hands on Zeke, the things I'll do to him are gonna be straight *unholy*.

"Oh, speaking of Zeke—Coach's having the preseason party Saturday. Zeke, Manny, and me'll be closing the store that night, and I wanna do something for him after 'cause I know he'll be bummed about missing the party now that he's off the team. I got an idea, so make sure you're free Saturday. Deets later. Ciao, bitch!"

"Girl, bye," I said, rolling my eyes. As soon as the call ended, my phone buzzed with a text from Trevor.

Trev: Hey wyd fri night??
Trev: There's this artsy theater and they're playing this movie the fountain. It's like sci-fi romance and weird and like 100% ypipo
Trev: buuuut i kinda love it
Trev: never seen it on the big screen
Trev: U wanna go? Lmk it's @ 8. I can pick u up
Trev: I mean, if thats ok???
Me: Sure! I'd love to!

As if he even needed to ask. I spent the rest of the night plotting out the lie I was going to tell my parents, texting back and forth with Cara so she could help me sell my alibi. It was risky, breaking my parents' rules so close to my birthday, but I hadn't felt as excited about anything as I did about seeing a movie with Trevor. I fell asleep that night with a stupid smile plastered on my face, and as I drifted off, I felt like I was flying.

chapter thirteen
IMOGEN

"And where are you going dressed like that?" my dad asked in a loud, edged voice just as I was about to walk out the door. I had completely forgotten he was back in town. He was sitting at the kitchen table, which was covered in a new, disassembled script. Dozens of pages were laid out, marked up with highlights, Post-its, and thick Sharpie strikethroughs.

"Me and Cara are going to a movie, and then we're going to make plans for my birthday. If it's too late when we're done, I'll probably just spend the night over there," I said, and made a mental note to text Cara all the details of my lie.

"Huh. Don't see why you need to look like *that* to go sit in a dark movie theater," he said.

I was wearing a tank top under a thick button-up sweater and a pair of warm leggings, along with black lipstick and a pair of gold hoop earrings. In other words, an entirely normal outfit.

My father had a lot of fans around the world, but I wasn't one of them. A good actor, a not-so-good dad. He was "pursuing his craft," he'd said a thousand times. That was why he had missed my last two birthdays, why he wasn't around for my middle school graduation, why I hated talking to him, and why he used rules to make up for his absence. That way, he was still "man of the house" or whatever. He was the one who'd decided I couldn't date until I was sixteen, as if he had any knowledge of or involvement in my life to begin with, and now he had the nerve to police how I dressed?

"Okay," I said in a flat tone. "Well, I'm going now."

"You better watch it," he said, raising his voice. "I won't have disobedience in my house."

I wanted to laugh. God, I wanted to laugh so hard, right in his face. *His* house. That he was never in. But if I did, I wasn't going anywhere, and I *needed* to see Trevor. I wanted so badly to break, but I bent instead and made myself small. I bowed my head and murmured an apology. I'm not sure what I said because I didn't mean any of it, but it was good enough for my father to nod approvingly and return to memorizing his lines. As soon as I was out of the house, I pressed my gloved hands to my mouth to muffle the sound as I screamed as loud as I could.

Me: Don't come 2 my house

Me: My dad's in a mood

Me: I'll meet u down the street

Trev: Bet, I'm in rays truck

Trev: Bring a warm coat

Trev: You ok??

Me: Yeah. I'll tell u abt it if u want

Trev: Only if u want

I walked to the corner of my block and saw Trevor idling in a pickup truck. He didn't see me, not yet, and I got a chance to watch him look himself over in the mirror. He licked his thumbs to smooth out his eyebrows, flared his nostrils in the rearview mirror to search for errant boogers, and checked his teeth for clingers.

Me: I can see u

I watched him check his phone, and then he looked out at me, mouth agape, and I started laughing. As I approached, it felt as if I were in a dream, as if I was being pulled to him by some invisible force. When I got to the passenger door, he reached over and opened it for me.

"Sorry, it doesn't open from the outside. Ray said he's gonna get it fixed. But, uhh, hey. Wow, you look nice. You smell good too. Shit, was that weird?"

His nervousness was cute, and surprising. When we walked home Wednesday afternoon, he'd seemed so smooth, so confident, but now all his nerves were showing, and it made me like him even more.

"Nah, it wasn't weird. Thank you," I said. "You look nice too. Nothing between your teeth, nothing in your nose, but you knew that already."

"Hah, can't believe you saw that," he said, rubbing the back of his neck with his hand.

"Better than seeing boogers up in them nostrils," I laughed, buckling myself in. "You didn't tell me *Wolverine* was in this movie. Boy, that's all you had to say. Man is *fine*, as far as White men go anyway."

Trevor let out a big laugh. "Yeah, he's great in this movie. It *is* pretty weird, just to warn you. I saw it during . . . during a hard time in my life. It's got as much to do with grief as it does love and the lengths someone'll go for the person they care about. And the visuals are insane. Super psychedelic. The director, he's the same guy who did *Black Swan* and *Requiem for a Dream* and—"

Trevor paused and looked over at me. I was resting my head on my hand, just looking at him. I could've sat there and listened to him nerd out about movies for hours.

"I'm just going on and on, sorry," he said.

I shook my head. "I like it. I like hearing about the things you like," I said, my heart thumping so hard I felt it in my throat. "I haven't seen that second one, but I did see *Black Swan*. Movie was creepy, but I liked it."

Trevor nodded and chuckled. "He's a weird guy, yeah. *Requiem*'s nuts. Marlon Wayans is in it, it's a dramatic role, and he *kills* it."

"Hol up, *Marlon* Wayans? Marlon '*White Chicks*' Wayans?"

"The one and only."

"Damn, now *that* I gotta see."

"Okay, so, like, did he find the Fountain of Youth or what?" I asked Trevor as we exited the theater and stepped out into the late winter chill. "He did, right? But then . . . how . . ."

"I mean, you can take it however you want. I don't believe in souls or past lives or anything, but I like to think they were two people, reincarnated, who kept finding and loving each other, fighting death to be together. But you could also make the argument that it's not even that literal and that the whole movie's more like . . . like a parable or a myth," Trevor said as he got into the truck and opened the passenger door for me.

"I prefer the first interpretation. Much more romantic," I said as I got inside. Every hair on my body was standing on end, pointing toward him, and had been for the entire movie. Our arms had been so close on the armrests, almost touching. Once, we reached for the popcorn at the same time, my hand brushed against his, and I felt like I was about to explode. I wasn't sure if he noticed how I was feeling, and I had no clue if he felt the same way. I read and wrote romance, but somehow, I still wasn't any good at reading feelings.

Trevor grinned. "Yeah, thought you might. So, uh, how late can you be out? You got a curfew or something?"

"Why?" I asked, even though I knew what my answer was going to be no matter what he said.

"I wanna show you something. It's a secret. It'll take an hour to get there. Think you can stand being around me that long? I think you'd appreciate it, but mostly, I just like hanging out with you and don't feel like going home yet."

I practically melted into a puddle. "Hey, as long as you're not taking me to your secret murder spot, I'll go anywhere with you," I said.

Trevor smiled. "I'm not. Pinky promise," he said, offering me his finger. I nodded and wrapped mine around his. "Dope. Let's do this."

We sat in silence—the most comfortable silence I'd ever felt—

as we drove out of the city proper. I gazed out the window, watching the city give way to the suburbs. Eventually, the smooth, paved streets were replaced with bumpy gravel roads and we bounced and rumbled across the rocks until we reached a near-empty patch of land and the remains of what had once been a baseball field. "All this way for . . . a baseball field?" I said.

Trevor laughed, parked the car, and grabbed two thick blankets out of the back seat. He motioned for me to follow him and headed toward the visitor dugout, its roof—and little else—still intact. "Ray—my dad showed me this place. His granddaddy played ball here. I didn't know baseball was in my family. My mom's folks, they were really into one thing and one thing only: the Lord, which I'm not too keen on," Trevor said.

"Same," I said. "No thanks to all that."

"Phew. So, apparently, he was in the Negro Leagues and played here." Trevor wrapped himself up in one of the blankets and took a seat on the beat-up wooden bench. I sat as close to him as I could without actually touching him.

"Folks booed him. Called him nigger. Made him fear for his life, Ray said. But he kept playing because he loved the game. Ray took me here the day after I arrived. He's trying. To be my dad, I mean.

"That was two weeks ago, and I've already been back a couple times by myself. I was out here one night when there was no moon, and I could see the stars brighter than I thought was possible this close to the city. Mostly, though, I come out to listen to the quiet. Sometimes, the wind blows through the holes in the dugout and whistles like some kind of deep flute. Like a ghost, but not spooky. More, comfort. Like the sound's got you cradled up in it. It's the first place up here I've fallen in love with. The ice and the snow and the cold, I'm not used to it, but there *is* something beautiful to it. The way the world disappears beneath it all. That's what I mean, the quiet."

I imagined being carried aloft by flute song, lifted into the sky by a rushing, humming wind. I imagined standing out in the middle of the field in the dark night, gazing up at the stars and the planets and the nebulae so very far above, holding Trevor's hand, listening to him talk for hours. I loved the sound of his voice, the rhythm of his words, the images that got stuck in his mind and the way he described them to me.

"Do you know the stars? I mean, the constellations and stuff?" I asked. "I had a telescope when I was a kid, but I haven't used it in a long time."

"Some. The main ones. It . . . was one of the only things I remember my mama teaching me. She always loved the sky, whether it was day or night. Sometimes I think it's 'cause that's where she wanted to be—high above the world, above all of this, because something down here made her hurt in a way she couldn't tolerate."

"Where's she now? Back in Houston?"

"Yeah, sorta. She died," Trevor said. "It's why I'm in Chicago now, with Ray."

I gasped, then kicked myself for my reaction. "I'm so sorry, I didn't . . . I didn't know. I shouldn't've brought it up."

"Hey now, don't need any apologies. She wasn't a very good mom. And you reminded me of a *good* thing. That's the other reason I come out here. Now that she's gone, I'm trying to remember her better parts."

I looked up at the sky, quiet, dazzled by all the stars I could see now that I was out of the city.

"Can I ask about her?" I asked after a few minutes. "You can say no."

"'Course you can," he said.

"What was her name?" I said, my voice cautious.

"Gabby. Gabrielle Anne Cook. The name fit, too, 'cause she could throw *down* in the kitchen. She had this jerk chicken that'd blow your mind. She had a good sense of humor, too. Quick and sharp with her wit. She talked herself out of a lot of trouble. And into a lot more."

"And she never talked about Ray?"

"Never. Not once. I might as well've been Jesus himself—born immaculate. Just appeared in her womb and in this world, no dad, no big. I've been wondering, ever since she went, what happened. But Ray doesn't know, and I can't ask her. All I know is that she and him met when Ray was in his doped-up days, after he wrecked his knees. He didn't say, but seeing as pills is how she went out, I imagine pills is how they met.

"Shit, I'm sorry," Trevor said. "That was a lot, wasn't it?"

"It wasn't," I said. "Can . . . I give you a hug?" He nodded. I scooted over toward Trevor and hugged him tight.

"I'm so sorry that happened to you," I whispered as he wrapped his arms around me too, and when we let go, I didn't scooch back to where I'd been.

"What about you? You said your dad was in a mood?"

"It's nothing," I said. Nothing I could say about my dad held a candle to what Trevor'd just said about his mom.

"Didn't sound like nothing," Trevor said, nudging me with his elbow.

"I mean, in comparison—"

"If you don't wanna tell me, that's fine, we can talk about something else. But me and my mom? That's an old story. I had a long time to get ready for her end. Besides, could use a change of subject." He smiled.

I turned and looked at him, his warm brown eyes, his perfect smile. "You sure?"

"I am." He nodded.

"Okay," I said, and took a long, deep breath. "He's just an asshole. Like, straight-up. He thinks he's hot shit because he's on this hit show now. He's always been kind of a dick, but his ego has gotten huge, so now he's a dick times a thousand. The only upside's that he's gone a lot for shoots and press tours.

"I don't get how my mom's dealt with him all this time. I bet he secretly makes her miserable. He definitely makes *me* miserable. He thinks he can just fly in and start barking orders when he hasn't been around for more than a day at a time in weeks. Months! Claims he's the man of the house with all his stupid, patriarchal rules. Like, he was the one who said I couldn't date until I turned sixteen!" I said. "And tonight, he had all sorts of things to say about my outfit. Ugh. Sometimes, I wish he'd just drop—"

I clapped my hand over my mouth. "Sorry, I didn't mean . . . I'm an idiot. Sorry."

Trevor laughed. "Gen, it's *okay*. I'm sorry he sucks. And, hey, for whatever it's worth, I think your outfit's bangin."

"You're a dork," I giggled, and nudged Trevor with my shoulder.

"It's the truth," he said. "Do I look like I'm playing?"

I turned to face him. My eyes lingered on his mouth for a moment, and almost without thinking, I leaned forward and pressed my lips against his. When they touched, the entire world went still, quiet, dark. It was the exact opposite of my kiss with Zeke. The way I felt about Trevor—the way my *body* felt about Trevor—was an entirely different thing.

"Is . . . is it okay that I did that?" I asked.

Trevor laughed, wrapped his arms around me, pulled me to him, and kissed me again in the cold, quiet night.

chapter fourteen
ZEKE

"I'm like a walking, talking, fro-yo-hawking gender reveal party."

"Correct," Cara said.

I looked at myself in the mirror, clad all in baby blue and baby pink, a visor cap on my head. Awful. I'd tried the uniform on a few days earlier when I picked it up with Cara, but this was the first time I was actually *wearing* it.

"I've tried for *years*, bro, but the old man won't even consider another color scheme," Manny said. "I even suggested we do the colors of Puerto Rico's flag and he shot *that* down. You ever in your whole-ass life heard a Puerto Rican turn down showing the flag? Something's wrong with him, for real. Got our asses looking like we work in a damn nursery."

"The thought of you taking care of a bunch of babies is terrifying," Cara said.

"Please, like I haven't been taking care of my baby siblings since first grade."

"Like that day you sent me a dozen Snapchats 'cause you couldn't make them Easy Mac, right?" she said as she headed into the back office.

"It's *Easy* Mac. You just read the box, dude," I said.

"This is the thanks I get, Zeke?" Manny said. "After getting you this job?"

"Yeah, this *awesome* job," I said. My first day was a bust. It had been an unusually slow Saturday—twelve customers in seven hours, and I still had an hour to go until close. I couldn't help but think about all the things I'd rather be doing, or what the team was up to.

It was the last weekend before the start of the season, which meant that Coach had everyone out at Vincent's: Braejon halfway through housing two dozen boneless wings by himself, with more on the way. Rinky-Dink eating those sorry-ass cauliflower wings that didn't deserve to be called "wings." Uncs coming through to wish us a good season, mostly 'cause they always had money on the games. Coach introducing everyone to Trevor and giving a speech about how the year was going to be tough without me, but they were still going to take home the trophy and do me proud.

At least, that was what I hoped he was saying. I hoped someone was thinking of me while I was standing around, bored out of my mind, with only Manny and Cara and the strange thoughts that bubbled up when I had nothing to do.

Case in point: "We had a dozen people in here tonight and not one of them stayed a second longer than they had to. Go to an ice cream spot, guarantee you they got butts in seats. What is it about fro-yo that makes people wanna just get in and out?" I asked.

"You ever thought about that?" I continued. "Like, there were ice cream parlors, you know, but no one's ever heard of a fro-yo parlor. Or remember when we had ice cream socials and everybody got to make sundaes and splits and all that? No one's ever had a fro-yo social, and if they have, people definitely weren't excited about it, not like they would be for an ice cream social. Maybe people think ice cream's still a treat? And frozen yogurt's just, like, diet ice cream, so nobody's interested, not like that. That's my theory."

"Zeke, if you're gonna show up to the Yo high as the sky, you gotta share. Them's the rules," Manny said. "What, you got your pops's pain pills or something? Split that shit, homie."

"Zeke do drugs? Hah!" Cara let out a bark of laughter from the office, then slid into the room on a wheeled office chair. "Sweet little Zekey-poo doesn't even like cursing. As if he's gonna pop pills," she said as she stood up, walked over, and pinched my cheek.

"Ow!" I pinched her back. "How do you like it?"

"Oh, you wanna go?" She lunged for me with her free hand, dancing her fingers down my sides to tickle me into submission.

I wasn't going down without a fight. I knew her weak spot was right above her knees. I squeezed her there, and Cara shrieked with laughter as her light brown face turned bright red. She got away from me, jumped back into her chair, and rolled away, the two of us breathing heavy. Cara had a sly grin on her face, taunting me. I was about to lunge again when Manny whistled.

"Quit flirting, we got customers," Manny said as he washed the windows and nodded at a Jeep that had just pulled up outside.

"We're not flirting," Cara and I said in unison.

That was all we had time to say before Raquel Damaris and Niecy

Adams—two juniors at our school, both on the basketball team—entered the store. Raquel always looked fly. Her nails were painted a gleaming gold that matched the soles of her shoes and the bangles around her wrists. Niecy was one of those girls who'd developed early, so she learned to be fierce to protect herself 'cause she knew the world wouldn't. That was what Cara always said, anyway. I just knew Niecy'd fight at the drop of a hat if you gave her a reason, and she'd win, too.

"Oh shit, I forgot my man was working here," Niecy said in a stage whisper, her eyes on me. "Girl, how I look?" She adjusted her tank top, pressing her (sizable) breasts up. Cara sucked her teeth and left the floor to take inventory in back.

"Welcome to Fro-Yo Jojo," I called out, acting like I hadn't heard every word. Niecy'd had a crush on me for the longest, so I had a lot of practice ignoring her affections. "What's good, ladies?"

"Hiii, Zeke," Niecy said, giggling as she approached.

"Niecy Nice, what can I get you?"

"Oh, you know *exactly* what I want." She leaned forward on the counter.

I heard a loud cough from the back.

"Well, cups are over there," I said, pointing toward the fro-yo machines. "So go on, help yourself."

"And if I want something *hot*?" Niecy said.

"Look, we're closing soon, so are you gonna get something or not?" Manny cut in. He didn't look back at her, so he didn't see the hateful look Niecy gave him.

"Yeah, yeah, we hear you," Raquel said, and headed over to the machines. Niecy stayed at the counter, making eyes at me the whole time, until Raquel returned with two respectably toppinged towering spires of frozen yogurt. Niecy paid for both and, before she left, wrote her number on a napkin.

"In case the Imogen thing doesn't work out," Niecy said. She slid the napkin to me and blew a kiss.

"Girl, you so thirsty, come *on*," Raquel said, and dragged Niecy out of the store.

"*Finally*," Cara said, peeking her head out from the back office. "Niecy's voice is like a fork scraping against a plate."

"Oh, come on, she's not *that* bad," I said.

"*Bzzt!* Wrong! And what the hell is that?" Cara squinted at the napkin on the counter. "Did that trollop leave her number?"

That finally got Manny to set the squeegee down and look away from the windows. "*Trollop*? The hell's a trollop?"

"It's back-in-the-day for busted-ass ho. I saw it in one of Imogen's old White-folks books," Cara said as she walked up and grabbed for the napkin.

"Hey, back up!" I pulled it away just before she got her fingers on it.

"You're . . . not going to keep it, are you?" Cara said, eyes narrowed.

"Why not?"

She opened her mouth, and in a rare moment of restraint, stopped herself and took a breath. "You know what? Fuck it. Fine. But you gotta clean the bathroom."

"What? Why? Just 'cause she gave me her number?"

"Nah," Manny chimed in. "Rules. How the old man tests new hires. Fresh meat's gotta make the place sparkle or it's your ass because—"

"'A man is only as good as his first impression,'" Manny and Cara said in unison.

"Oh, and it's gonna be a doozy. Homie who came in couple hours ago?" Cara said. "He stay having the mudbutt squirts something fierce!"

"Loose-ass Lucas." Manny shook his head sadly. "I worry for that man."

"It can't be that bad," I said. Cara and Manny glanced at each other and laughed.

When I stepped inside the bathroom, I realized right away that it *was* that bad. No, it was *worse*, like a port-a-potty at a music festival. The tile was movie-theater sticky, my every step accompanied by a loud, wet squelch. The toilet seat was covered in brown streaks, and the bowl was so speckled with poop flecks that it resembled chocolate chip ice cream. There were even a couple smears on the wall next to the toilet somehow. When I came out of the bathroom, Cara and Manny laughed.

"Look at his face!" Manny snickered as he rolled the mop and bucket my way.

"Told you. Gonna need these," Cara said as she set down a large plastic tote of rubber gloves, face masks, safety goggles, a damn *hazmat* suit, a dozen different types of sponges and brushes, and a bevy of different cleaners.

"And remember," Manny said. "It's gotta *sparkle*. And you can't come out here till it's done, got it? It's a health code thing. Can't have you tracking nasty all around the shop."

I sighed. "Got it." I suited up, grabbed the mop and my supplies, and reentered the hellscape that was the Fro-Yo Jojo bathroom.

I could've been eating wings. I could've been at the batting cages. I could've been out with Imogen, wherever she was. But I had made my choice, and I was going to stick with it because my family needed me to be a man and that was what men did. I learned that from Pops.

When I finished, my arms were tired as shit *from* shit. I felt like I was never going to smell anything but Lysol and disinfectant for the rest of my life. I had put two pairs of gloves on, just in case, and carefully peeled off the outer pair. I unzipped the top half of the hazmat suit, then removed the second pair of gloves. I scrubbed my hands and arms in the spotless sink and backed out the bathroom door, balancing the tote atop the mop bucket.

"Yeesh, you guys weren't kidding. It was all kinds of nasty—"

"SURPRISE!"

I jumped and knocked the tote to the ground. My nasty gloves hit the floor with a wet *thwap*. The mop bucket almost spilled too, but I caught it just in time. I turned around to see Manny, Cara, and Imogen gathered behind the register. A spread of wings, ribs, mac and cheese, and potato salad from Vincent's sat on the scale next to a projector displaying the Blu-ray menu for *The X-Files: Season 5* on a screen on the opposite wall.

"Imogen? What are you—you all scared the hell outta me! I almost spilled piss water everywhere," I said.

"We wanted to do something special tonight," Imogen said. "We know it's tough, being here instead of with the team. You haven't really talked about it, 'cause you keep a lot inside, but we want you to know that we see you doing a lot. So, we just thought, tonight we can celebrate you and all you've done for your mom and dad."

"Blah blah blah feelings feelings feelings," Cara jumped in.

"Let's get to it already! C'mon, the last thing I saw was Mulder shooting himself—"

"And she won't shut up none about it either, for real," Manny muttered.

"I gotta know if Mulder's fucking dead or what!" Cara said.

"Okay, okay, just chill," I said, and grabbed a plate. "Was this your idea?" I asked Imogen.

"No, it was all Cara's idea. She planned it all out, even the bathroom."

"Even the bathroom?"

"You didn't think that was really all shit, did you?" Cara asked, laughing.

"Wait, what?"

"I blended up chocolate chips, threw them in the bowl, and fixed them on there with this spray. Mixed corn syrup in water and splashed it on the floor to make it sticky. Stink bombs from Axel for the smell."

I stared at her, dumbfounded.

"I'm telling you, cuz. Me and you. Haunted house. Ten bucks to get in. We'll make a killing," Manny said.

"You also said we'd make a killing selling Tía Alma's tamales on the side of the road," Cara said.

"Your ma made all them things, and you only made, what, thirty dollars?" I laughed.

"Look, Tamales Ta-Day wasn't my best idea. But a haunted house is different. Just for a few days, a couple weeks, something like that."

I turned to Cara. "You hear him? 'A few days, a couple weeks,' like those are the same thing."

"Fine. Don't come to Manny with the Planny asking for a little scratch when I'm rich," he said.

Imogen groaned. "Manny with the Planny? That sounds—"

"Catchy? I know. So, you gonna press play or what?" Manny asked me.

I shook my head, laughing. "Anything to shut you up. Thanks, you guys. I mean it. You're the best."

Cara stepped up and gave me a hug. "Of course, you ding-dong, I—we got you, always."

I hugged her back, hit play on the projector, and took a seat between Cara and Imogen. The theme song kicked in. Imogen moved her fingers in the air like she was our conductor, Manny came in whistling the high notes, while Cara and I hummed the main rhythm in perfect unison. We watched two episodes, learning almost immediately, much to everyone's relief and no one's surprise, that Mulder was fine.

"Now I can sleep easy. Thank goodness," Cara said, yawning, as we cleaned up.

"Yeah, you better rest up for the party," I said. "You got one week to get ready for the bash of all bashes."

"So, you gonna tell me about the surprise?" Imogen asked, her arms folded.

I glanced at Manny to see if he'd said anything, but he shook his head. *Phew.*

"Nah, girl, it's called a surprise for a reason. You'll find out when you find out. Believe me, it's gonna be good."

chapter fifteen
IMOGEN

I watched from the front door as my parents got into their Uber. My mom was beach-ready, wearing a long, flowy dress and a sunhat on her head, while my dad was on his phone trying to take care of some last-minute business before their vacation was officially underway. He had promised my mom radio silence come sundown on Thursday and his time was running out. Despite my dad's *many* misgivings about leaving me home alone and his long lecture about what I wasn't allowed to do and who wasn't allowed to come over, I knew they were too eager for a vacation together for that to stop him from leaving. Between my dad's shooting schedule and my mom's exhibitions, it had been a couple years since their schedules had allowed for a vacation. I hoped that was part of why he'd been such a dick lately and that he'd come back a little less . . . well, just a little *less*, period. I stood on the stoop, waving as they left. My parents were hidden behind tinted glass windows, so I wasn't sure if they waved back, or if they were even looking at me, but I still waited for the car to round the corner and vanish into the sunset before I pulled my phone out.

Me: Annnd they're gone!!

Me: Four days of FREEDOM

Manny: Yeeeeeee let's GO

Manny: These playlists got playlists

Manny: Ima dj the fuck outta this party

Cara: You better cuzzo

Cara: I'm tryna turn UP

Cara: SATURDAY SATURDAY SATURDAY

Manny: SABADO GIGANTE

Zeke: It's gonna be THE party, believe me

Zeke: Got it all planned out, best bday yet

Me: So . . . what's the surprise

Zeke: Lol gen u been asking all week.

Zeke: 2 more days. U gotta wait n see

Me: Zeke, it's MY birthday

Me: C'mon I hate surprises

Zeke: Promise you're gonna love this one

Zeke: Guaranteed

I sighed. Nothing. After a week of my probing and needling, Zeke hadn't dropped any hints. Time was running out; I needed a new approach. I hadn't wanted to involve anyone else, but I was out of options. Cara seemed just as in the dark as I was. I thought about asking Trevor to eavesdrop on Zeke and the team, but I didn't want to throw him into my mess, not when we were just figuring each other out. Which left Manny. I remembered the way Zeke had glanced at Manny that night at the shop. I was sure Manny knew *something*, but his commitment to Zeke was legendary—it was the only time Manny kept his mouth shut. But what choice did I have? I put on my coat and boots, grabbed my headphones, and stepped out of the house, locking the door behind me.

I had made all sorts of guesses to Zeke over the week that he shot down. Zeke wouldn't even tell me if I was hot or cold. It wasn't a Cameo from Sam Heughan in character as Jamie Fraser. He wasn't having the party catered by Umi Kara, an upscale sushi restaurant I was obsessed with but had never visited. They weren't Beyoncé tickets either, but that was always a long shot. I didn't have the nerve to ask him if he was planning the one surprise I wanted the absolute least. It wasn't lost on me that I was about to become "officially" dateable; Zeke's surprise very well could be him making a move on me in front of everybody, and that filled me with terror.

Thankfully, Manny was about to clear everything up. And I wasn't leaving until he did.

I knocked on Manny's front door, and after a loud pitter-patter of footsteps too small and wild to be Manny's, his six-year-old sister, Almanita, opened the door and slashed at me with a plastic light-saber. I dodged out of the way and backed away from the door.

"Immygen!" she shouted. "You wanna play wightsabers?"

"Nita, leave her alone," Manny said as he bounded down the stairs. "Sup, Gen? Didn't realize you was comin by. You wanna see the playlists?"

I ignored Manny and addressed Almanita. "Hey, Nita, Manny'll play lightsabers with you if you let me and him talk alone for a minute, okay?" I said, then glared at Manny and added, "*Outside.*"

Manny cocked his head. "Wait, what? Why?"

"Okay! Manny, outside!" Almanita shouted as she scurried under Manny's legs, shoved him out the door, and locked it behind him.

"That little—" Manny hissed as he spun around and started banging on the door.

"Almanita will open the door when I say we're done, won't you, Almanita?" I called out.

"Yeah! Then wightsabers!" Almanita shouted from inside, waving her lightsaber in front of a nearby window to show she was serious.

"This is against the Geneva Convention. Cruel and unusual punishment, you know," Manny said, shivering. "Fine, what do you want?"

"Oh, you know why I'm here," I said.

"Um, to visit your friend? To place your bets for the game on Sunday? The Trevor/Zeke shake-up's been wild for the odds."

Manny was Hampton High's unofficial bookie and had made himself a decent chunk of change off the Panthers' unexpected success the previous year.

"Manny. Get serious, okay?" I said, angrier than I intended. "Sorry. I'm just stressed." My voice caught in my throat, as if I was about to cry. Manny's grin vanished.

"I'm sorry, Imogen, I didn't realize—I told Zeke I wouldn't say anything, but, like, if it's got you like this . . . You're putting me in a really awkward position, Gen," Manny said in a low, serious voice as he ran a hand through his hair.

"*Please*, just tell me what he's planning. Is it going to be cool? Expensive? Is it going to be embarrassing? Do I need to be worried? Do I need to dress differently? Am I going to, I don't know, get dirty? Should I wear sneakers? This is why I *hate* surprises," I said, the words tumbling out of my mouth.

Manny looked down at the ground and sighed. "If I tell you, you swear you leave me out of it?"

"I swear. I don't snitch. You've set off so many stink bombs, put viruses on so many school computers, and I've never, ever said a word. Never will, either."

Manny chuckled. "*Forgot* about the viruses. The one yelling 'Stop looking at porn' was hilarious. Got Axel's ass in so much trouble. You remember—"

"*Manny.*"

"Okay, okay," Manny said, pacing back and forth on the stoop, rubbing his arms to warm himself up. "Just keep in mind I told him—I've *been* telling him—it's a really bad idea. I've been trying to talk him down, okay? I just want you to know."

"It's what I think it is, isn't it?" I asked. I *knew* I was right to worry.

He nodded. "He's . . . he wants a big spectacle because he's gonna declare his feelings for you and ask you out. Not much of a surprise, if you ask me."

"*Fuck!*" I shouted. "Ugh, I knew it!" Manny's eyes went wide—I never said the f-word. "Manny, you *have* to stop him." My voice was taut with panic. "Please."

"I told you—I've been trying. But you know him. Plus," he said as he narrowed his eyes at me, "let's all be honest here: it's not like you made it any easier with the goddamn kiss. I mean, how the hell'd you think that was gonna go? You *know* how he feels. You *been* knowing. So you kiss him and now you're upset he's got feelings?"

I dropped my head in shame and started drumming my fingers against my leg. "It . . . was a bad idea. I just had to know. If I felt romantic about him or not."

"Gen, I could've told you that you didn't. Just 'cause I'm not interested in dating or romance or whatever don't mean I don't know what's going on. I see more than any of you. I know how Cara feels about Zeke. And I know about you and Trevor."

I froze up. "What . . . what about me and Trevor?"

"You got it bad. Have since day one. And I get it, not one of us is into books like you two. He got that look—that smart, wise, knows-something-about-life look you get sometimes, when you're in that whole other world inside you no one knows about. Trev's like that too. Makes sense."

I stared at Manny, mouth open. Trevor and I were both attracted to each other, but that wasn't why we'd clicked so fast, so hard, I realized. It was because we both had these hidden worlds, these what-if places inside us made of our dreams and fantasies, because reality just wasn't good enough. Zeke wasn't like that. He was practical, grounded, anchored. I didn't want to be weighed down by the real. I wanted to fly and leave my cares behind.

"Surprised? You ain't the most subtle tool in the shed, Gen. Like, compared to Zeke, you're a ninja—he's as sneaky as fireworks—but you're still making waves and I'm the lifeguard. I see it all."

"Manny, first of all, you're mixing way too many metaphors.

Second, you haven't said anything, have you? About Trevor?"

"Of course not. That's on you. If you *really* wanna stop this surprise from happening, you gotta tell him you and Trevor are a thing. That's the only way he might back down. And even then, I dunno."

"Look, we're not a thing," I said. Which was true. We had kissed. We texted some after that, about the movie, about how he beat Coach in a spicy wing contest at the preseason party, about different books and movies we wanted the other person to check out. Some nights, we fell asleep texting each other, and on the nights we didn't, we told each other good night. But, no, we weren't together.

"Yeah, okay." Manny snorted.

"If I say something now, it'll ruin everything. It'll be so awkward at the party between him and Trevor and—"

"Hold up," Manny said. "Zeke didn't invite Trevor. I know, 'cause he gave me the guest list."

"Yeah, uhh, I invited him," I said.

"Imogen," Manny said, his face in his hands. "Are you serious right now? You invited the guy you're crushing on to the birthday party organized by the guy who's got a crush on you. Fuck me, you really did want this to be like some Netflix shit. Drama and everything, goddamn."

I stomped my foot hard on the concrete. I hated being called dramatic. "I should be able to invite anyone I want to *my* birthday party. If there's drama, that's on Zeke, not me."

Manny laughed. "Convenient. Way I see it, you got two options. Either you uninvite Trevor or you're straight up with Zeke *before* the party. Otherwise, you're asking for a shitshow."

I clenched my jaw and pressed my nails into the meat of my

hands. "Why do *I* have to do it? How come I have to change my life because of *Zeke's* feelings? How come he just gets to do what he wants?"

Manny stared at me, working his jaw. There was more he wanted to say, but he held his tongue. "Fine," he sighed. "Fine. I'll double down. I'll press him harder, get him to call off the surprise. But I can't guarantee anything, Gen. If this blows up in your face, don't come blaming me, got it?"

I hadn't realized how tight my body was until Manny agreed and my muscles relaxed. "Thank you," I said, and hugged him. "Thank you, thank you, thank you."

"But you owe me. You owe me big. I'm talking bit-part-in-one-of-Brian's-movies big."

"Dad would never go for it, you know that."

"Well, not with that attitude!" Manny said.

I rolled my eyes. "I'm counting on you, Manny," I said.

"You wanna come in, warm up before you go back?"

"No, I'm okay. I want the time to think," I said. "But thank you. Again."

"You're welcome, but you better think quick. Ain't much time left."

chapter sixteen
ZEKE

I couldn't tell if I was more excited or nervous for Imogen's party. From the moment I woke up Saturday morning, I felt the two feelings battling inside me, twisting my stomach into knots.

"Not hungry?" my mom asked.

"Me?" I said. "Or Pops?"

"Wish I was," he sighed at the plate of French toast in front of him. "Two weeks since my surgery and I still got no appetite to speak of."

"I meant you, Zeke. You look like you're about to burst out your skin. Can't even sit still," my mom said. She was right; my leg was bouncing like a piston and I couldn't find a comfortable way to sit to save my life.

"It's the big day, Nessa," Pops said. "Ain't that right, Zeke?"

"Oh shoot, I completely forgot. I've been so tired I—" She cut herself off. My mom hated talking about how tired she was in front of my father. She didn't want to make him feel any worse than he did already. "Oh, I'm so excited. I can't wait for this to be official!"

"Been a long time comin," Pops said. "Nice, romantic story to tell our grandkids someday."

Any other day, I would've told them to stop. I would've cringed at their commentary on my love life. But they could neither dampen my anticipation nor calm my terror. Nothing could.

"You need anything for your big night? Gas money?"

I shook my head. They still didn't know about my job and wouldn't for as long as possible. I told them I wasn't playing in the season opener because Coach wanted to try out the new guy, which gave me a week to figure out how to break the news to them. Ma'd get sad that I felt I needed to work, Pops'd be heartbroken I put baseball aside on account of his illness, and it was just easier for everyone not to tell them, not yet. One thing at a time.

"I'm good. I've been saving up for tonight," I said. "Besides, it's just a few of us going out to eat, no big."

My parents both laughed and looked at me like I was crazy.

"We *all* know that's not what you got planned," my mom said.

"I don't know what you're talking about," I said, crossing my arms.

"I know my son. My son doesn't do small or subtle," Pops said. "And I heard you and Manny talking about playlists."

"You think we can't put two and two together? Gen's parents are on vacation until Monday. Awful good time to have a party, Samson, don't you think?"

Pops nodded. "Sure is, Nessa," he said. He and Ma both had smug looks on both their faces.

I rolled my eyes. "Okay, fine, yeah. Imogen wanted a big party for her birthday. I've been planning it since my birthday. It's gonna start at eight and—"

"Question," my mom interrupted. "There gonna be drinking? Weed?"

I thought about saying no. I wasn't sure how they'd react. They might try to break it up, or tell Brian and Jean, or—

"We'll take that pause as a yes," my mom said. "Look, we're trusting you, okay?"

"Okay, yeah, but Manny doesn't do that stuff, not really. And Rinky-Dink doesn't at all, so he's gonna be on guard duty."

"Then it's on the three of you to make sure no one drives home, got it? And you watch them boys, make sure all the girls stay safe. You do that, Jean won't hear a peep from us," Pops said.

"And we don't like Brian, so no worries there," my mom laughed. "I'm off tonight, for once, so I'll be home. If anything happens, promise you'll call me, okay?"

"I promise. Trust me, it's gonna be great," I said. The fear turned into anticipation. I found my appetite and wolfed down the three lukewarm slices of French toast on my plate, then three more. "It's gonna be perfect."

chapter seventeen
IMOGEN

"Fine, I'll tell him you went to get your nails done or something," Cara told me. "But you *can't* be late, or Zeke's gonna flip shit and then he's gonna blame it all on me."

"I won't," I said as I buckled myself into Trevor's passenger seat. "We'll be there by eight thirty at the absolute latest, I swear. But we have to leave like, *now*."

"*Fiiiiine*," Cara said, throwing her hands up as she walked away.

I nodded to Trevor, and we zipped away from Cara's house, racing toward Evanston. Diana Gabaldon was having a reading and signing event at six thirty p.m.; it was a forty-five-minute drive if we got lucky, and it was already six, so we needed to hurry. Trevor had found out about it at the last minute and asked if I wanted to go, and I said yes without a second's hesitation. He thought it was out of my love for *Outlander*, and I was happy to let him think that. It wasn't a complete lie. I was beyond excited to see Diana Gabaldon in the flesh, but neither she nor Trevor were why my heart was racing in my chest. Now that I knew what Zeke's surprise was, I was eager for any opportunity to delay my arrival. That I got to spend more time with Trevor was just icing on the cake.

"Thank you," I said after a couple minutes of quiet.

"For what?"

"For finding out about this. And taking my mind off this dumb party. This is the best birthday gift I could ask for."

"You don't need to thank me for that. What kinda monster would I be if I heard about this and *didn't* tell you? I'm real sorry we're gonna miss the reading," Trevor said. "You okay, though? I thought you were excited about your party."

What Manny had told me, he told me in confidence, and I hadn't shared with Trevor exactly what had me so worried. My leg wouldn't stop bouncing, I kept cracking my knuckles, and every couple of minutes, I had to remind myself to relax and breathe. I kept feeling phantom vibrations from my phone in my pocket and pulled it out every few moments to see if Manny had any updates. He was up against Zeke's legendary stubbornness, but I still held out hope that Manny could convince him to change his mind and cancel the surprise.

"Yeah, just . . . nervous. About the party. I almost don't even wanna go."

"I'd be nervous too," Trevor said. "Huge party in my own house with a whole bunch of teenagers acting a fool? Shit, what if folks start tryna get fresh in your bed?"

I laughed. "Like, this is what I wanted and what I asked for, but . . ." I trailed off, debating whether or not to tell Trevor everything.

"Hey, you say the word, I'll get you out of there. I'll kill the music, throw everyone out if I have to. It's your night, first and foremost, and I'm gonna be there for you. I promise," Trevor said. He reached over and took my hand in his—he was so *warm*—and gave it a squeeze. "Let's talk about something else: tell me what happened after the second book, so I don't look like a fool in front of everyone."

I snapped to attention and turned to face Trevor. "You want me to summarize the *whole* series?"

"Sure. We still have half an hour."

"That's seven books. There's not *nearly* enough time," I said, shaking my head, idly stroking his hand with my thumb.

"Hey, if you don't think you can do it—"

I laughed. "Boy, please." I talked him through each book. We finished book seven as we pulled into the parking lot of the bookstore. I texted him my detailed summaries of books eight and nine while we were in line, afraid of speaking, even quietly, and spoiling the books for someone else. By the time we reached Diana herself, Trevor was more or less caught up, and I was grateful because I was too lost in awe to say much of anything to her besides my name. Trevor paid for the book, while I stared, mumbled, and nodded as she formed words in my direction. Trevor had to direct me away from the table, his hands on my shoulders.

"'To Imogen Eleanor Parker: For where all love is, the speaking is unnecessary,'" Trevor read, and laughed. "You didn't tell me she was funny, too."

"Ha ha," I muttered. "Let's all make fun of Imogen. I must've looked like such a dingus."

"Nah, she laughed. She thought you were cute," Trevor said, then added, "*I* think you're cute."

Jordan K. Casomar

I wanted to kiss him. I had wanted to kiss him since he picked me up. I also had a feeling I'd want to kiss him the whole way back. But I knew that if I did, the party was going to be even more uncomfortable. I had to wait until after I told Zeke how I felt. It was only right. But when, on the way back to my house, Trevor put his hand on my thigh, I curled my hand around his. The radio played, but we didn't talk. The speaking was unnecessary.

As I was staring out the window, I realized I hadn't checked my phone in almost two hours. I pulled it out of my purse; I had one text.

Manny: Sorry gen. I really tried

chapter eighteen
ZEKE

"Lights here, here, and here," I told Braejon and Rinky-Dink, pointing around Gen's living room. The furniture was pushed up against the walls to make room for the dance floor. Manny was getting his sound equipment set up against one wall. The kitchen table in the next room was covered in red cups and liquor, courtesy of Braejon's full beard, deep voice, and exquisitely crafted fake ID.

"Yeah, yeah, got it," Braejon said as he climbed up the ladder. Rinky-Dink was on the ground, holding it steady. "You need to chill, bruh. You ain't ever been like this, not even in the finals."

"This is a lot more important," I snapped.

"Off the team for two weeks and you're saying this shit? Better not let Coach hear," Braejon said, shaking his head. He peeled the backing off the light and pressed it onto the drywall. "Aight, Dink, move me."

"Uhh, that's really not safe," Rinky-Dink said.

"Nigga, you want to come up here?"

"You know I can't reach."

"Yeah, so move the goddamn ladder, smart-ass. Let's get this done before Zeke gets on my *last* nerve."

Yeah, I was being a little impatient, but I needed everything to be perfect. The lights had to be angled just right, so that when the big moment came, it felt like something in one of Imogen's romance novels. We were running behind; it was seven, the party was supposed to start in an hour, and even accounting for CPT, we had ninety minutes at most for Manny to get the sound working, for Dink and Braejon to get the lights set up and programmed, and for me to put the fragile stuff somewhere safe. It seemed like plenty of time, but I couldn't count on it. I hoped for the best, planned for the worst.

A sudden feedback whine cut through my thoughts, so loud and surprising that Braejon almost lost his footing. I let out a tremendous sigh of relief as he steadied himself.

"Man, these fucking speakers. The hell'd they even find these," Manny muttered to himself as I approached.

"Yo, you good?" I said, only a little sharper than I intended.

"Zeke, miss me with your bullshit right now. I'm fixing it, just chill."

"Sorry, man, just nervous."

"You shouldn't be."

"I know, I know. It shouldn't feel like such a big deal, but it is."

Manny looked up from his computer and narrowed his eyes at me in, to my surprise, anger. "I meant you shouldn't be nervous because you shouldn't *do* this."

"This shit again?" I scoffed. "You've been on this all week, trying to get me to change up. To *not* give her the party of her dreams. To *not* make her feel as special and loved as she deserves to feel. To *not* tell her how I feel. I'm tired of hearing it."

Manny shook his head. "She hates being the center of attention," he said as he looked me in the eyes. "Zeke, she *hates* it. She doesn't even like being called on in English class, when she's the best in the whole damn school."

"This is different. She wanted this party, to be the center of attention just this one time. It's what she wants," I said.

"The party? Sure. Your 'surprise,' though?"

"She's always reading romance novels, and not just those *Outlander* books. She says she loves *X-Files* for the tension between Scully and Mulder. She wants grand gestures, to be swept off her feet. That's what I'm going to do."

"Oh, so she *told* you this is what she wanted? I didn't realize you'd asked her!"

I glared at Manny. "No offense, bro, but you're kinda the last person I'd take advice from on dating and romance," I said.

Manny's voice got low. "Offense taken, asshole," he said, a little heated.

"This is what girls want, man. Trust me. I've read it online and in books—"

Manny snorted. "Since when do you read books?"

"—and from Braejon, who gets *all* the girls," I said, ignoring him. "This is how you get out of the friend zone."

Manny groaned so loud and so sudden, for a second I thought something was really wrong.

"This 'friend zone' bullshit again?" he said.

"It's not bullshit!"

"Yes, it is."

"So, when you are super into someone and you ask them out and they say they just wanna be friends, what do you call that?"

"Normal."

"The friend zone," I shot back.

"The hell've you been reading? You turning into one of those red-pill incels? God, I hope not. Just because someone you're into isn't into you, that doesn't mean you're in some stupid zone."

I had heard enough. I got loud and in Manny's face. "Okay, so if you know so much, why's the friend zone bullshit? Tell me, Mr. Know-It-All."

"Like, it's not one or the other, man," Manny shouted. "It's not friends or fucking. Sometimes it's *just* friends. You don't get to have more than what they wanna give you! If someone just wants to be friends, they didn't *do* anything to you. No one *put* you anywhere. Like, it's not a matter of the right time or the right words or the right moment. All it means is that they don't wanna date you and that's it! You don't have a chance with every girl just because you want them. Some girls you'll never, ever have a chance with, Zeke!"

"Tread lightly, bruh," I said as I glared at Manny, my fists balled up at my sides. A long silence passed between us. I kept opening my mouth to speak and losing my words right after. After a while, Manny closed his eyes and took a deep breath.

"I don't wanna fight, man. You're nervous and tense and shit, so let's just take a breath, okay? I'm not trying to . . . I just don't think this is the right way to do it, okay? Why not after the party? When it's just you and her? Take her somewhere you can talk and be alone. That'd go over better with her."

I did as he asked and took a deep breath, then I shook my head. "I'm sorry for snapping at you, man. But it's gotta be tonight, man. It has to be—it's *going* to be perfect. But I need your help. I need to know you got my back."

Manny took another deep breath—or let out a deep sigh, it was hard to tell.

"Yeah, man," he said, not meeting my gaze. "Yeah, I got your back."

"Thanks, Manny. It's gonna be perfect. You'll see."

I was interrupted by a loud crash and a yelp of pain.

"Ugh, what now," I said. Manny and I ran to the kitchen and saw Rinky-Dink sprawled out on the floor, surrounded by fragments of porcelain that had once been two fine china teacups. He was rolling back and forth, holding his hand and wincing as blood trickled down his wrist.

"What happened, man?"

"I need a towel or a Band-Aid or something," Rinky-Dink said.

"I got it, hang on a second," Manny said.

"I said, what happened!" I shouted.

"Nigga, I got hurt, that's what happened! I was standing on the counter putting some lights up, and I slipped and fuckin hit the cupboard and the damn cups fell out. That answer your fuckin question? Goddamn," he said.

I'd never heard Rinky-Dink curse so much, and he almost never called anyone a nigga, on account of the fact that he grew up in a White household. The word sounded almost alien in his mouth.

Manny rushed back into the room with a plush red towel and tossed it to Rinky-Dink. "Yo, where's the Band-Aids? You know this house, right? I don't know where shit's at here."

I didn't hear him at first. I felt so very far away, staring down at the blood and the broken dishes. The party was a mess already, and it hadn't even started. But I could still fix it. It wasn't over yet. It could still be perfect.

"Zeke!" Manny yelled. "Wake up, and get this man some goddamn bandages, come on!"

"Oh yeah, sorry," I said, snapping to attention. I ran to the first-floor bathroom, grabbed the first aid kit from under the sink, and gave it to Manny. "I'm gonna get all the fragile stuff upstairs so this doesn't happen again."

"Jeez, not even a 'How you doin?' or 'You good, fam?'" Rinky-Dink muttered.

I ignored him as I grabbed a cardboard box and filled it with the rest of the china from the kitchen cabinet. The dishes rattled loud against each other on the way upstairs, as if they were as nervous as I was. It didn't help that I was going into Jean's studio, the only room with its own key and, thus, the best place to stash things. After I had set the china down, I was going to bring the vases and lamps up from downstairs. Some were worth thousands, a fact I was well aware of because Brian couldn't buy nice things without bragging about their price, and it would be a complete disaster if one of them broke instead of just the partial disaster the party was shaping up to be.

I pushed open the door to the studio and stepped into the one messy, chaotic room in the whole house. The floor was covered with drop cloths, frames rested up against the walls, and a massive canvas dominated one wall of the room. It was . . . red. Just red, from top to bottom. I never liked going into Jean's studio, partly because I felt like I was peeking into Jean's mind in ways I shouldn't, but mostly because I never *got* her art, and that made me feel equal parts stupid and uncomfortable. I set the dishes down and left the room, avoiding the painting, and felt my phone buzz in my pocket.

Cara: Ok so, heads up I'm omw

Cara: Buuut Imogen's not w me

Me: Wait wdym she's not w u

Cara: She had 2 get her nails done

Me: And??? U didn't go w her?

Cara: Hell no. The smell gives me migraines

Cara: Her nail lady squeezed her in last min

Cara: So yea

Me: Wtf cara cmon

Cara: She'll be there at 830

Cara: What's the big deal?? Not like it's a surprise

Cara: Why's it matter how she gets there?

Me: Cause that was the plan

Me: This has to be perfect

"Everything's fine, Zeke. It's gonna be fine. You got this," I whispered to myself as I shoved my phone back in my pocket, sat down on the top of the staircase, and took a few breaths to calm myself down.

chapter nineteen
IMOGEN

"**W**ell, shit," Trevor said.

We were stuck in a long line of unmoving brake lights, as far as the eye could see. In the distance, the evening sky was full up with the flashing lights of well over a dozen emergency vehicles.

"Looks like an accident," Trevor said.

"I hope everyone's okay," I said, secretly happy for the delay and wishing we'd been the ones in the wreck. That would've been preferable to the car crash that was going to be my party. I glanced at the clock on the stereo. It was already eight thirty, and Cara was going to be pissed. "How much longer?"

"Another thirty minutes, if Google Maps ain't lying to me."

Maybe I could make myself sick? Pretend I've got awful motion sickness, make myself throw up. That could work, right? When Trevor's not looking, I could—

"You gonna let Cara know?" Trevor asked, interrupting my train of thought.

I nodded and fired off a quick text to her.

Me: Ran into traffic, be there in 15 sry

Cara: GIRL

Cara: U said 830

Me: I kno I kno sry we're hurrying

Hurrying was the last thing I wanted to do. I considered texting her again to tell her that we'd just been rear-ended. It'd be easy to convince her that we'd gotten into an accident, what with all the dings and dents on Ray's truck, but I didn't want to make Trevor an accessory to my lie. I couldn't see any way out of this without either involving Trevor or lying to him. I already felt bad enough that he didn't know what he was walking into. God, I was an idiot. I shouldn't have invited him, I shouldn't have waited to talk to Zeke, I shouldn't have let this get as far as it had gotten. Manny had been right, and now, time was running out.

The traffic jam cleared faster than I'd hoped. I pretended to listen as Trevor talked excitedly about the party, but my mind was elsewhere. My whole body went numb when we pulled off the highway.

"You, uhh, have all your stuff with you?" Trevor asked. "We're almost there."

"Oh, right," I mumbled. "Uh, yeah, no time to go by Cara's to get ready, guess I'm changing in here." I unbuckled my seat belt and reached behind me to grab my bag.

"I won't peek, don't worry," Trevor said with a laugh. "I'm a regular Southern gentleman."

"Huh?" I looked at him and realized he was flirting; my brain was going so slow. "Yeah, uh, I bet you are," I responded awkwardly. *Oh my god, Imogen, pull yourself together!* I turned my back to Trevor, took off my coat and top, and slipped a tight-fitting red dress over my head and down over my butt.

"Can I look yet?" Trevor asked.

He had his hand up to the right side of his face to block his view—a gentleman, indeed. I reached over, lowered it, and when I did, he almost rear-ended the car in front of us. *If only,* I thought. Nervous as I was, I couldn't help but smile. "Make us even later than we're gonna be, all you'll ever get to do is look," I said.

Trevor moved his hands to ten and two, kept his eyes on the road and *only* the road, signaled every lane change, and drove the speed limit, his head on a swivel for the police. Google Maps' prediction was exactly right; we pulled up to my house at nine on the dot. By then, I could tell the party was alive and well. The music was thumping loud, multicolored lights danced behind the drawn shades, and the unmistakable smell of vapes and Swisher Sweet blunts was faint on the wind.

I kicked off my boots, shimmied out of my leggings, and slipped my feet into the heels I'd packed. Then I lowered the visor mirror to check my makeup and took my time reapplying my lipstick. I dug around in my bag, looking for more things to do, but there was nothing left.

"Goodness gracious, you look incredible," Trevor said as he took me in. "I feel like I should've spruced up."

"Don't even. You're lookin all kinds of good, and if we weren't already late, I'd make us late." I grinned. He had on a monochromatic outfit of different greens with gold accents—a gold watch on his wrist, a gold chain around his neck, and gold laces on his green Jordans. His fit and the look on his face, the smile at the corners of his lips, the wonder in his eyes, and the plainly visible desire were enough to make me forget Manny's bad news, if only for a second.

"Remember: it's your night. Anything you need, I got you, promise." Trevor put his pinky out, and when I wrapped my little finger around his, I fell even more in love with him.

I knew, right then, what I needed to do. I needed to march into the party, find Zeke, and tell him the truth: Trevor was the one for me and that was that, consequences be damned. It couldn't wait until after the party, and it certainly needed to happen before his surprise. *You can do this, Imogen.* I took three long, deep breaths—in with the blue, out with the red—and climbed out of Trevor's truck.

"Hey, would you mind if we walked in separate?" I asked as we approached my house. "Just because of everything with Zeke," I added. "I need to try and talk to him. I know it's kind of weird, but—"

"Imogen Eleanor Parker, what'd I just say? Your night. I got you, girl, no sweat," Trevor said. "I'll be right behind you, enjoying the view."

chapter twenty
ZEKE

Cara came up to me at eight thirty to tell me that Imogen was fifteen minutes away. I found it a little weird that she'd be so late to her own party, but I wasn't stressing. Still, when eight forty-five came and went and she still hadn't showed, I tried my best to hide my growing irritation, unlike Cara.

"I can't believe this shit! She said eight thirty, and now it's almost nine! I'm pissed! We had a deal," Cara said, a little tipsy already.

"What do you mean, a deal?" I asked.

"Oh," Cara said. "Just . . . that she wouldn't be late. That was the deal. I need a new drink. You want something?"

"Not until Gen gets here," I said, and shook my head.

Cara let out an exasperated sigh. "What about you, Manny?" she asked.

"I'm good, cuzzo," Manny said.

"God, she better hurry her ass up. You two are no fun," Cara said as she walked off.

As soon as Cara was out of earshot, Manny turned to me. "Okay, she's almost here. I'm just gonna say it again, man. You may not wanna hear it, but I'm fuckin right. This ain't the time or the place. Don't do it. Not unless you wanna ruin the whole night."

"Man, don't."

"I'm telling you, Zeke. I swear, I'm telling you, with all my heart, I think this is a *bad* idea."

"Yeah, whatever." I rolled my eyes. "Just kill the music when I give you the signal."

"No," Manny said.

"No?"

"For your own good. No."

"Don't mess with me right now, Manny."

"Please don't do this."

"*Do it,*" I growled. "You said you had my back."

"Fine. Don't say I didn't warn you," Manny said as he put his headphones on and turned away from me.

"Fine yourself," I said, knowing he couldn't hear me, and looked out at the party. There must've been fifty, sixty people, at least. The dance floor was packed. The lights shifted slow and soft through the color spectrum, the room heavy with shadows and alluring darkness.

Dark as it was, though, I couldn't miss when Imogen walked in. When she stepped through the front door, it felt like everything stopped. Time, the music, reality itself—it came to a halt for that one perfect moment as she entered, sexy as hell in a red dress. My mouth went dry, my heart started thumping, and I felt a bead of sweat run between my shoulder blades and down my spine. For that second the world was paused, I was afraid. I knew what I wanted to say, I knew what I had to do, but I couldn't take that first step toward her.

"Head in the game, Zeke. This is it. Go time, can't freeze up now. Bottom of the ninth. We're up a run. Slugger on the plate. You know what to do. Time to play ball, Ladoja," I murmured to myself. "Game time."

And just like that, everything unpaused, and the world started moving again. I took a breath to steady myself and pushed my way through the crowd to her.

"Welcome home and happy birthday, Gen! What do you think? Is it the party of your dreams or what?"

She looked nervous, almost uncomfortable.

"Don't worry, it'll be spotless after! Guaranteed!"

She cocked her head in confusion. "What? No, that's not— Zeke, can we talk real quick? Upstairs?" Imogen said.

She hadn't said anything about the lights, the music, the decorations. "Oh, we'll go upstairs later, bet." I grinned. "But we been waitin on you, birthday girl, so let's get you a drink and start the celebrations! Birthday girl, comin through!" I shouted as I put an arm around her shoulder and pushed through the crowd.

"We got gin, we got tequila, we got . . . this nasty licorice shit that Manny says is good but, like, nah. You want some of that herb, we got that too, just ask Braejon," I said, leaning close to her so she could hear me over the noise.

Her lips were so close to mine. I wanted to make a move. She was right there. But I couldn't. Not yet. I had a plan, and even though the night hadn't gone exactly the way I wanted, now that Imogen was at the party, it was time to get back on track. And as soon as she got a cup in her hand, it was time to execute.

"Zeke, for real, I need to talk to you," Imogen said, and grabbed my arm. She pulled on me, trying to get me away from the party. "*Please*, Zeke. It's important."

"C'mon, Gen! Can't it wait? Everyone's been waiting for you. Let me get you a drink!" I tried to guide her back toward the kitchen. She planted her feet and stood firm, but she was the guest of honor and was swarmed by people eager to see her.

"Daaamn, girl, you *in* that dress! Where you get that?"

"Happy birthday, Imogen! That sweet sixteen!"

"Birthday fit on point, I see you!"

I left her to be questioned and complimented as I made her a drink and used the opening to text Manny.

Me: It's time

I put my phone away and returned to Imogen's side, drink in hand. "Gin and juice," I said as I handed her the cup. "Hope it's not too strong."

"Listen, Zeke, there's something you need to know. I'm—"

Out of the corner of my eye, I saw Manny look up at me from across the crowd, and for a moment, I didn't know what he was going to do. Maybe he didn't either. Maybe he still thought he was right. I was about to head over to him to do it myself when the music began to fade out. I grinned and gave Manny a thumbs-up.

He shook his head, set the mic on the table, and folded his arms. Cara was standing next to Manny. She said something to him, and when he replied, she turned and scowled at me, then left the room.

"Hold that thought, okay? I gotta do something real quick," I told Imogen, then headed toward Manny. I walked up, grabbed the mic, tapped it to make sure it was on, then I climbed up onto the table and cleared my throat. "I'm sorry to interrupt, but we're not just here to get buck wild. We're here to celebrate someone's birthday. A very special someone: the one, the only, the incredible and incomparable Imogen Eleanor Parker!"

The room exploded in applause, whoops, whistles. The crowd nudged her forward until she was standing in the center of the dance floor, lit up by the spotlights around the room, all eyes on her. She looked nervous as hell, which was understandable, everyone's eyes on her. I had to do a double take, though, when I noticed Trevor a little ways behind her. I hadn't invited him, so what was he doing here? But I didn't have time to think about that—I had a plan to execute.

"We'll get back to the party in a second. I promise I won't take up too much time, but I've got a surprise for Imogen. Something I've been wanting to do for a long time. So, Imogen, everyone, can I have your attention, please?"

chapter twenty-one
IMOGEN

"So, Imogen, everyone, can I have your attention, please?" Zeke said. He was standing atop the table, careful around Manny's equipment, and waited for the crowd to calm down before continuing. I hardly felt the hands of the crowd around me on my shoulders, nudging me forward, my feet heavy as anvils. I must have looked like a baby giraffe, uncharacteristically awkward and uncertain in my heels. I hadn't even taken a sip of my drink yet. I chugged it then, grateful for the warmth blooming in my belly and the way it dulled the world around me as Zeke opened his mouth to continue.

"Imogen, we've known each other since we were kids. You've always been my best friend, the only person who could bring me out of a funk no matter what. When Pops got his diagnosis, you were the first person I told. You were there for me right away. You've been there with him during his chemo, not just to help me and my mom, but because you love Pops, too. He's been there for you, and now, you're there for him. It means a lot to us. To me. More than you can imagine. But how my family feels about you, how you feel about my family, that's not what I'm up here to talk about."

Fuck, Zeke, don't, I thought. My face got hot. The crowd was abuzz with whispers and laughs, whistles and *oooooh*s. I had never been so embarrassed in my life.

I stared at Zeke, my face fixed in fear, his eyes full of desire and victory and love. That was what made everything so difficult— what I saw in his eyes truly *was* love. The way I felt around Trevor, how he made me feel light, how he gave me the best kinds of shivers, how I wanted to hear his thoughts on anything and everything, how I delighted in making him laugh, how I hadn't even known I could laugh as hard as I did when I was with him—that was how Zeke felt about me. In that moment, from the way he was looking at me, I could tell. I wasn't just someone he wanted to get with. I wasn't *just* someone at all to him, and he truly believed this was what it took to win me over.

"This won't go on long—it's a party, after all—so I'll just say this," Zeke continued. "Gen, when we're together, you make me feel like I'm flying. Like I'm weightless. I have a feeling it's the same for you. I know your folks've always said you couldn't date till you were sixteen. Well, as of today, you're sixteen, so let me ask you the question I *been* wanting to ask you."

Zeke straightened himself up and cleared his throat. He looked right at me, so happy, so expectant, and reached a hand out toward me.

"Imogen Eleanor Parker, will you be my girl?" Zeke said.

Manny was shaking his head from behind his DJ table, his face in his hands. I didn't see Cara anywhere. The air was heavy, the room almost silent, but for a few scattered whispers. Everyone was staring at me, waiting, and it took everything I had not to crumple into myself under the scrutiny.

"Can . . . can we talk about this somewhere else?" I said in a hoarse voice.

"*Oh shit,*" someone said.

"Huh? What'd you say?" Zeke said, still grinning.

"*Girl, do it!*"

"Can we do this somewhere else?" I said. "In private?"

"*Oh, this gon be good.*"

"Why? What's wrong?" Zeke said, his face falling.

My legs were shaking. My entire body was hot. Sweat rolled down my forehead. There was something heavy on my chest and I couldn't breathe.

"Gen? You all right?" Zeke asked.

Of course I'm not okay, I didn't have the breath to say. *Not by a long shot. Not with everyone staring at me. Not with the weight of your feelings made heavy by the years, our parents, everyone who's ever commented on the two of us together, everyone who's asked when we were gonna get married and what kind of wedding we'd have and what kind of dress I was going to wear. It's all too much. I don't want it. I don't want you.*

I didn't know I was falling until I felt arms underneath me, holding me up.

"Hey, girl, I got you, you're okay," Trevor said.

I looked up at him. At the worry on his face, his nervous smile, his Texas-sun-dark skin. He made everything better. He made everything melt away. He made me weightless. I wanted to be lifted up, not pushed down, and that was the difference between

Zeke and Trevor. Trevor listened. Zeke didn't. Trevor wanted me to be happy. Zeke wanted *himself* to be happy. At my request, Trevor would've whisked me away from there without a second thought. But Zeke? Even as I started to panic, even as I asked for a minute to have a private conversation, leaving never crossed his mind. Nothing did, except *his* plan, *his* surprise, because I was *his* girl. Except I wasn't his girl. I wasn't and I never would be and if he didn't want to listen to me, then I had to do something to *make* him listen. Something I had wanted to do all day.

I pressed my lips against Trevor's, my eyes closed, and a loud gasp filled the room, followed by the loud squeak of a pair of sneakers screeching to a halt. When I pulled away and opened my eyes, I saw Trevor stunned into stillness, his eyes wide but still wanting; Zeke, statue-still, jaw-dropped, and ashen-faced; and a whole room of folks looking at me, hands over their mouths like I'd just killed someone, as I realized what I had just done.

Why did all my mistakes involve kissing?

Trevor helped me back to my feet, and I turned to Zeke. His bottom lip was quivering, his eyes dim and tear-wet. The light I was so used to seeing in his eyes was gone. I hadn't seen him look this crushed and empty and hollow since the day he found out about his dad's cancer.

"I . . . uh . . . um . . . I guess, happy birthday," Zeke said, just before he ran out the house. I heard a car door slam shut, and by the time I'd reached the front door, Zeke was gone.

chapter twenty-two
ZEKE

What the fuck just happened?

"Stay cool, Zeke. You're okay."

How could she do this to us?

"Eyes on the road, Zeke. Keep it together. Almost home," I said to the empty car.

I wiped my face with the sleeve of my nice jacket—all black but lined with gold silk decorated with black fists—that I only busted out when I needed to look all kinds of fresh. Now it was smeared with snot, a streak of white across the fabric. It was going to need to be dry-cleaned; Ma was going to be mad.

What are you gonna tell her?

I pulled onto my street, rolled up slow to the curb, parked, and turned the engine off. The lights inside were low, but I could still make out my parents on the couch, bathed in the flickering light of the TV.

I wasn't ready to go inside and face them. It was cold but not freeze-your-balls-off cold, so I leaned the seat back as far down as it could go, closed my eyes, and waited for the tears to stop.

It's Trevor's fault. Country boy thinks he can come up here, swoop in on my girl. Bet he got her thinking he's a better ballplayer and all kinds of nonsense. Shoulda seen this coming, shoulda known he was no good.

"I'll just say the party ended early 'cause Imogen got sick," I told myself. "That'd work, right? No, 'cause then Ma'll reach out and ask if she's okay. If she needs any medicine or ginger ale. Might even try to go over there since her folks're still gone, and then I'm *really* screwed."

You're screwed no matter what.

"I could tell them someone called the cops. A noise complaint. But that's the kind of thing Ma'd definitely ask Mrs. Parker about. And if Brian found out about that, he'd go completely nuts."

There are no good options, man. She's not into you, everything's ruined, get over it.

"I could just tell them the truth? But they're gonna wanna talk about it, and that's the last thing I wanna do."

No wedding bells, no cuddling in bed together, no next kiss.

"Shut up," I said to myself. "She's just . . . she was overwhelmed. And Trevor, he's just . . . he's just the new thing. She'll get over it, bet. Girls date the wrong guy all the time because they're scared of their real feelings.

"Yeah," I said, suddenly more animated, eager to believe myself, the windows fogging up as I talked. "It happens *exactly* like this in all those shows and everything. The main character tries to get the girl they love to admit her feelings and then the girl freaks out, does something she doesn't even *mean* to do, realizes she messed things up bad, and faces her feelings.

"So, all I need to do is stay the course, be the top nigga I am, and she'll come to her senses, 'cause there's no way she'd choose him over me. She'd be crazy not to choose me. I've been there for her since jump—"

A quick, loud rapping on the passenger window scared me half to death.

"You *best* not be gettin freaky in front of our house," my mom said, standing there in her thick Pepto-pink terry-cloth robe. The window was closed, her voice muffled, but I heard her words loud and clear. The power of moms, man.

"Why're you back so early?" my mom asked me as I got out of the car. "It's barely past eleven. Didn't expect you home till late-late. Gen in there?"

"She's not, and, uh, there was—some kids got into a fight. Someone started throwing hands and broke some stuff. Imogen got all kinds of pissed and kicked everyone out," I said.

Nice one.

"Even you? Wasn't tonight the big night?"

Shit.

"Oh, she just, umm, you know how Brian gets. I think, I dunno, she got sorta nervous about him getting mad. And her anxiety, so—"

My mom put a hand up to stop me.

"What?"

"Zeke," she said.

"Ma, it's cold, and you're in your pajamas and your slippers. Let's get inside."

"*Zeke,*" she repeated.

"You're always tellin me I'ma catch a death of cold or whatever, so let's go," I said, pushing her forward. Strong as I was, she didn't budge. All of a sudden, she weighed ten tons.

"Boy, you better get those hands off me. Trying to push me around, you musta lost your whole mind. Now, I won't tell your father or ask you questions, not tonight. But I want the *truth*."

I sucked my teeth and walked toward the front door.

"You're really going to just walk away from me?"

"I don't even know what you're talking about!"

"You think I don't know how you look when you've been crying? I've wiped away more of your tears than you have, so don't stand here and lie to my face about something you been talking about all year."

I froze, my hand on the ice-cold doorknob. My eyes started to well up as my mind traveled back to Imogen's house, to the moment she kissed Trevor.

How could she do this to me?

"Ma, I love you, but you don't know what the hell you're talking about. I told you what happened, and that's it," I said.

I didn't wait for her reply. I turned the doorknob, walked inside, marched up the stairs to my room, and slammed the door. I expected her to chase after me, to yell at me to get my butt downstairs and apologize for my attitude, to take my keys and my phone, to do *something*. But a few moments later, I heard her come inside, lock the front door behind her, and that was it. No footsteps, no shouting, no nothing, until my mom unpaused the movie and the sounds of *The Equalizer* filled the air.

I needed to listen to some music, something to block out all the bad thoughts. Definitely not anything that reminded me of Imogen or was the kind of music you listen to when you're sad and all up in your feelings—the absolute *last* thing I wanted. I pulled out my phone to open up Spotify and realized I hadn't looked at my phone since just before my speech. I'd placed it on Do Not Disturb right after I'd texted Manny to turn off the music because I didn't want any interruptions.

Time to assess the damage, I guess, I said as I unlocked my phone. It'd been barely an hour since everything went down, and I already had over a hundred messages and notifications.

Someone had captured the entire thing—on me like a *Maury* cameraman from the moment I got up on the table to the moment I ran out the room—and posted it with the music from that show with the old guy who made *Seinfeld*, the one in all the memes that sounds like what you'd play at a clown's funeral. They had posted it from their Finsta, so I couldn't tell who was behind the camera. The video ran right up until Trevor kissed Imogen, then froze and zoomed in on my horrified face, and added in that voiceover clip, "It was at this moment that he knew he'd fucked up."

It wasn't the best idea, but I kept scrolling. It seemed like the whole school'd come out of the woodwork to clown on me with an endless supply of GIFs and memes.

Will Smith saying, "Oh damn!"

Wee-Bey Brice looking like he just discovered the meaning of life.

Chris Pratt, before he went wrong, wide-eyed and jaw-dropped.

Jordan Peele dripping wet with sweat.

Homie with the red Solo cup walking away.

Crying Michael Jordan.

Crying Michael Jordan with my face Photoshopped in.

All the classics, one after the next.

I tried to laugh at them. I tried to pretend it wasn't about me, that all of this had happened to someone else, but that didn't work at all, not even a little. It still hurt too much. I still felt sick to my stomach and so, *so* angry. My jaw hurt from clenching too hard. I wanted to break something, to scream at the top of my lungs, but the best I could do was punch my pillows as hard as possible. It helped a little, but not enough.

I scrolled past my texts from Manny, Cara, and Imogen—I wanted to read them last—and started with some from the team.

Braejon: Hey bruh, man that was fucked up.

Braejon: U good? U need anything, B got ya back fam!

Dink: Hey dude. That was rough.

Dink: You need someone to talk to, let me know.

Dink: I've been there. Rejection and all, I mean.

Axel: Yoooooooooooo

Axel: We just showed up and wasn't no party

Axel: But TX answered the door like ???

Axel: U kno he's like, @ yr girls???

Axel: Where the party @ now?????

Axel: Hmu bout the new spot

Axel: Oh n yovani says u a bich jajaja

They weren't as bad as I expected. I thought Axel at least would lay into me a little harder, and I was grateful he didn't. It made looking at Manny's messages that much easier.

Manny: Hate 2 say i told u so

Manny: But i fkn told u so dude

Manny: Hmu we need 2 talk.

Manny: Lmk yr okay, k?

Manny: Don't do anything crazy

Manny: And stay off insta

Manny: It's gonna b okay dude

Manny: Zeke

Manny: Z E K E

Manny: Ezekiel Amal-up-in-my-feelings Ladoja

Manny: Don't make me come over there

Manny: Don't make me spam u either

I didn't want to respond to Manny, not yet, because I knew he was gonna come back with a storm of texts trying to get all up in my business, so I moved on to Cara's.

Cara: U ok? Stupid question, ofc yr not.

Cara: Who would be after that?

Cara: Don't need to text back or nothing

Cara: Just want u to know I'm here for u always. Hope u know that.

Cara: No matter what

Cara: I'll cover yr shift tomorrow so don't worry about that.

Cara: I'll tell jojo you're sick or smth

Cara: Ima come check on you in the next couple days

Cara: And I won't take no for an answer so you better open the door

Cara: If u wanna sit and watch xfiles

Cara: Don't even need 2 talk, I'm in

Cara: If that'd help you feel better, just lmk ok?

Cara: ♥ talk soon?

For all her bluff and bluster, Cara was a softie at heart. She didn't show that side of herself to a lot of people. Just me, mostly. I had forgotten about work altogether, so her covering my shift was a relief. And drowning out everything that had happened over the past several hours with a marathon of Mulder and Scully? Sounded like just the thing I needed.

Me: Thanks c

Me: Don't really feel like talkin now

Me: But yeah, soon

Me: 👍 to xfiles marathon

And then there were the ones I was dreading most: the messages from Imogen. I tapped on them, expecting the worst, but there wasn't much to them. They were short, to the point.

Imogen: Zeke, I'm so, so sorry about what I did. I'm not proud of it. It wasn't right that I did what I did during such a big moment, right in front of you and everyone else. It wasn't the respectful, mature thing to do.
Imogen: Instead, I did the opposite, pretty much the worst thing I could do, and I'm so sorry. You're my best friend, Zeke, and I really, really don't want that to change. I want

you in my life. I hope, one day, you can forgive me.

Imogen: Please don't take this out on Trevor. He didn't know that was going to happen. I didn't even know it was going to happen! I just want us to be okay. You mean so much to me, Zeke, and I care about you so much. Please say something so I know you're okay?

"Say something? What is there to even say?" I said. "'Oh, hey, I'm okay, just recovering from getting stabbed in the back. Had my world shattered but, sure, I'm doing just fucking fine.' Not like I was just embarrassed in front of the whole school!"

I stared up at the ceiling, listening to explosions and gunfire coming from the TV downstairs. They just could not get enough of Denzel taking care of business. I wondered if Denzel'd ever had problems like this. I bet not.

My stomach growled. I had been too nervous to eat before the party; now the leftover pulled pork in the fridge was calling my name too loud for me to resist. I slipped out my bedroom and tiptoed down the stairs.

"Ooh, get him, Denzel. He bad," I heard my mom say as I approached the kitchen.

"Y'all just wait till he gets that nail gun! Gonna be cleanup on aisle nine on y'all's asses," my dad said as I started looking in the fridge for food, waiting for the loud parts to make my own noise. I was pulling the Tupperware out when—

"Zeke," my mom said, and I jumped, almost dropping the container on the ground. She gestured for me to take off my headphones and I did, resting them around my neck.

"Shoot, Ma. Scaring me half to death," I said, forcing a laugh.

"Are you okay?" she said, and she wasn't laughing.

"I'm just hungry," I said.

"I'm serious, Zeke. Are you okay?"

"Bring him over here," my dad said, his voice barely audible over the TV. Ever since he started chemo, I'd hated being near my dad, hated looking at him. It always felt like so much of him was missing, and every time I saw him, my memory of him started missing more and more too.

"I'll make you a plate. Just go over and sit with your father," Ma said.

I sighed, then headed over to the armchair next to the couch and faced forward, focused on Denzel, not my dad.

"Gen's birthday was tonight," my dad said.

I didn't say anything.

"Know you've been waiting for this for a minute."

I was quiet, still.

"And then I heard you and your mama fightin out front. So, what happened?"

"Everything's fine," I said.

"Everything's fine, huh."

"Yeah, that's what I said."

"Don't think just because I got cancer, you can talk back to me. Best check your attitude, Ezekiel."

"Sorry, Dad," I muttered.

"I don't know what happened tonight. Don't need to know neither. But you ain't a quitter. I didn't raise you to be a quitter. You don't see me quittin either. I hurt, boy, all damn day. I hurt, and I'm tired, and I know why you try your damn hardest not to look at me because I do the same thing. I look like a skeleton. Like someone took all the meat off my bones and left me with nothin. You love her, right? But you're gonna give up 'cause this one thing didn't work? What kind of sense does that make?"

"You don't get it," I said.

"I don't get what?"

"She . . . there's another *guy*, Dad. And I'm just . . . she said I was her best friend and she doesn't want that to change. Those were her exact words," I said, louder than I intended. "So, what the hell am I supposed to do with that?"

I looked up at my dad through tears I hadn't realized were there. Despite how much he'd changed in the last year, his eyes were still the same, and when he reached his hand out to squeeze my shoulder the way he did before every one of my Little League games growing up, the way he did before my final game of our almost-championship season, he felt just as strong as he used to. He felt just as everything as he used to.

"It's okay, Zeke," he said. "Did you tell her how you feel? I mean, really tell her?"

"I gave a whole speech in front of everyone and—"

"That's not what I'm sayin, son. I'm sayin, did you tell her and *only* her how you feel? The two of you. Eye to eye, without a whole mess of people around. 'Cause that's different. Some girls don't want that kind of attention. I know your mama wouldn't. If I'd tried that, she'd've pulled the nearest fire alarm and run out the room screaming. Can't be putting people on the spot like that."

"So . . . what do I do?"

"You go talk to her," my dad said after taking a long sip of water, wincing as he gulped it down. "Just the two of you. Heart-to-heart. Tell her how you feel. Just be you. Not Zeke Ladoja, the star of the team. Not Zeke Ladoja, whose dad's got a bad case of butt cancer," he said with a short, dry laugh that got me to smile for the first time since the kiss.

"Just be Zeke. No speeches. No performance. Just you. You're a man now. No need to hide behind fancy words and grand gestures. All you need's you. I've known that girl a long, long time, and let me tell you—I think there's something there. Always have. But you gotta be willing to *fight*. Got it?"

I jumped up from my chair and gave my dad a big hug. It didn't bother me how insubstantial he felt in my arms. Sick or not, he was my dad and he was right—I couldn't give up without a fight.

"Now, sit down and hush up. Denzel's boutta mess these folks in this Home Depot *all* the way up."

I let him go and settled back into the armchair. "Why do you guys keep watching this movie anyway? You've seen it like a million times."

"Boy, were you not listening to a single thing I said? If somethin's real good, if somethin's *quality*, you stick with it. You come back to it. Nessa! Denzel's got the nail gun! Better hurry on in here!"

"You know I'm already comin," she said as she hustled into the room, handing me a plate with a pulled pork sandwich and a side of greens, before snuggling up with my pops.

We watched Denzel get downright vicious in an off-brand Home Depot. And I had to admit, it *was* pretty damn good.

chapter twenty-three
IMOGEN

I woke up in my bed on top of my comforter, still in my dress from the night before, my shoes off, a blanket over me. When I sat up, it felt like my whole skull was about to implode, which meant that, unfortunately, everything that had happened the night before wasn't all just a bad, bad dream. The last thing I remembered was lying on the couch, sobbing into a pillow as Trevor and Manny cleaned up.

My phone was on my nightstand, along with a glass of water, a bottle of Gatorade, some Advil, and a handwritten note.

Mornin, Gen, the note read. *I bet you're not feelin too well. I got you some things to help. I know the drill, used to do the same for my moms. Not that you're anything like her, I mean. Anyway, last night got a little crazy, huh? I want to talk about everything when you feel better, 'cause this might cause some problems. But now, deep breaths, drink this water, chug this Gatorade, pop those pills. Everything's gonna be okay. Be kind to yourself.*

P.S. You sleep cute.

I realized I was holding my breath and let it out in a big exhale. I was so relieved Trevor didn't hate me for what happened. I was already so mad at myself, I couldn't handle Trevor feeling some kind of way too.

"God, what were you *thinking*," I said to myself. My voice was scratchy and on the verge of going out from crying so much.

I sighed and grabbed my phone. "Time to assess the damage, I guess," I said as I opened up my message thread with Zeke. I had vague, patchy memories of writing the message I sent him after a couple shots of what little alcohol was left. Zeke had read my messages last night, but he hadn't responded, and it was almost noon.

I jumped over to Instagram and groaned when I saw my feed full of memes making fun of Zeke. They were going to make everything so much worse. There were some about me, too, but not many. People went after me in the comments instead. They called me a ho, a slut, a tease, a bitch, and I wasn't sure they were wrong. I scrolled through my feed and messaged each and every person who had posted something about Zeke, asking them to stop. Yeah, it was kind of a pathetic thing to do, and it most likely wasn't gonna work at all, but I couldn't think of a better option.

After sending a few dozen messages, I rolled out of bed to change into some pajamas. The moment I stood up, the pain behind my eyes got knife-sharp, and I buckled to the ground. Just like the night before, right before I fucked *everything* up.

"No, none of that, Gen. Remember what Trev said. Be kind to yourself," I said, my voice whisper-quiet, even though I knew the house was empty. I used the wall for support as I left my room and started down the hallway. It was bright from the near-noon sunshine coming through the skylight. The curtains had been drawn in my room, so the sudden shift into a bright world made my headache even worse. I closed my eyes, guiding myself to the railing and the staircase, and opened them to descend the stairs. When I did, I gasped.

The place was *spotless*, as if no one had ever been there. The dance floor had been disassembled, the pieces neatly stacked in a corner of the room. The floor had been steam-mopped, the wood warm and glowing from the fresh clean. The couches were back in their original positions. There weren't any loose cups or broken glass, no stains or scuffs. I wasn't sure if it was because the party ended early or because Trevor put in the work, but the morning-after mess I was expecting just wasn't there.

I made my way to the kitchen, hoping that my headache'd get better if I ate something, not that there was much to eat. Peanut butter on toast was going to have to do. I tossed two slices into the toaster oven and took a seat at the kitchen table as the machine tick-tick-ticked away.

Me: Trev

Me: Did u srsly clean my whole house???

Trev: Morning, miss lady

Trev: Wasn't just me. Manny helped, it was no big deal

Trev: How u feelin?

Me: Like crap

Me: I can't believe u did that!!

Trev: Course I did. U had a tough night, least I could do

Me: U aren't mad at me?

Me: For putting u in this situation?

Trev: I mean wouldve preferred for things to go different

Trev: Will this make being on the team harder? Yes

Trev: But I can't be mad at u

Trev: The way u make me feel

Trev: It'd take a lot more'n that for me to b mad

Me: Omg u have to stop

Me: Thank u for being the best

Trev: Haha the best? Nah

Trev: U heard from Zeke?

Me: No . . . he left me on read

Me: I feel so bad

Trev: I mean it wasn't great

Trev: But Manny said he tried to tell him.

Trev: And u tried to talk 2 him b4 it happened yeah?

Me: Yeah

Trev: So u coulda handled things better, sure

Trev: But Z set himself up for a bad time.

Trev: Didn't listen to u or respect yr feelings.

Trev: Evry1 said it was a bad idea so idk how much of its
on u

The toaster oven dinged. I set my phone down to grab my toast and started spreading the peanut butter on when I heard a loud knock at the front door that scared the hell out of me.

"Shit!" I shouted as I dropped the knife. It was just a butter knife, but I jumped back like it was the sharpest blade ever forged.

The knife smeared peanut butter on the bottom of my pajama top before landing on the freshly cleaned floor with a sticky *schlap*. "Damn it, Trevor just cleaned this."

I grabbed some paper towels, wet them under the faucet, and started rubbing at the peanut butter on my shirt on my way to the door. I glanced out the window and was surprised to see Zeke. I opened the door and looked out at him, stunned.

"Hey, Gen," he said. "Can we talk?"

"Uhh," I said. "Um, yeah. Come in, I was just—"

"Peanut butter toast," he said, slipping his shoes off as I returned to the kitchen. "I know."

"Hah, yeah. So, uh, you want somethin to drink?" I grabbed a rag and squatted down to wipe up the peanut butter on the floor. I felt his eyes watching me and my every movement.

"Sure. You got juice?"

"Orange and apple, what you want?"

"Is it that clear apple or is it that cloudy stuff?"

"The second."

"Then, yeah, gimme that."

I grabbed a glass from the cupboard, poured the juice, and joined him at the table. An awkward silence moved into the room. I hadn't been able to read his face at the door. The sunlight had made the snow blinding bright, and I couldn't look at him without feeling like someone was sliding a red-hot needle into my eye socket. Now that we were inside and the headache had dulled to a throbbing, pulsing vise closing on my temples, I saw his eyes were bloodshot, as if he hadn't gotten much sleep, as if he'd been crying all night. I hoped that meant my apology had landed well and that the hangover was going to be the worst part of the weekend.

"Crazy, you got it cleaned up so fast," Zeke said to break the silence.

"Oh yeah," I said. "So . . . uhh, so what's up?"

"Promise to let me say my whole thing?" Zeke said.

"I mean, yeah. For sure. That's fair." My breath was stuck in my chest, frozen still in my lungs as I waited for the other shoe to drop. Maybe he was here to apologize and make peace and be my best friend again. But could he bounce back that fast?

"Okay," Zeke said, taking a breath. "Last night wasn't cool. I really messed up, and I'm sorry. I put you on the spot and put all our business out in the world. I sprung that on you all at once and that's not okay. I ruined your birthday party. I realized last night that I never actually planned it for *you*. If I had, things woulda gone different, but I realized, nah, I planned that for *me*."

The trapped breath escaped me in a long, slow, quiet exhale. I sank into my chair as muscles I didn't know I had started to unclench. Even my headache started to ebb away.

"I did bad, I know. And I'm hurting, too. That's the hardest part—the person I wanna go to when I'm struggling is you. Always been you. Called you first when I found out about my pops. Called you first when we made finals. Nobody I trust more than you. You mean more to me than damn near anything in this whole world, and I'm so sorry I hurt you."

I was crying. Like, blubbering. Big ol' tears rolling down my cheeks. *This* was the Zeke I knew. The boy who was so kind and good and giving, who I trusted with my life, who was there for me no matter what, and it was such a relief to know that he understood. That we were going to be okay.

"Thank you. I really, really, really needed to hear that. You're like my rock, Z. I still have the voicemail you left to help talk me through my panic attacks.

"And I'm sorry too. Like, I *also* messed up, you know? I just . . . I guess I panicked? I shouldn't have done that. And in front of everyone? I can't imagine how that made you feel, and I'm so, so sorry. I've seen all the stuff on Insta, it's all so mean, and I hate that people are doing that to you. I told a bunch of them to stop."

Zeke held up a hand. "Nah, it's okay. I can handle it. But, yeah, that's what I wanted to say. Oh, and I wanted to give you your birthday present."

"Bruh, you don't need to give me *anything*. Save the money for your moms or something."

Zeke shook his head. "No way, Gen. Birthdays are sacred, you know that. So, here." He got up from the table, went over to his bag, and pulled out a thick, rectangular package a little smaller than a shoebox. It was crimson, and my name was elegantly written across the top in a gold ink that matched the thin golden string tied around the package. "Go ahead, open it."

I tugged the string loose, unwrapped the package, and gasped. Inside was a beautiful, leather-bound copy of the first *Outlander* novel. The cover was beautifully designed, gold etched against the book's deep green—absolutely gorgeous.

"Go on, open it up." Zeke grinned.

I opened the cover, savoring the best smell in all the world—

the musty scent of a fresh book—and squealed in delight when I saw Diana's signature staring me back in the face.

"Zeke! You didn't—this is amazing, but . . . wasn't this expensive?"

Zeke shrugged. "I've been raking in good tips at Fro-Yo Jojo this week, for one. And, besides, it's your birthday. Like I'm not gonna come correct. It's no photo album, but—"

I got up from the table and hugged Zeke tight, cutting him short. I felt a wave of relief wash over me that was very short-lived, because when I went to end the hug, he pulled me toward him, his head crooked just so, his eager lips advancing.

"Yo, yo, hold up," I said, pushing myself away from him. "What the hell, Zeke?"

Confusion flickered across Zeke's face for a brief second, then he tried it again.

"Hey!" I shouted as I shoved Zeke as hard as I could. "What are you doing?!"

"But we just . . . I thought we just talked through this. I love you, Gen. I'm sorry I made a mess of your birthday, but I'm gonna make it up to you, starting tonight. I wanna take you out on a date. I made reservations and everything," Zeke said, cheerful but confused.

I stared at Zeke, truly shocked, and backed away from him. "Are you . . . Zeke, are you serious?"

Zeke looked as confused as I felt. "What do you—am I serious? Of course I'm serious. Like, are *you* serious? Imogen, I do *everything* for you. I got you this gift 'cause I *know* it's your perfect, dream gift. I listen to all your problems, do my best to cheer you up when you're having a bad day. Every time your dad tore you down, I helped build you back up. You're always with me. We *been* hanging on to each other. You play-fight with me, you tease me—everyone knows it. Everyone sees it. Our folks do. All our friends. Even strangers on the street," Zeke said, his voice rising. He paused and took a breath. "I get that you're scared, but—"

"Scared?" I shouted. "Scared?! Scared of what?"

"Of how you feel about me. About letting yourself fall in love with me for real," Zeke said, like it was a fundamental fact of the universe.

"You have lost your whole damn mind," I said. "You're my best friend. I love you so much. But don't get it twisted: I'm not scared of being with you—I don't *want* to be with you. I just don't. Please, go." I walked to the front door and opened it. A gust of cold air rushed inside, but I was too angry to feel it.

Zeke froze up, and his eyes went wide and empty. "Whatever. Know what? Fuck it, I'm out. Maybe you have, but I'm not giving up on us," he said as he walked out the door.

I slammed it shut behind him, then curled up on the floor and sobbed as I tried to register what had just happened.

chapter twenty-four
ZEKE

The moment I walked through the doors of Hampton High Monday morning, I felt like Tupac, all eyes on me.

"Chin up, son, there's gonna be others," Alvin, the security guard at the metal detector, told me as I came through. "You gonna be aight. You a king, you gonna find your queen."

"What a shame. I was really rooting for the two of you," Mrs. Dionne said as I passed the front office.

"I think you should fight for her," Ms. Limm added. "It works in all the novels!"

It was still early and the hallways were quiet, mostly empty, save for the occasional teacher or custodian, all of whom gave me long, irritating, piteous looks. Mrs. Koons from government. The Chinese teacher, Ms. Hui. Mrs. Bella from choir. I knew it was pity, too, because everyone'd made the same face when word about my pops started going around. Folks I'd never talked to in my whole life had that pity face on when they told me how sorry they were, how much they admired my father, how hard it must be for my mom. It got real old real quick.

It's gonna be a long day, I thought as I hurried through the halls to the locker room. I wasn't on the team anymore, but I still went to morning workouts when I could. I heard voices and the clank of weights from far down the hall, but the second I entered the weight room, everything went quiet.

I started to look around the room, but Braejon cut in. "You good. Trevor ain't here, chief."

"Nigga, I'm lookin to see what ain't covered in your nasty sweat," I lied, mean-mugging Braejon and the twins and the four other players in the room. I heavied a bar up and lay down on a bench. "Yovani, spot me?"

"Got you," he said.

I saw Braejon look at the rest of the room and shrug. "Anyway, I was saying, after the party, me and Renee—" Braejon started to say when he was interrupted.

"We gonna ask Zeke about what happened with Imogen or—" an out-of-breath Rinky-Dink said as he stumbled into the weight room.

"Dink, come on, man." Braejon slapped his forehead.

Dink looked right at me and put his hand over his mouth.

"Yovani," I said. "You gonna spot me or what?" He had stopped mid-stride when Rinky-Dink entered.

"Yeah, sorry," Yovani said as he got behind the bar. "But bro, *are* we gonna talk—"

"Talk about what?" I said. "There's nothin to talk about. Why don't all of you mind your damn business?"

"Homie, the whole stoic don't-feel-shit kinda man?" Axel said. "Ain't the way anymore."

"Even the grimiest nigga around'd feel some type of way, gettin curved like that in front of damn near everybody they know," Braejon said. "Plus, you know what Coach says: 'Weight room's a safe space and an honest space.' We your boys, man, we got you, so out with it. You mad?"

"I'd be mad as hell," Axel said.

"You won't ever have to worry, Axel, ain't an ounce of game in your whole body," Yovani said.

"We're twins! We got the same body, dipshit."

"Oh yeah?" Yovani said, stepping away from the bar and toward his brother.

"*Yovani,*" I hissed, the bar shaking in my hands.

"My bad, Z," Yovani said, darting back to the bar.

I racked the weight and sat up. "I swear, ain't nobody more gossipy than a room of dumbass niggas," I said. "Look, I went over there yesterday and—"

"The *day* after the party? Nigga, no, you *didn't,*" Braejon said.

"Glug glug glug," Axel said.

"Boy's thirsty!" Yovani followed.

"I wanted to tell her how I felt, without all the pressure of everybody watching and without the alcohol."

"Shit couldn't wait a day?" Braejon said. "As your elder, I gotta say: that's some dumbass shit."

"*Anyway,* how'd it go?" Rinky-Dink asked.

"She was confused about how she felt between me and Trevor, but she still loves me," I said. It wasn't even a flat-out lie—Imogen *did* say she loved me. And she *was* confused about her feelings for me. "She's my girl. I know it. You guys know it. I just gotta get Texas outta the picture."

Yovani and Axel glanced at each other and snickered.

"You two got something to share with the class?" Braejon asked.

"It's probably better if you don't know," Axel said.

"Plausible deniability and all that," Yovani added.

"Big words for you, Yo," Braejon laughed.

"What are you . . . ?" Rinky-Dink asked. Boy couldn't help but be late to the point, every time.

"We make Trevor think twice about swoopin in on your girl," Yovani said. "Make it in his best interests to break up with her."

"You mean, like, bullying him?" Rinky-Dink said. "Nah, that's fucked up."

"So's seducing away your homie's girl," Axel said.

"He's our teammate!" Rinky-Dink shouted, and looked at me. "What if he quits? Without you or Trevor, we're—"

"Just think of it like we're jumping him in, Dink. No one's gonna hurt him or nothin," Braejon said. "Just a little something-something, a message."

A few of the other guys were nodding their heads in agreement.

"Come on, Zeke," Rinky-Dink said. "This is messed up. I mean, we did that anti-bullying thing back—"

I held up a hand to cut Rinky-Dink off. "Hey, I'm not gonna tell anyone what to do. I don't wanna hear about it." I smirked. "What happens, happens. I don't know nothin bout nothin."

"Got you loud and clear. Lock and key, my man," Braejon said as he dapped up the twins. "Dink, you ain't gotta do shit, but you *better* not say shit either. Lock. And. Key. You got it?"

Rinky-Dink nodded, then looked at me with pleading eyes. *Zeke, don't do this,* they said. I felt a pang of guilt in my chest, but only briefly, as the image of Trevor and Imogen kissing surged to the front of my mind. I broke eye contact and lay back down, hands on the bar, smile on my face, ready for another set.

chapter twenty-five
IMOGEN

"I'm not feeling well, I swear," I told my mom. "That's why I didn't go to school yesterday. I'm sorry I didn't call you, but I didn't want to bother you on your last day of vacation."

"Mm-hmm, is that so?" my mom said, and arched an eyebrow. "'Cause you sure don't look sick to me." She touched my forehead. "No fever."

"Mom, *please*, I never ask for anything. Can't you let me stay home, just this once?" My voice hit a register I rarely used, only when things were dire. That got her to pause. She looked at me, eyes narrowed.

"What's going on with you? You're hiding something," she said. "What is it?"

I looked away. There was no way to explain what was going on without also mentioning the party, Zeke, or Trevor. "I'm not hiding anything, I just . . . don't feel good, okay?"

"Is that Cara trying to talk you into skipping school to smoke weed and get lit or whatever?"

I held in a snort of laughter. I didn't want her suspicious *and* mad.

"No, jeez. I just . . . whatever. It's fine, I'll just go. Please don't tell Dad I skipped yesterday."

"Long as the school doesn't call me again to tell me my daughter's not where she's supposed to be, we don't need to tell your father a thing. Are we clear?"

I nodded. "We're clear," I grumbled, trying to keep the attitude out of my voice.

All weekend, the attention had been on Zeke, but on Monday, everything changed. I'd woken up yesterday morning to dozens of notifications flooding my phone in real time.

> hampton ho
>
> smh bitches out here stay curvin real niggas
>
> cheatin ass slut
>
> fuckin tease bitch
>
> this y u can't trust black women, them hoes aint loyal

Most of the posts were from usernames I didn't recognize, but there were some from a few girls who'd always been down bad for Zeke and resented me for the "hold" I had on him.

Niecy Adams, she said in one of her Stories, "I knew she was one of them girls who plays games. I *knew* it. I can always tell which ones are shitty like that. She one of them girls who loves to string along a buncha niggas so she can hedge her bets and tie onto the richest one, just like her sellout-ass mama and her Tommin-ass pops."

Raquel Damaris was going in on one of her Stories: "So, as everybody knows, ol' triflin-ass, goody-two-shoes, rich-bitch, movie-star-daddy Imogen Parker's been playin our boy Zeke. Star of the school. *Fiiiine*-ass nigga. Quit playin ball to take care of his daddy with cancer. Boy wants to give her the world and she goes and steps out on his ass in front of *errybody*," she said, followed by a clip from *Coming to America*, the part where the old woman on the subway tells Akeem, "If you're really a prince, I'll marry you."

U think u kno a person, one of Zeke's teammates wrote. *And then they do some 2faced fuckshit like this.* The likes were racking up like points on a pinball machine.

Even kids from across town who Zeke'd beat the brakes off last season were laying on the hate. There was no end to it, one post after another.

I would've kept scrolling until my eyes bled were it not for the sound of several small thumps downstairs. I rushed out of my bedroom and saw streaks of egg yolk trailing down the front windows. I poked my head out the door and saw a trio of whooping, hollering boys tearing off down the street in a car I didn't recognize.

"What a great start to the week," I said as I grabbed a washcloth from inside and wiped the windows down. It couldn't wait, not unless I wanted my parents finding out. I was cleaning the yolk off the window when I heard the squeal of the school bus rounding the corner. I ducked inside before it got too close, and as it passed, I saw faces pressed up against the bus's windows, looking for me, ready to say something. It was barely audible from inside, but I heard a muffled voice yell out, "Fuck you, bitch!" as the bus rolled by.

That was when I decided to skip. If it was that bad before I'd even reached school, I didn't want to know what it would feel like once I was actually there. I scrubbed the windows clean, then I turned my phone off, got back in bed, and distracted myself by reading the new *Outlander* novel Trevor had bought me, *Go Tell the Bees That I Am Gone*, and writing my way out of my reality.

I didn't turn my phone back on until late that night, and I almost wish I hadn't. The ratio of cruel, hateful messages to kind, supportive messages was about twenty to one. I tried to only look at the good ones, hard as that was.

Dink: Hey Gen. It's 2nd period, haven't seen you yet.

Dink: Assuming you aren't coming to school today.

Dink: I know it's pretty rough on the gram right now

Dink: If you need anything, just lmk okay?

Dink: You've always been cool w me and just a nice person period.

Dink: You don't deserve any of this.

Dink: So yeah, just wanted to say that. Hope yr all right.

Trevor: Missin you at school today.

Trevor: Trust me, you made the right call not showing.

Trevor: People been messin with me all day, makes me wish I skipped too.

Trevor: Anyway, I hope yr all right.

Trevor: Lmk you're ok, ok?

Trevor: I can get yr hw for you

Trevor: And don't let people get you thinking that this is
all on you

Trevor: Cause it ain't. Hope you got some rest today.

Trevor: See you tomorrow? I hope? <3

There were a few texts from Zeke and Cara, too, but I didn't feel like reading them. I couldn't handle that, not yet, not after his visit over the weekend. I was still pissed at him, at the thought of even interacting with him. As for Cara, I wasn't angry, just scared. Now that I knew exactly how she felt about Zeke, the entire situation felt awkward. I kissed another guy in front of the guy she was real into right after he declared his love for me in front of her and everyone else. That had to feel weird, to put it mildly, and she and I needed to have a conversation that I just wasn't ready for.

On Tuesday morning, I left early so as to avoid all the crowds, and because I needed to talk to my teachers about missing class the day before.

Thankfully, it wasn't too cold out. The worst of winter was past, the temperatures were climbing, and I didn't spend the whole walk with my teeth chattering. The downside, though, was that the snowmelt made every car a potential disaster—all it took was someone veering a little too close to the curb, and you'd end up sprayed by the nasty, oily water pooled on the sides of the road. And it certainly seemed like there were enough people who were pissed off at me that it wasn't unreasonable to think someone might splash me in filth on purpose, so I kept my hood up and my face hidden.

Lo and behold, maybe ten minutes into my walk, a car swerved toward me, sending a wave of muckwater my way. I jumped back, almost throwing myself into the snow, and narrowly avoided the splash zone as they sped off. I looked around, embarrassed, and spied an old man across the street peering at me from behind the blinds, his nosy eyes magnified by his thick-lensed glasses, who disappeared as soon as he noticed me looking his way.

When I was in sight of the school, I saw Trevor rush out of the building in his gym clothes. He looked pissed and was carrying his backpack in one hand and a canvas tote bag in the other that read WOMEN OF THE WORLD UNITE! He was heading for his truck, and I followed after him.

"Hey, Trev? You okay?" I asked when I caught up to him at his truck.

He smiled when he saw me, though a cloud quickly settled over his face. "Nah, I'm not okay," he said, uncharacteristically angry. "They hid my keys yesterday. And today, well, first of all"— he tossed his emptied backpack, the cloth soaked dark, into the trunk of the pickup—"that's not water! That's from the boys' bathroom by the library. The middle stall, to be exact. So now I gotta carry everything in this stupid bag Ms. Limm gave me. Not that I don't want women of the world to unite or nothing, but all my books were in there. But that's not even what's got me pissed off. I can deal with all that. I'm new, I gotta get jumped in, that's just how it is."

"You want to get in the truck?" I asked. It was still early and there weren't many people, but Trevor was angry and loud, and the few folks who were around were starting to look our way.

Trevor nodded and climbed in, opening my door for me once

he was inside. "What's really got me mad? When I got my bag from the toilet just now," he said, "I saw carved into the metal door, 'Trev's mom a dead junkie.' And that's crossing the line." He paused. "And the thing is, I've only told you and Zeke about my mom. You didn't say anything, did you?"

My jaw dropped. "Of course not! I'd never do that. I'll tell Mr. Randall, he'll fix it."

"So, if you didn't, then . . ."

I considered what he was saying. "No, Zeke wouldn't do that. I know things are bad with him right now, but he's still a good person. I mean, he led the anti-bullying squad in middle school."

"So, you think that Zeke, the leader of the team, doesn't know that his boys are messing with me, the dude who stole his girl. C'mon now, Gen."

"I was *never* his girl—"

"Tell that to him," Trevor murmured.

"—and Zeke, he's just not like that."

"No disrespect, but I don't think you know him as well as you think you do."

"And you do? You've only known him—and *me*—for a couple weeks," I spat. I regretted my words as soon as they left my lips. "I'm sorry."

Trevor sighed. "It's okay. It's a lot. Let's both just take a breath, yeah?"

My eyes hummed hot with tears. I reached for his hand and squeezed tight.

"It's really hard, Trev. Like, what do you do when someone

who's so important to you, who's almost like a part of you, just . . ." I didn't know how to finish that sentence.

"Only thing to do is talk to him, I guess? I saw him in the gym, so I know he's here."

I let out a big sigh. "Yeah, yeah, I know. Just needed someone else to say it. This is going to suck." I straightened up in my seat, took out my phone, and texted Zeke.

Me: Can we talk? Meet me at my locker?

Zeke replied with a thumbs-up and I put my phone back in my pocket. "Okay, here goes . . ."

I heard Zeke's duffel bag before I saw him. It was this cheap, old Nike bag made out of the raspiest nylon on the face of the earth. Soon as I heard it, I took a deep, calming breath and readied myself. He rounded the corner with a smile on his face that quickly disappeared when he saw the frown on mine.

"Hey, Gen," Zeke said as he came in for a hug. I stepped back, held my arm out.

"Don't, Zeke."

"Oh, so I can't even hug my best friend now?" He narrowed his eyes.

I ignored his question. "You . . . you didn't say anything to the guys about Trevor's mom, did you?"

"What about his mom?"

"About her having died of drugs."

He gave me a blank look.

"Someone scratched something hateful about her into one of the stall doors in the boys' bathroom."

"What's that got to do with me?"

No surprise, no empathy, just hardness. "I want you to lay off Trevor, okay?"

Zeke stepped back. "What are you talking about? I didn't do—"

"People took his keys. They put his backpack in a toilet. He didn't tell that many people about his mom, and he knows I'm not doing it." I gave him a pointed look.

Zeke backed away, holding his hands up. "You serious? That was the first thing we connected on, and it was deep—his mom's overdose, my dad's cancer. You *really* think I'd say something like that?" He looked at me with such sad, disappointed eyes.

"I just . . . Okay, so, then it's gotta be someone on the team, right? The twins, maybe? I mean, this sounds like their kind of thing. Can you talk to them, tell them that he's cool?"

"So, is this what you wanted to talk to me about?" Zeke said after a short pause, his voice cold as stone. "Trevor? That's it?"

"I know it's a little awkward right now, but Zeke, you're still my best friend. That hasn't changed. And right now, I need my best friend's help. Will you talk to them? Please?"

"Oh, that's what best friends are for? I thought that all best friends do is *embarrass you in front of the entire school*. I don't have anything to do with what's going on with Trevor. You think it's the team? Talk to them yourself," Zeke said as he stormed away.

chapter twenty-six
ZEKE

"What about Naimah?" Manny said. "She that Angela Davis–type junior. She *been* feeling you. What's that put us at?"

I sighed and ignored him. When I'd gotten the job, I was excited about working with Manny, goofing and laughing all day, but in the six days since the disastrous party the previous Saturday, the only thing he wanted to talk about was how I could move on, why I should move on, and who I should move on to.

"I *said*, what's that put us at?"

"Oh, you thought I cared?"

"We got *seven*, for your information. Seven whole other girls down bad for you. And that's just off the top of my head. We haven't even looked at your DMs, and don't act like they ain't been poppin off since."

"Am I really gonna have to listen to four more hours of this?"

"Shit, wouldn't be nothin new, didn't listen to me before, either. If you had, you wouldn't be up in this mess."

Manny wasn't wrong; I *should've* listened. If I had done it right the first time, me and Gen and no one else, we'd be together. But I failed spectacularly and sealed myself into the friend-zone tomb.

He wasn't wrong about my DMs, either. My inbox was filled with girls comforting me, striking while the iron was hot. But they were no Imogen.

"So, Naimah?"

"I mean, she's cute and—"

"Cute, bro? *Cute?* I've heard from multiple sources that she's, quote, 'a certified b-b-baddie.' And she straight-up told me that she's had a crush on you since, like, third grade. Some story about a broken pencil and you grabbed her a new one. I quote, 'Maybe now that he got those blinders off, he'll see what's *been* waiting for him.' End quote."

"I barely even remember that," I lied. Of course I remembered. I had a crush on her too back then, before my first kiss with Imogen changed everything. "She sounds kinda clingy."

"Man, fuck off. You been reading those stupid-ass messages from those hotep assholes?"

The messages Manny was referring to were from men—not boys, but grown men—showing up in my inbox. They were the older brothers, the cousins and "cousins," the uncles and "uncles" of the Hampton High student body. They sent me links to this wack fake doctor dude who talked about women like they were prey and he the hunter. They told me to "never trust (a) pussy." They said I couldn't let that nigga clown me like that, make me look like a little bitch. And every last one of them called women *females*.

"Bro, no, those guys are fucking nuts. I'm just saying she's no—"

"She's no Imogen. Yeah. Got it. So, what's your plan? You gonna let your peepee shrivel up from disuse while you wait for Imogen to come around? It's never happening, bro. You *gotta* see that by now."

I shook my head. "Nah, man. You'll see. Love wins out."

"Yeah, it does, and that's why she's with Trevor," Manny said.

I clenched my hands into fists and was about to deck him when the bell over the door jangled and a woman entered.

"You're lucky," I said to Manny as I relaxed my fists, forced a smile, and turned to face her. She had on big sunglasses, a fur shawl, big pearl earrings, and makeup that was too bright for her pallid skin and her bleach-scorched blond hair.

"I'm lucky, *and* I'm taking my lunch," Manny said, slipping out the back door a moment later.

"Welcome to Fro-Yo Jojo, ma'am," I said in a cheery voice. "Fill your cup up as much as you like, and when you're done, we'll weigh it over here!"

She ignored me and mumbled to herself as she swirled a long, poop-like chain of peanut butter yogurt. I watched as she tried to pour toppings into her cup, but she spilled more onto the floor than she did into her cup.

"Excuse me, ma'am, you need any help?" I asked in my lightest, Whitest voice.

"Was I talking to you?" the woman snapped. I guess it wasn't White enough.

"My apologies," I said through gritted teeth.

She quivered her way on up to the register with her yogurt.

"Here, let me take that from you and put it on the scale," I said, reaching for her cup.

She slapped my hand. "I can do it myself, don't need your dirty hands all over it," she said. As she tried to place the cup on the scale, it shook out of her hand and landed on its side, spilling its contents out all over the counter.

"Look what you did," the woman shrieked.

"I'm sorry, ma'am, that's on us," I said. It wasn't worth the argument. "Go ahead and get whatever you'd like."

The old woman shuffled over to the machines. "I swear, this place was so much better when the Edwins owned it. Before all you riffraff moved in and ruined the neighborhood, so now it's just a buncha wetbacks and jigaboos," she mumbled, loud enough for me to hear.

I hadn't heard someone say "jigaboo" in a minute. I was so caught off guard by the word that it took me a second to register everything she'd just said.

"I'm sorry, what did you say?"

"I didn't say anything," she said, though the smirk on her face said otherwise.

"Ma'am, this is a private business. We can refuse service to anyone, and right now, I'm refusing service to you. You need to please leave. Now. Manny! Can you come up here?"

"You said I could get another cup!" she said as she started dispensing more yogurt.

"Ma'am, you clearly said two racial slurs. You need to leave," I said. I was gripping the wood of the countertop so hard, my knuckles were changing color. *Today's really not the day, lady.*

"But I'm a paying customer!"

"That was before you called me a jigaboo," I said. And then the anger rolling around in my head over the past week erupted. "You know damn well the truth is that I didn't touch your damn cup. You know I heard what you said. I'm not gonna listen to some racist hag talk to me like that. Either you get out or I escort you out."

"I've been coming here since I was a little girl, before you people took over and ran this city into the ground," she said.

"Lady, I don't give a shit about how things were in the covered wagon days, all right? I got better things to spend my energy on than the stupid things tumbling out your mouth. So . . ." I came from around the corner, snatched the cup out of her hand, and threw it in the trash. "Get *out*."

That was when I saw Manny standing in the front doorway, wide-eyed, a burrito in one hand and a soda in the other.

"Everyone's going to know how I was harassed and assaulted by some thug who works here," she said, shuffling her way toward the door.

"Go, tell your old friends, you'll all be dead soon, see if I care!" I shouted at her as she went past Manny and out the door.

Manny looked at her, then me. "Dude, what the fuck was that?"

"Man, I don't know, she was on some next—"

"Not her, man. *You.* You can't talk to customers like that."

I rolled my eyes. "You didn't hear what she said, so you—"

"It doesn't matter what she said. This is my dad's business. My *family's* business. Something like that could tank us and the store.

193

You can't just wild out on someone like that, especially an old White lady."

"Seriously? She called you a wetback. Called me a jigaboo."

"A what?"

"Jigaboo. It's . . . it's old-fashioned nigger."

"Man, you get called worse every time you play up north. You shut that shit out. Same thing."

"You don't get it."

"What if she called the cops? What if they lit you up? It's not worth it, man."

"No!" I shouted loud. It must've caught Manny off guard, because I saw him flinch. "You can miss me with that mess. I shouldn't have to just let racist shit happen."

Manny sighed. "Sorry, man, you're right. Just . . . the old man's gonna be mad as hell. I'm sorry that happened. But I also know you're not *really* pissed about that lady or what she said—you're pissed at Gen."

I glared at him, fists balled. "You don't know shit."

"I don't? You haven't said anything to me all week about her, so here's my guess. You went over to Gen's the morning after the party because, I dunno, maybe Pops gave you some spiel about chasing love, never giving up, all that. You stayed up all night planning out what you were gonna say, how you were gonna make it 'tender' and 'special,' how to slip a little apology in there even though you can't just *slip* apologies in anywhere—a real apology's an apology and nothing else. Maybe you got her a gift or something. So, you went over there, armed with all that, and she rejected you. So, all week you've been going to sleep mad, waking up mad, showing up to school mad, and now you're at work mad too. How'd I do?"

I had been ready to punch him, but I relaxed my fists about half-way through his uncannily accurate monologue. "How did you . . . ?"

"I'm your best friend, dude. I know you. You *can't* take this shit out on customers," Manny said.

"You don't—she came up and asked me to do Trevor a big favor. You'd be pissed off too."

"What'd she want you to do?"

"Talk to the team. He says they keep messing with him, ever since the party."

"And did you?"

"Why? I don't have anything to do with it," I said, glancing up at the ceiling.

Manny groaned. "Homie, I've been trying so hard to rock with you throughout all of this. I'm your boy, man. Even when I knew this whole thing was a bad idea, I still backed you up at the party, because we're like blood. We'd always clown and roast on each other, but, shit, we was always honest, right?"

I held a hand up to stop him. "You're saying I'm lying."

"Bro, what? Of course you are. If you had nothing to do with it, if you weren't getting something out of it, you woulda said yes to her because you're not an asshole. Well, you weren't. And even if you *really* didn't have anything to do with it, they'd do what you say and you know it. So, yeah, you're lying. I get you lying to Gen, but I just don't get why you're lying to me."

"I . . . I just . . . " I searched my brain for the right words and came up empty.

Manny walked over to me and reached a hand up onto my shoulder. "Zeke, my guy, I know this hurts. The only way for it not to hurt is to let it go, man. I'm telling you, there's a thousand girls in a ten-mile radius who'd love to love you. You got your pick, dude. Someone out there's everything Imogen is and more."

I let out a long breath and tried to send my anger with it. I knew Manny was right. I couldn't just keep beating my head against the wall. "It's just . . . we have so much history. We've been friends forever. Like, who else—"

"Fucking *finally*, progress! Look, man, the Imogen in your head's perfect, but no one's perfect . . . 'cept Janelle Monáe and ya boy right here," Manny said, his voice full of gleeful relief. "So, throw that shit away and let's think about all the girls you know you think's fine. We'll make a list. Like, your top ten."

"Isn't that a little . . . misogynist?"

"We're not *ranking* them. It's just a list of ten in no order between you and me."

"Uh, sure. Okay, Naimah. Her cousin Kalissa, who's about to graduate. Lily."

"White-girl Lily?" Manny said, confused, as he took notes on his phone. "With the thick back-in-the-day pioneer braid?"

"Yeah, yeah," I laughed. "I don't know, man. Just somethin about her. What's with the commentary?"

"My bad," Manny said, holding his hands up. "Proceed."

"Rochelle. Dinah. Kirsten, too."

"Okay, that's six, four more."

"Nadja. Zaza. Oh, Chaunte, of course."

"One more. Last of your top ten Hampton High baddies. Imogen excluded."

"Well." I paused. "Cara, I guess."

"Tall junior Kara? Weird choice, seeing as she's gay, but okay."

"Nah, man. *Cara* Cara. You know? Your cousin? Our friend?"

Manny looked up at me from his phone. "You serious right now?"

"No cap, Cara's fine as fuck, Manny. I know you—"

"Gross. Nope. Next," Manny said.

"What? Come on."

"I'm not putting her on the list. Next," he said flatly.

"Why? 'Cause she's kin?"

"I said *next*."

"Why, you know something I don't? She not into me?"

Manny let out a sharp laugh, then quickly covered his mouth.

"Yo, what was that?" I asked.

"Just, uh, the thought of the two of you made me laugh," Manny said, looking away.

"I thought we wasn't lying," I said. I folded my arms and narrowed my eyes at him.

Manny returned my gaze. "I'm *not* lying," he said. He wasn't going to budge.

"Fine," I said.

"So, what about Rina? You and her *stay* vibin. I'll put her down. I can work with this. I'll crunch the numbers."

Manny, the Nate Silver of Hampton High, was off to the races. He left me alone on the floor while he created a spreadsheet of pros and cons, noted his observations from past interactions with each girl, estimated the likelihood of success with each girl, and delivered a breakdown of his analysis a couple hours later.

I nodded along to his presentation, but I couldn't shake the feeling that Manny was hiding something. Something about Cara . . . and me?

"In conclusion," Manny said, "of the ten possible matches, your greatest chance at long-term success is with Naimah and Zaza. Physical compatibility is high across the board. Naimah's fun, expressive, open with her feelings, which would help you feel and express your own. Zaza is very sweet and grounded and intentional. She would sit with you during, say, a long chemo session without a second thought. Both have asked me—multiple times—how to win you over, so I have it on good authority that they are interested. Your thoughts?"

"Pretty comprehensive." I yawned. "Today's been a long day. Let's just clean up and get outta here. I gotta think on it. Appreciate the presentation, though. Thorough as always. You need a ride tonight?" I dapped him up.

"Nah, the old man's coming to get me. Wants to make sure I 'lock up right,' like I haven't been working here since I learned to read."

"So just a few days then, huh," I laughed as I started sweeping.

"Real funny," Manny said as he gave me the finger. "Season opener's tomorrow. You comin?"

I shrugged. "I don't know. I kinda want a break from everybody, the way this week's gone. And I don't want to take attention away from the team, you know?" Really, I didn't think I could stand to see people cheer for Trevor, not after what had happened, but I kept that to myself.

"I feel you. There'll be other games. Plus, it's just Rock Isle. Can't even make money betting on the game, they're so bad, so it's not like you'd miss much. Take a break, dude. No people eyeballin you, nobody whisperin bout you and Gen."

"Yeah." I nodded. "Yeah, maybe you're right."

"*Maybe?*" Manny laughed. "Please."

Two hours later, the store was closed. I waved to Manny and Jojo as I left, then I got into my car. I couldn't stop thinking about Cara.

Me: Hey u goin 2 the game 2mo?

Cara: Ya yr coming right???

Me: Ehh, idk

Cara: What???

Cara: U sick or smth?

Cara: Since when do u miss games?

Me: Kinda wanna break from ppl tbh

Me: You still wanna do that xfiles marathon?

Me: instead of goin 2 the game?

Cara: !!!

Cara: Shiiiiiit yeah

Cara: Mom and ray got a saturdate

Cara: So I was gonna smoke + xfiles neway

Me: Yo thats crazy

Cara: What is

Me: I smoke

Me: I watch xfiles

Me: We got so much in common

Cara: Lololo

Cara: Come over like four

Cara: Bring snacks. Good ones, ok?

Cara: None of that hummus shit.

Cara: Like CHIPS. CANDY. Got it??

Me: Lol I got u girl don't worry

chapter twenty-seven
ZEKE

"Look, I'm not saying T-1000 is Mulder-level, I'm just saying homie came in with big shoes to fill and he doesn't get enough love," Cara said.

We were on our third episode already. The air smelled of weed but only a little, thanks to Cara's well-made and well-used sploof. We were sitting on the couch—well, "sitting" might've been a little strong. We were slouched deep into the cushions, our bodies more like gelatin than anything else. Cara in her pajamas, wrapped up in a knitted multicolor blanket, me in a terry-cloth bathrobe that Cara had snatched from some fancy hotel, the table before us a bountiful spread of Oreos, sour-cream-and-onion chips, gummy bears, and a whole bunch of pink Starbursts.

I came correct.

"Man, he'll always just be T-1000 to me. Villain. To the bone. Can't rock with him, just can't," I replied.

"You're such a dork," she said, extending a leg out from under the blanket to kick me.

"See, that's where you messed up," I said as I caught her foot and dragged her over to me. She let out a shriek, then went for my sides.

"Who messed up now, huh?" she said as she danced her fingertips along my waist. It took everything I had to calm down enough to squirm away.

Once I was out of her reach, I sprang at her, grabbed her wrists, and pinned her down. "Still you."

The two of us were panting, a little sweaty, tangled up in the blanket, and looked at each other for a brief moment before Cara grabbed my face and brought my lips down to hers. I felt a jolt race down my spine when our lips touched and felt her hands on my body, on the places where our skin wasn't separated by fabric. I leaned into the kiss, which might've lasted all night had I not knocked over Cara's piece and spilled weed all over the table.

"My bad," I said, looking over at the mess.

"Butterfingers over here," Cara said, her arms around my neck.

"Should we . . . ," I began to say.

"Nah, stay with me right here," Cara said. She put a hand on my face and turned my gaze back to her. "So, what's going on here?" she asked, her eyes a twinkling smile. "Because, you know, I want to do more of *that*."

"Yeah? Me too," I said, surprised at how much I wanted her, and came back in for a kiss.

"Hold up," she said. She took a breath. "I'm into you, always have been. Always figured it was a lost cause because of Imogen, so damn if this isn't a great surprise."

"But you never said anything?"

"Would you have if you were me? Listen, I'm no side chick. I'm not your sad-boy rebound. So, straight up, what is this? What's going on here?" Cara said.

I sat up to face her and took a second to think. Cara was right in front of me. One of my best friends. She was beautiful. I always liked being with her. Maybe . . . "Yesterday, I was at the shop with Manny. He was telling me I needed to move on. Wanted me to make a list of all the girls I was feeling and was feeling me back. So, I brought you up, 'cause you're a baddie—"

"This is true." Cara grinned.

"—which Manny didn't like at all. But it got me thinking about you. And once I started, you were all I thought about. You're the one who comes to all my games. The only one I texted back the other night, the only one who texted to see how I was doing and nothing else. You planned that surprise at the shop. I mean, you filled a toilet up with fake poop for *me*," I said, both of us laughing. "The party was the wake-up call I needed. I'm with you, girl. If you want me. I know I'm—"

"Finally! I've been waiting *so* fucking long for you to get it!" Cara said, her face split wide with a smile.

"Was the wait worth it?"

"We'll just have to find out," Cara said as she ran her hand down my body and bit her lip. "But not now, 'cause my mom and Ray'll be back soon and I'm pretty sure that if you don't leave immediately,

Jordan K. Casomar

things're gonna go further than they should 'cause *damn*."

She led me to the front of the house. Her hips had me in a trance, and it took every part of me to not jump her then and there. We lingered for a while at the door after I put my coat and boots on, Cara in my arms, her heartbeat quick and thunderous against my chest.

"I *really* like you, Zeke. Probably more than I should. And my brain is telling me it's too soon, but fuck my brain, I want what I want. Just don't screw me over, okay? I just . . . promise me that this isn't about her. About getting back at her, about replacing her, anything like that," Cara said.

I had never considered that angle, because there wasn't anyone at our school who could hold a candle to my connection with Imogen. Except for Cara, I realized, and somewhere in the back of my mind, a little voice began whispering what-ifs.

"It's about you and me. Not her—us. I'm not gonna screw you over, I promise," I said . . . and hoped that would hold true.

"Zeke. What the *fuck*," Manny said as he got in my car on Monday morning, clearly pissed.

"I know, I'm sorry I'm late. Probably would be quicker to just walk, but what's the point of having a car now if I'm not gonna drive us once in a while?"

"Man, it's not that. Not even a little."

"Okay, then what? What's wrong?" I asked, realizing a moment later that he wasn't just pissed—he was pissed at *me*.

"Cara, dude? Cara? She wasn't on the list. I told you no! That's my cousin, bro! First, y'all weren't at the game. And then I'm across the street, up in my room, and I see you out my window leaving her place at like ten at night with a damn skip in your step! My *cousin*, man?"

Oh. That.

"Okay, Manny, I was gonna tell you about it, but it just happened, man. We were hanging out, and there was this moment, and I dunno. Did you know she's had a crush on me since forever?"

"Yes, dude. That's why I didn't want her on the damn list."

I looked at him, confused.

"She's had it bad for you, and I knew that she'd go for it no matter what," Manny said. "But I know you're still stuck on Gen. It'll *crush* her. And not just her, but our whole squad. This shit with Imogen's already done enough damage. I told you, there's so many girls, and you just have to pick the one that'll cause the most problems. Fuck!"

I had never seen Manny so mad. There were bulging veins on his temple and his neck, his leg was bouncing like a jackhammer, and he kept clenching and unclenching his fists.

I put a hand on Manny's arm. "Listen, okay? I like Cara. For real. I didn't know I did and then we were hanging out, and all of a sudden, it hit me. It was like love at first sight, man."

"Zeke, if you take advantage of her, if you start playing with her—"

I started shaking my head as we pulled out of his driveway. He didn't say a word the whole drive. I'd never heard Manny stay quiet so long. Once we reached the school parking lot, I turned to Manny, put my hands on his shoulders, and looked him right in the eyes.

"I get it. You don't trust me. I wouldn't trust me either. But this *is* real, Manny. Like, it felt different with her than it does with

Imogen. It felt . . . nice? Easy?" I said, smiling to myself as I thought about Cara. "I'm not gonna mess this up. I swear it, on Pops."

He didn't say anything as he got out of the car and started for the front doors. Right after we stepped inside, Manny turned and pointed a finger at me. "You better not."

In truth, I wasn't as sure as I seemed. I'd barely seen Imogen since our fight the previous week, and I didn't know how I'd feel about her when I did. But I *wanted* to feel different, so didn't that count for something?

"And don't think we're—"

Our conversation was interrupted by Braejon throwing open the doors behind us with a loud bang. Behind him came the sound of several loud, boisterous, and familiar voices.

"Panthers! Listen up!" Braejon boomed as he entered the building. The entryway went quiet as students and staff alike turned to Braejon. "Let's give it up for the one, the only, the bad-bad brother *cook*ing up a storm, your star: Trevor. COOOOOOOOOK!"

Trevor entered the school held aloft by the hands of Axel, Yovani, and Dink, followed by what looked like half the school, everyone whooping and hollering, clapping and cheering as the procession made its way down the hallway. Just before they cleared out, I grabbed Braejon and pulled him aside.

"Zeke, man, you shoulda been at the game! A shutout! Trevor, he never missed. Every hit was a damn *hit*, my guy, like Barry Bonds, ball way the hell outta here. Incredible. Dude can *swing*. They had to stop the damn game 'cause he had the runs like diarrhea, Zeke. We gonna take him out, team style. He don't know shit about shit up here yet, so we gonna learn his ass some. Want in?"

"So, what, everyone's buddy-buddy with Texas now?" I said under my breath so no one but Braejon could hear. "Flip on me *that* quick? After what he did to me? I don't care if he's the best player to ever walk the earth. And let's be real—it was Rock Isle Academy. They barely know what baseball is. It's why I was cool missing it."

Braejon looked at me sideways. "Yo, you *still* on that? Homie, that was, like, weeks ago."

"It's been nine days."

"Shit, really? Still, he paid his dues. Besides, word is you was with Cara this weekend, so we figure, you move on, we move on. Plus, that was before we saw him in game mode. You gotta see him play, Zeke. I wish I was getting held back so I could play with the both of you next year. It's gonna be *nasty*. 'Cause, yo, he ain't the best in the world but, shit, he just might be the best my Black ass has ever been around."

I gave him a look.

"Uh, on the plate, that is," Braejon quickly added.

"One good game erases him making me look like an idiot and stealing my girl?"

Braejon shrugged. "Bruh, if she'd been your girl, she'd've been your girl. He didn't steal nothin. You got a perfectly—I *do* mean *perfect*ly—fine girl now, so focus on that. On your dad. Not this old shit with Trev, man. New shit, like we always say."

"New shit" was our team motto, and we said it after every game. It kept us humble after easy wins—every single game was new shit, anyone's game to win or lose. It kept us up after losing the finals—we had made it where no one thought we'd ever go, that's that new shit. And this year, the new shit was going to be us holding the trophy.

Well, them *holding the trophy,* I thought.

"Aight, Z, I need to catch up with them and Coach," Braejon said, backing away down the hall. He pointed at me just before he disappeared out of sight. "New shit, Zeke. Don't forget."

Yeah. New shit.

chapter twenty-eight
IMOGEN

Cara: Uhh, know its late and we got school 2mo

Cara: but I gotta tell u smth. Might b a lil weird??

Cara: U up? Lol

Me: ???

Me: You okay?

Cara: I hooked up w some1

Me: Oooo

Cara: Someone named ZEKE

I sat up and turned on a light and read Cara's text again. My best friend—former best friend—had hooked up with my best girlfriend.

Cara: You there?

Cara: Don't hate me

I snapped out of it.

Me: What???

Me: I'm so happy for you!

Me: Tell me everything

I waited for Cara's response to come, but it was taking too long, so I FaceTimed her.

"Texting is too slow. Give me the whole story! How'd it happen?"

"Well, he came over Saturday. That's why we weren't at the game. So we were watching *X-Files*, and I don't know, there was just a moment—Wait, you sure this ain't weird? Doesn't bother you?" Cara asked, her face rippling with worry.

"Girl, no! Why would it? It's not like that, at *all*."

"I know. It's just . . . always been 'Zeke and Gen.'"

"Cara, on god, I could not be happier for you and him. Wish it'd happened sooner. The two of you are so good together. You've always been able to get him to slow down and take a break. He needs that," I said, overjoyed.

"So, even though he's almost like your ex?"

"He's *not* my ex," I snapped. "Sorry, that . . . wasn't for you. Now that I'm 'officially' able to date, my parents keep asking about Zeke. It's tiring. He's so . . . Oh, sorry, I guess this *is* kinda weird, huh?"

"A bit, yeah," Cara said with a laugh. "Maybe—"

"Maybe we need to just have everyone clear the air," I interrupted. "We should do a double date!" The words flew out of my mouth before I could give them a second thought. I mean, I hadn't talked to Zeke since our fight earlier last weekend. We didn't have any classes together and I had been avoiding him in the hallways, and as far as

I could tell, he was doing the same. But that hadn't stopped me from thinking about him and how we could put all of this behind us.

"Uhh, what? You mean, me and you, Zeke and Trev, together at one table? Is someone threatening you? Do you have a brain slug inside your skull?"

I gagged. "Disgusting."

"Imagine the longest booger of all time," Cara began, a big grin on her face. "It'd feel *so* good, getting it out."

"You're not wrong, but you *are* weird. And yes, I mean all four of us at a table together. It'll be . . . like a restart!" I said. Even though I was so angry with Zeke, I still missed him. I missed his jokes. I missed talking to him about his dad and how he was holding up. I missed him because he was my family. And now that it seemed like he was moving on from me, maybe this was how I got my family back?

"I think this is insane. You really want this?"

"For sure," I said, though I wasn't sure at all. Did I really want to spend time with the guy who was doing nothing to stop Trevor's harassment? Would Trevor? Despite all that, I allowed myself to feel the tiniest bit of optimism. "Don't worry! It's gonna be great. Trev literally told me earlier today that he wants to bury the hatchet, so, yeah, let's do it!" That was another lie, for now. I'd win Trev over.

"And you're *sure* you're okay with me and Zeke?"

"*Cara.* Yes. I'm okay, you're okay, you two are okay."

"I still think this is a crazy idea. Like, *really* crazy," Cara said, eyes narrowed and wary.

"Look. Real talk? Every night since he and I had our fight last weekend, I've dreamt me and Zeke were friends again, joking and laughing like nothing ever happened, and every morning, I've woken up sad that it was just that—a dream. But it doesn't have to be, right? Can't we just try it? Please?"

Cara let out a long, loud sigh. "Okay, fine, sure. But no fancy places, 'cause Zeke's saving up," she said, then blushed. "Sorry, you already know that."

"It's *fine*. All of a sudden, big bad Cara's a soft little puddle? Since when are you—"

"Double date's off, girl, bye," Cara said as she pretended to end the call.

"It's just cute," I told her.

"I won't tolerate this reckless slander. Okay, I gotta sleep. Time to have nightmares about this double date. See you tomorrow?"

"A-yup. P.S. still so happy for you, okayyy bye," I said, waving at Cara.

The call ended on a still of her face, triple-chinned and mid-eye-roll that I screenshotted to torment her with later. I turned the light off and lay down to go to sleep, but my thoughts kept me up for hours.

Over the next few days, I tortured myself thinking about a double date, going over every possible scenario again and again. I wanted this to work, and I said as much when I floated the idea of the double date to Trevor when we were hanging out at his place after school on Wednesday.

"Let me get this straight," he said. "You want me and you to go on a double date with Zeke and Cara? Trevor Cook and Imogen Parker on a double date with Cara Ramirez and Zeke Ladoja, of Chicago, Illinois. I have that right?"

"Oh, come on, quit playing," I said.

Trevor let out a long sigh. "Look, I think I've been really chill about everything. I wasn't thrilled that you kissed me in front of all those people. The stuff about my mom really pissed me off, but thankfully, that seems to be over and done with. The last couple weeks've been harder than I'd like, but I got to be with you and that made it all worth it. Still, Zeke ain't been what I'd call welcoming lately. So, believe me when I say: a double date would be a disaster."

He opened his mouth to say something more, but he was interrupted by the sound of the front door opening. I heard the thump of Ray's limp on the floor above as he approached the basement door.

"Trev, you down there?" he shouted from the top of the stairs.

"Yes, sir. And Gen, too," Trevor answered.

"Figured, unless you started wearing little wedge shoes all of a sudden," Ray laughed. "Gen, you want a plate?"

"Oh! Uh, sure. Is that okay?" I asked Trevor. He squeezed my hand and smiled.

"Just let us know when to come up," Trevor yelled.

"Yep, yep," Ray said, and closed the door.

Trevor turned to me. "So, yeah, this double-date idea? Sorry, Gen, but—"

"Trevor, please," I begged. "I really, really want this to happen. Can you at least tell me *why* you think it'd be a disaster?"

"I know for a fact that Zeke's still angry with me. When the team paraded me through the halls, he had this look on his face, Gen."

"But that's normal, right? I mean, he was just jealous that you were getting the attention that he used to get," I countered.

"No, Gen—it was definitely more than jealousy." He paused. "Look, people aren't messing with my stuff, and the weight room's not as awkward since then, so *maybe* he's coming around? But do you honestly believe that Zeke wants to spend time with the girl he loved for years and the guy she's dating?"

"Well, he has Cara now, so—"

"Gen, c'mon."

"What, you're worried about you and Zeke getting into it?"

"No, I'm worried about *you* and Zeke getting into it. 'Cause I know you're mad too. You just put it all in your writing instead of out in the world."

I was quiet. I couldn't disagree with that.

"I'll do it, for you. If you want it to happen, I'm there. But I wanna know why you think it's so important. What do you want to happen?"

It was a good question, one that took me a while to answer. "I was going to say I wanted things to just go back to how they were, but they weren't that great before, either. I just . . . I want everyone to be happy and connected and friends."

"I know you want everything to be cool between everyone, but it hasn't even been two weeks since the party. It's too soon," Trevor said.

"I know it sounds naïve or immature, but I don't know what else to do. I hate this feeling, Trevor. Not having Zeke in my life, knowing he's upset at me, it's like a part of me's missing," I said. "Look, just do me this one favor, and then I'll do one for you. We can even—" I grabbed a piece of paper and started folding it, smaller and smaller, until it was a dense, compact square. "Favor token. We pass it back and forth."

Trevor perked up at the word "token," his nerd neurons firing away. "Hold up, how come *you* get to start with it?" he said.

"Uhh, 'cause it was my idea? So: token? We have a deal?" I extended my pinky finger.

He looked at me, clearly fighting a smile. "Fine, fine, yeah, we got a deal. I'll go. Gimme that damn token."

"Nuh-uh, I'll give it to you at the date and not a second before." I grinned. "So you don't wiggle outta this deal."

Trevor laughed. "You cutthroat as all hell. I love it. But on the real, if he tries to start anything with me or if he goes off on you, I'm not gonna let it stand, fair?"

"Fair." I nodded.

That night, I texted Cara to let her know Trevor was down. Now all we had to do was get Zeke on board.

Cara: U rly sure this is a good idea?

Cara: Cuz idk the party was only like 10 days ago

Cara: It hasn't been that long

Me: I honestly think so!

Me: It'll be good for all of us.

Me: Even if ppl get upset, better than not talking, right?

Me: Like the only way out is through

Me: We can't just act like its nbd

Me: Ur always telling me to stand up for myself

Me: To not keep things in

Cara: Wowwwwww

Cara: Ur gonna play it like that huh? Use my words against me

Me: :))))))))

Me: Do u disagree?

Me: Radical honesty and all that

Cara: Ughhhh noooo

Cara: Fine. I'll talk to z. No promises tho

Cara: What T say

Me: He didn't wanna at first

Me: But I gave him a favor token

Me: Now I owe him one

Me: Little to no questions asked

Cara: A favor token????

Cara: He gonna use that for butt stuff

Cara: U kno that right??

Me: Cara lol

Me: He's not like that.

Me: And he already told me what he wants

Cara: Ooooo

Cara: He wants u to do butt stuff to HIM

Me: No u freak lol

Me: He wants me to play D&D w him and dink.

Cara: Um excuse me

Cara: Out of everything

Cara: Wwow

Cara: And that's ur man?

Me: Lol stop. It'll be fun.

Me: So! Double date. Vincent's on Sat at 7?

Cara: It's Thursday right

Cara: Lil baked atm tbh lmao

Me: No, Cara. It's Wednesday.

Me: Three days, ok??

Cara: Aye-aye captain

Cara: I'll b there or b squared

Cara: Equals c squared

Cara: Equals d's nuts

Cara: Lmaooo

chapter twenty-nine
IMOGEN

Vincent's was *the* spot. You wanted ribs, you wanted catfish, you wanted a milkshake, you wanted some crab legs, you went to Vincent's, where you could get it all. It was my favorite spot for people-watching. I liked to sit at one of the picnic tables, pretending to eat while eavesdropping and eavespeeping on the slicked-up brothers looking fresh, putting out feelers for girls; the kids dragging already-stubby crayons across the paper that covered their table; the half-dozen older women in the corner booths playing cards and drinking wine and gossiping about who was steppin out on who. That was what made the place so great—it was for all kinds of folks, all kinds of talk.

Including two (former?) best friends talking their way through the tail end of a very, very awkward couple of weeks, I hoped.

Trevor and I arrived first, and the hostess seated us. Trevor put a hand on my leg, which was bouncing like a jackhammer. I kept rereading Cara's texts from the past few days, looking for any comfort, any sign of how things would go tonight. She'd asked Zeke the same night I asked her.

Cara: He said he needs 2 think abt it

Cara: But he said he misses hangin w u too

Cara: and he wants to talk bball w T

Cara: So maybe it'll be fine??

Cara: I'll let u kno more when I kno

On Thursday, Zeke and I made eye contact in the hallways for the first time in a week without one or both of us quickly averting our gaze, and that left me hopeful. And then, finally, Friday afternoon Cara texted me a thumbs-up and I felt relieved. For a few minutes, anyway, because then reality began to set in. There was no backing out. It was happening. With every passing minute, the date growing ever closer, my anxiety grew and grew.

"How are you so calm?" I asked Trevor.

"I'm calm 'cause that's what you need me to be," Trevor said, and kissed me on the forehead. "I'm here for you. Not Zeke, not Cara. Just you. So, whatever you need tonight, okay?"

"Okay, new question: How are you so perfect?" I said, pressing myself into him.

"Ahem," Trevor coughed. "I think you're forgetting something?" He held his hand out.

I stared at his palm for a moment before I realized what he was talking about and laughed. I fished the favor token out of my bag and placed it in his hand.

"There we go! Faerûn, here we come! Now, look alive, they're here,"

Trevor said, nodding to Zeke and Cara, arm in arm, walking our way.

It was my first time seeing them out together. As a couple. Dating. I felt my face grow hot, but I didn't know why.

"Here goes," Trevor whispered right before they reached us.

"Oh, you got that *good* good top on, okay! I see you," I said to Cara, standing so I could hug her.

"You *got* to," she said, and gave a little spin.

"Zeke," Trevor said.

"Trevor."

Zeke didn't say anything else, just sat down and hid his face behind the menu. I glanced at Cara, and she shrugged.

"Hey, Zeke, how's your dad?" I asked. I knew Samson was doing fine; I had just visited him during his chemo a couple days before.

"He's okay. Doing better," Zeke said, still behind the menu. He sucked his teeth as Cara snatched it out of his hands. "Hey! I wasn't done!"

"Like you don't know this menu backward and forward."

Zeke crossed his arms and leaned back into the booth, doing his best not to look me in the eye. Every time I tried to make eye contact, his eyes darted away to the saltshaker, the specials menu, the rings on Cara's fingers—everything and anything except me. I waited for Zeke to say something else, but he didn't. A quiet came over us once again.

"Uhh, I—so, Zeke. You watch the game earlier?" I asked. "I saw Cara there, but I didn't see you. Coach said you always recorded the games, so I figured—"

"Yeah, I was busy," Zeke said.

"Zeke . . . ," Cara said.

"Cara gave me a recap," Zeke said. He turned his gaze to Trevor and gave him a small grin, the first sign of warmth I'd seen from him all night. "Heard you was blastin 'em. They got a decent pitcher, too. See, I knew you could play."

Just then, a server walked up to our table. He was holding a tray with four glasses of water, and he looked nervous, like maybe it was his first shift. He grabbed one of the glasses of water, disturbing the balance of the tray, and spilled the other three onto our table and, more specifically, all over Cara.

"Bruh, you kidding me?" Zeke said as he jumped to Cara's defense. He pulled a stack of napkins out of the dispenser on the table, handed some to her, and started sopping up the water on the table.

"I'm so sorry. Shit. Uhh." The server pulled a towel stained with dried barbecue sauce and meat grease from his waist and offered it to her.

Cara was dabbing at her shirt with a napkin. She paused, looked at the towel, then the server, and gave him a look as if he had lost not only his mind, but the minds of his ancestors, too.

"Bruh, if you think for one second I'm gonna take that nasty towel and dry myself off with it, yo, you got another think coming," Cara growled.

The server made himself scarce as another employee arrived with towels to clean up the mess.

"Man, this is why I hate dressing up," Cara said. "I'm gonna go to the bathroom to try and fix this."

Trevor raised his hand like we were in a classroom and said, "Ray always keeps white tees in the car. Says you never know when you're gonna need spare shirts. I know a T-shirt ain't as fashionable as the top you got, but, hey, it's dry?"

Out of the corner of my eye, I saw Zeke roll his eyes.

"If drying it doesn't work, I'll take you up on that. Thanks, Trevor," Cara said.

Trevor glanced at me and Zeke. "Maybe I'll go grab one now, just in case. I'll be right back, boo," he said, squeezing my shoulder as he got up from the booth.

"You good?" Cara asked Zeke. He nodded but stayed quiet. She turned away from him, mouthed *good luck* at me, and headed for the bathroom.

Of the night's many awkward silences—and the night had only just begun—this one was the worst, not for its length, but its weight. It felt like gravity had changed on me all of a sudden and I was being pressed into the ground by the weight of the words unsaid between Zeke and me. I had to end it.

"I'm really glad you're here tonight," I said, hesitant. "You two seem happy."

"We are," said Zeke, who *still* had yet to look me in the eye.

He was giving me nothing, and I made the mistake of trying to fill the silence. "I'm really glad. I'm so happy for you and her, Zeke! I mean, I've had a feeling for a while that she liked you, so it's awesome it's finally happening. She's so happy, I can already tell. I was worried for a second there—"

"Worried?" Zeke said. Finally, he looked me full in the face, and I found the intensity of his gaze hard to bear. His whole vibe was a rubber band ready to snap, and I had to avert my eyes. "Worried about what, Imogen?"

"Well, I was . . . just, let's forget it. It's not—"

"Let's not. What were you worried about?" he said again, his voice a little louder.

"I just . . . I was a little worried that—" I hesitated. "That you were just doing this to make me jealous or something."

Zeke gave a dry laugh. "Why, you jealous?"

"Zeke, c'mon. I was worried for my friend. I don't like you like that," I said. For a moment, Zeke's angry mask slipped, and I saw the deep hurt in his eyes.

"Yeah, you've made that pretty clear," he said. "But, unlike you, I don't string along people I'm not interested in. I prefer to be, y'know, honest?"

I bristled at the accusation, but I didn't want to push back and get into a fight. It was supposed to be a night of healing. "Zeke, it doesn't have to be like this. This sucks. I hate this. I hate not talking to you," I said. "We're both happy with other people. Can't we move on? Get back to how things were?"

"God, you have such an ego. You ever think that maybe *I* didn't want to talk to you? You're not even the one who got hurt. You were just fine, you and Trevor, just—"

"Leave him out of this, Zeke. This is between you and me and that's it."

"Says the girl accusing me of using Cara."

"I never accused you! I was just worried! Cara's amazing. She deserves someone great, and you, Zeke, are great. Is it so wrong to just want the best for my friend?"

"'The best for my friend.' You hearing yourself, Gen? Were you thinking about 'the best for my friend' when you threw yourself at Trevor and made out with him in front of everyone? 'Cause, yeah, that was just 'the best' for me," Zeke said.

"I'm *sorry*, okay? I freaked out," I said, tears burning in my eyes.

"People freak out every day without embarrassing and emasculating their friends."

"Then what's it gonna take, Zeke? What's it gonna take for things to be okay?"

"Too late. You already fucked everything up, Gen, so stop trying or you're gonna make everything worse," Zeke said. "I'm done with this."

Zeke stood up from the table just as Cara was exiting the bathroom.

"Didn't have any paper towels and I didn't wanna use toilet paper, so I had to spin the air dryer—yo, what's going on?" Cara said, confused.

"I can't do this," Zeke said. "I'm done, let's go."

"But—"

"Cara, I'm sorry, it just got a little heated and—" I started just as Trevor returned.

"Sorry, the pack was fresh, so it's still got that new shirt smell," Trevor said, oblivious as he opened the pack of shirts and handed one to Cara, only then noticing she and Zeke were standing and putting on their coats. "Huh? What's up?"

"We're leaving," Zeke said as he started forward, shoving Trevor out of his way. The folks around us were glancing between Trevor and Zeke, some clearly hungry for a fight and disappointed there wasn't one. Cara gave me an apologetic look, but I waved it off, and she followed after Zeke.

"What was all that?" Trevor asked me, sliding into the booth.

"He's . . . he's still so angry at me. You were right. I don't get why he agreed to come if he was just going to be so mean."

I looked to Trevor, but he didn't have an answer to that.

"God, why did I think this was a good idea? What the hell is wrong with me? I keep making all these stupid decisions that just blow up in my face and hurt everyone around me. I'm so stupid. I'm such an—"

"Hey, Gen, look at me," Trevor said. He put his hands on my shoulders and turned me toward him. "You're not stupid. You took a chance. And, hey, it wasn't going *terribly* at first. Hell, he and I were about to have a civil conversation for a second there. I mean, I'm not gonna lie and say I think it was your *best* idea, but you're a romantic. You want happy endings. You want everyone to feel okay. That doesn't make you stupid."

"Well, it sure doesn't feel that way," I said as I leaned my head against Trevor, who wrapped his arm around me, and allowed myself to cry.

"Uh, sorry, bad time, but, um, are you ready to order or . . . ?"

I opened my bleary eyes and saw the server standing there, shifting from one foot to the other like a kid about to pee his pants.

"Actually, we're gonna head out," Trevor said. "C'mon, Gen, let's go, okay?"

We walked out the front door and into the cool night air. I could smell Zeke's cologne, faint, lingering in the air. I was starting to hate the scent.

chapter thirty
ZEKE

"What the hell was that?" Cara said as she slammed the passenger door.

"We got into a fight," I said. "And I didn't want to be there anymore. That's all."

"Oh, *that's* all?" Cara scoffed.

"Look," I said, my volume getting away from me. "I tried. I gave it a shot. I was talking to Trevor, that was all right. But then she—I wish you hadn't left me alone with her."

"Zeke, don't even. Don't put this on me. That was about you and Gen, didn't have shit to do with me being there or not," Cara said. The car went silent as we pulled out of Vincent's parking lot.

I knew she was right. It wasn't her fault at all. It wasn't even Imogen's fault. Mad as I was, I knew she wasn't *really* trying to start something. It was just a lot easier to get angry than it was to have a real conversation with Imogen about the fact that she had hurt me, deep. Cara had nothing to do with it. I glanced over at her; she was looking out the window, watching the streetlights pass by overhead, her arms folded across her chest.

"Hey, I'm sorry. That was unfair," I said. "Just 'cause I'm mad, that doesn't give me the right to take it out on you. I'm really sorry."

"Damn right you are," Cara said. "It's okay, this time. That was your one warning, got it?"

I nodded. "Loud and clear. You mind if we drop it for now and talk about it in the morning?"

"Fine by me," Cara said as her stomach growled loud. "Last thing I'll say about it: boy, you couldn't've waited till I got some ribs? Damn!"

We laughed, the tension of the night melting away. "You wanna order something and watch—" I started to say.

"Read my mind. What are you feeling? Thai? Burgers? Pizza? I don't do Ethiopian food. Don't like the textures. Too soft. But I'll eat basically anything else."

"Tacos?" I said as I pulled into Cara's driveway.

"Tacos." Cara smiled, and we headed inside. The house was quiet.

"I'm betting my mom is at Ray's place, knowing Trevor was supposed to be out for a while," she said.

Cara plopped down on the couch, grabbed her laptop off the ottoman, and waved me over. I crouched by the armrest so I was behind Cara and could see her screen.

"So, the places that deliver here are Taco the Town, which is way better than it has any right to be with that stupid-ass name; the Tortillery, which has some of the best tacos I've ever had in my whole human life, though they are expensive and fancy as hell; but the only real choice is—"

"Good-Ass Tacos," we said in unison. The place was practically an institution in Cara and Manny's neighborhood. All they made were, well, good-ass tacos, including this Korean fried chicken taco that'd ruined all other tacos for me.

"See, that's why I like you," Cara said.

"Oh, *that's* why? Not my very kissable lips?" I teased.

"I mean, let me give them a try," Cara laughed. She kissed me, and once we started, we couldn't stop. Our hands roamed all over each other. I had known Cara for more than half my life, but as our clothes came off, I found parts of her body that I had never seen, as if she wasn't beautiful enough. She had a trio of moles on her left hip; when I kissed and bit her there, she let out a rush of breath. Her back was sensitive, I learned; as I traced my nails against her soft brown skin, she twisted and squirmed and goose-bumped as her breaths got heavy.

Then she pulled away from me, got on top of me, and pushed me down. I learned just how much I liked the feel of her breath on my neck, her kisses down my chest, the weight of her on me, and the heat of her too. I reached a hand into her underwear, then looked at her for her permission. She nodded and let out a long, hungry sigh as she dug the nails on her left hand into my chest. I let out a little gasp as her right hand crept under my boxers.

She got off me to take my pants all the way off, then asked, "Do you have a condom?"

My heart skipped a beat and I nodded. "Uh, in my wallet. Coat pocket," I said. She raced over to the coat rack on the door and started rummaging through the pockets, which gave me a second to take a breath.

"Found it," Cara said, holding it up like a prize. "It's, uh, my first time," she said.

Contrary to popular belief, I had not had sex. I had dreamt of having sex. I had longed to have sex. But this would be my first time. I fumbled with the condom, only half-sure of what I was doing as Cara helped. "So . . . it's mine, too," I said.

"You trust me?" she said, kissing my forehead.

"I do. I trust you," I said, nodding.

"I trust you, too."

As she got on top of me, I thought, only briefly, about how I'd always imagined my first time would be with Imogen.

And then I didn't think of Imogen at all.

I woke up the next morning spooning Cara. She was all curled up, snoring softly. It was cute. Unlike my stomach's loud, gurgling growls. My stomach ached with hunger—we'd gotten distracted and never ordered the tacos. I hadn't missed dinner maybe ever, and I was definitely feeling it. I slid out of bed real quiet, rinsed myself off in the shower, checked for Cara's mom, then helped myself to Cara's kitchen. As I was finishing making omelets, she came downstairs.

"Uh, *excuse* me?"

"Shit, sorry," I said. "I thought it'd be okay to use the—"

"No, like, you're making me food. I usually eat a few Pop-Tarts or something from Pappy's, but you're doing all *this*." She sat down, and I placed an omelet in front of her, the steam wending its way up into the air. "It's amazing. You're amazing."

"Pfft, nah, it's nothing. I cook breakfast for Pops most of the time 'cause Ma usually needs more sleep, so . . ." I shrugged. "You know, whatever, ain't no thang for my girl."

Cara took a bite. "And it's actually *good*, too!"

I grinned at her. I had never cooked for anyone except my family, and I was surprised at how nice it felt. Frankly, I was surprised at how good *I* felt. I was afraid I was going to feel weird or guilty, but I didn't.

"I also wanted to say sorry for how I was on the date," I said after we finished eating, the two of us perched up on barstools at Cara's kitchen island. "I'm done, I'm over it. I've been living in the past, ignoring everything I got going for me in the present."

"Boy, you better be," Cara said, leaning her head against my shoulder. "So . . . are we gonna tell anyone?"

"About us? I don't see why not. Unless Lisette's got some rules that I don't know about," I said.

"Hah! No way, Mom's no punk-ass like Brian. Not like the rules really mattered anyway," Cara said offhandedly.

"Wait, what do you mean? About the rules?"

"You didn't know? That whole not-till-you're-sixteen thing? It didn't seem to count for Trevor. They were seeing each other a full week before the party."

"Oh yeah, I knew about that," I lied as my mind and body disconnected. My body stayed in Cara's kitchen and ate a second omelet. My mind, though, was racing. Gen lied about something huge to *me*. Me, of all people. First she made a fool of me at the party. Then there was the dig at me and Cara during the double date. And now I was learning that the entire reason I never made a move on her was a rule she threw out the window the very *day* she met Trevor—

"Then we're going public? You're good with that? Last chance before I start bragging to everyone." Cara grinned, too excited to notice the uncertainty in my voice.

"I am. Gen can believe whatever she wants, say whatever she likes. I know where I wanna be," I said, trying to make my statement sound like a casual aside, and kissed Cara's forehead.

"What do you mean?" Cara said as she sat up straight.

"About what?"

"About Imogen. What does she believe? What'd she say?"

"She was just—" I paused. In the seconds that passed, my mind raced ahead of me. I could leave it alone and tell Cara that she should talk to Gen. Or I could tell her Gen's exact words, that Gen said I was using her to make Gen jealous. I felt something break inside me. Not my heart—Imogen didn't have that power over me, not anymore—but something else, something darker I didn't have words for. All I knew was that, in that moment, I wanted Imogen to feel as bad as she'd made me feel. It was only fair.

"She was just what?" Cara asked. "Zeke, tell me. Now."

I made a show of hesitating. "You sure you wanna know?"

Cara nodded.

"Okay, well, when you went to the bathroom at Vincent's, she grilled me about us. She accused me of dating you to make her jealous, like that was the only possibility. That's why I got up and left. I didn't wanna listen to her anymore, I was just too mad."

It wasn't *exactly* a lie.

"What else did she say?" Cara said, gripping her fork tight.

Jordan K. Casomar

"She also kept asking me if we were happy. And I told her we would be, if it weren't for her causing problems. Between work, my dad, and all this shit, I'm exhausted, when all I wanna do is spend time with you," I lied. "It's not fair for you. I can't be a good boy-friend while still dealing with her stuff, you know? I don't know what to do, boo." I kissed Cara's hand.

"She said all that?"

"Pretty much, yeah. And it got me mad. I told her, not every-thing's about you and how you feel. I told her I was done with her and that I wanted to be with you, not to make her mad, but 'cause you make me feel . . . good. Like, comfortable. When I was after Imogen, I always felt a little on edge. Like I was doing something wrong. But not when I'm with you. If I was trying to make her jeal-ous, being with you wouldn't feel as good as it does," I said, unsure of what was true and what wasn't, and surprised at how easy it was to keep going.

Cara was blushing, grinning, and clenching her jaw. That was her in a nutshell—embarrassed, excited, and enraged, all at once, always.

"Okay, whatever, shut up with all that gooey shit," she said, her face unable to get any redder. "Gen needs to mind her own damn business. I mean, love that girl to death, but she gets her ego from her dad. She got main character syndrome, like she's one of those dudes in those books she's always reading and we're just side orders. Frankly, I'm tired of it. And now she's trying to get between you and me? After standing in our way for so long? Oh, hell no, fuck all that, she got another think coming."

In the back of my mind, I heard my father's disapproving voice, but I shut it out, drowned it out with my own anger. I didn't care anymore. Imogen had lied to me and embarrassed me at every turn. Who else knew she had been with Trevor before the party? Did Manny? Did *everyone*? Once again, I was the fool, joke's on me. Well, to hell with that.

chapter thirty-one
IMOGEN

Something was up. Cara wasn't responding to any of my texts. After she and Zeke left Vincent's, I texted her to say I was sorry. Later that night, I asked if she was okay. The next day, I sent her question marks—four in the morning, three in the afternoon—and before I went to sleep on Sunday, I asked her if we were good. No replies. Not a one.

As soon as I got to school on Monday, I headed for the band room. They were finishing up their morning practice, the door open, noise spilling out into the hallway. I peeked inside and saw Cara standing at a marimba, mallets between her knuckles like she was drumline Wolverine, and I ducked back before she could see me. I waited by the door, rocking on my feet next to the wall, for her to come out.

"Hey, girl," I said to Cara as she stepped out the door.

"Oh." She jumped. "Hey," she said as she started walking up the hallway toward her locker.

"Somethin up with your phone or what? I've been texting you all weekend."

She shrugged. "Guess I didn't notice."

"What's going on, Cara? Is it about the date? You were right, it was a terrible idea, but, like, are you mad at me?" I said, my chest tight.

Cara looked me in the face and rolled her eyes. "So, you're just going to act all innocent, huh?"

"What are you talking about?"

"I know what you said to Zeke. At the dinner. Just . . . can't you let me have this?" She opened her locker and rummaged around for her textbooks, turning.

"Cara." I grabbed her arm and held firm. "I don't know what you're—"

"You told Zeke you thought the only reason he'd date me was to make you jealous. Ring a bell? You kept asking if we were happy? You were worried I was making a mistake because you still think he's stuck on you, the great and wondrous Imogen," Cara said.

"What? I didn't—that's not what I said."

"Oh, come on, Gen. I mean, it's fine—I know you love attention, just like your dad, so just own it."

I gasped and balled my fists. I couldn't believe she'd just compared me to my dad—she knew how hard I tried to be the opposite of him. And I also couldn't believe that Zeke had twisted my words . . . or could I? Tears were leaking out my eyes. Not sad tears—angry ones. "I told Zeke he better *not* be using you just to make me jealous!" I shouted. "I don't care how Zeke feels right now. I was worried about *you*. That's all. I don't want him to break your heart."

Cara looked taken aback but quickly recovered. "How about you just *let us be*? You're always asking questions, poking holes. Or just keep it to yourself? No one needs to know how you feel about me and Zeke. No one," she said, slamming her locker door shut. As if on cue, the first-period warning bell rang. "Guess we're done here. Good talk, Gen!"

The crowd parted for Cara as she stormed away, then started to slowly disperse. Some grumbled as Cara left, disappointed at the lack of a fight, and more than a few booed and hissed at me as I stood there. I couldn't move, but I could feel my body. I felt my brain speed up past the point of no return. I felt my lungs fold in on themselves until all they could provide were small, shallow, gasping breaths. I felt my legs rattling, my knees knocking. I felt a familiar pair of strong, calloused hands on my back as the floor began to sway beneath my feet.

And then I didn't feel anything at all.

I was on a cot under a thin blanket in a small, white-walled, walk-in-closet-sized room, the lights overhead turned low. *My head hurts,* I thought. My memory was foggy. The last thing I remembered was waiting for Cara outside the band room. The door was closed, but I still heard soft, soothing lo-fi beats playing from a speaker on the other side of the door. While I was looking at the door, it opened and in walked Nurse Weeks.

"Welcome back, kiddo," Nurse Weeks said. She tapped something on her phone and the lights slowly brightened. "Heard you rustlin around back here. Water, ginger ale, or Gatorade? Need to drink something."

"Ginger ale," I said. "What happened?"

Nurse Weeks walked over to a mini-fridge and grabbed two ginger ales. "You had a panic attack and fainted. Woulda hit your head, but that new boy from Texas caught you as you was falling."

I couldn't help but smile as she handed me the can.

The nurse narrowed her eyes. "Girl, if you did this as some kinda made-for-TV stunt to get this boy's attention, so help me," she said.

"No, no," I laughed. "He's already my boyfriend. Don't worry."

"He better be."

"So, now what?"

"Well, how're you feeling?"

"A little tense and wound up, but fine."

"Do we need to call your folks?" the nurse said. "I tried earlier, but it just went to voicemail."

"Hah, don't bother," I said. "Do I have to go back to class now?"

"I can give you another hour, but then you gotta go. Should be right before lunch."

I nodded. "Can you turn the lights back down?"

"Sure thing, kiddo," the nurse said. I lay back down on the cot and stared up at the ceiling as the lights dimmed again, working out what I was going to say to Zeke.

Why did you lie about what I said to Cara? Too confrontational.

Are we ever going to be okay? Too apocalyptic.

Why are you being such a complete dick? Too real.

Maybe we just shouldn't be friends, then? Too unimaginable. At least, it used to be.

Laid up in the dim room, alone with my thoughts and my

anger, I started to wonder. Why was I hanging on to Zeke? Out of habit? Was all this trouble worth it? Why? Because it's what people expected, what everyone thought was going to happen?

I had all these memories of me and Zeke. Playing in his backyard during the hot, sweaty summers. Catching fireflies in our hands and watching them glow in the dark of our cupped palms. We found a bunch of frogs one afternoon when we were six and hopped like frogs for the rest of the day. Drove our parents crazy. Once, in eighth grade, we pulled an all-nighter to watch the sunrise with Manny and Cara. We all got the giggle fits around three in the morning and laughed nonstop until the sun peeked up over the horizon. Our abs hurt for days after. I had all these great memories, but could that good outweigh all the bad? I wasn't sure.

Nurse Weeks woke me up a little before lunch period began.

"Figured you might wanna miss the rush." She smiled. I nodded, grateful for the small kindness, and entered the cafeteria looking for Cara and Zeke, but I didn't see them, only Manny, a tray in his hand piled high with chicken nuggets.

"Hey, have you seen—" I started to ask him, flagging him down.

"Nope." Manny shook his head. "You okay? I heard about the thing this morning."

"Oh yeah. I'm . . . fine," I said. "How're you?"

"Aha, someone finally asks!" Manny grinned, though he wasn't joking, and headed toward a table. "You realize we haven't talked since the party?"

"Oh . . . uh, sorry," I said, following Manny. People were throwing glances my way, murmuring as I passed. I ignored them as best I could.

"Hey, it's okay, it's not just you. It's everyone. You, Zeke, my own cousin. You've all been so wrapped up in your drama, and I've been over here watching my best friends go off on each other and implode, and all of it over, what, some stupid crushes? That's how I'm doing, Gen. I'm sad. Thanks for checking in."

I winced, and Manny must have noticed, because his tone softened.

"I know it's not your fault, not entirely. I'd say, in order, Zeke, you, Trevor, Cara. Everyone's a part of it, so don't go blaming yourself for all the bad shit that's happening. Unless you really do love being the center of attention," Manny joked.

"Thanks . . . I guess?" I said with a laugh.

"What're y'all laughing about?" Trevor said as he set his tray down on the table and kissed me on the cheek. "This cool, Manny?"

Manny nodded. "Oh yeah, man, I don't give a shit what y'all do. I'm like Switzerland. I just want everyone to chill the fuck out. Anyway, pop a squat, I was just telling Gen how some of this is your fault," he said with a shit-eating grin.

"Manny thinks we're all being stupid—"

"Correct!" he said.

"—and that no one's to blame because we're all to blame."

"Nailed it!"

"All I wanted to know was if he'd seen Zeke or Cara! Manny, this is why we haven't talked," I said.

"Cause he's a smart-mouthed little shit?" Trevor said.

"Ding, ding, ding," I answered.

Manny flung a sauced-up chicken nugget at me, but I was ready and dodged to the side. I smelled the honey mustard as it flew past my face, almost grazing my nose, and into the jacked back of Tyson Devins, one of the top wrestlers in the state, a boy with the strength of many men. Tyson reached for the impact zone on his back and when his fingers came away yellow, he stood up and spun around, took one look at Manny's guilty face, and bellowed.

"Aw, hell, see y'all later," Manny muttered. He jumped over the railing behind him and raced toward the door. Devins crashed through a couple other kids as he took off in pursuit.

I didn't see Zeke after lunch, either. He wasn't the type to skip school, and that got me worried.

"He's probably just sick or something," Trevor said as we walked out the door at the end of the day.

"What if something happened with his dad?"

"If something happened, it wouldn't happen quick like this. And if something had happened to Samson, Manny'd know. You need to relax," he said, hugging me and rubbing my back.

"You're heading to the shop after practice tonight, right?"

"Yeah, Ray wants to show me how to make donuts. We boutta feast!"

"Oh great, then you can make me donuts whenever I want? Special orders, right?"

"Long as you got the dough," Trevor said, then busted out laughing.

I groaned, kissed him, then pushed him away from me. "Get

that corny shit outta here, good*bye*. Talk to you later." I waved as he headed off to the field.

I was still laughing about Trevor's cornball joke, right up until I turned onto my block and saw, parked in my driveway, Zeke's old Mercedes.

Zeke's car was ticking, its engine cooling as I passed it, so I knew he hadn't been there long. I took a deep breath as I put my hand on the door, exhaled, and stepped inside to see Zeke and my parents sitting on opposing couches in the living room, separated by a glass coffee table.

"Hey, Gen," Zeke said, a smile on his face.

"Umm, hi? What's going on? Why weren't you at school?" I asked, placing my coat next to his on the hooks by the door.

He ignored my question. "We were just waiting for you. I told them I wanted to talk to them about something," Zeke said.

My mom was thrumming with excitement. Even my dad was a little giddy. "About damn time, boy," he said.

"Zeke . . . ," I said, suspicious.

"Mr. and Mrs. Parker, I felt like it was my responsibility to tell you that not only has Imogen been dating someone behind your back since before her birthday," Zeke said, staring right at me, "but she's also having sex."

chapter thirty-two
IMOGEN

My house had never been quieter. Even in the depths of winter, on our snowiest, blizzardiest days, when the snowdrifts were taller than I was, and sound didn't carry anywhere—even then, there had never been such silence in the Parker household.

My dad's anticipation transformed into a near rage, held back only by his surprise. My mom's eager buzzing came to a sudden, sharp stop. Their heads turned to me, his brow narrowed in anger, her eyes wide in confusion.

"Sit," my dad said, pointing to the seat on the couch next to my mom. "Now."

I bowed my head and did as I was told. When I sat down, I looked at Zeke.

Zeke, please don't, I mouthed. *Please don't do this.*

He pretended not to see me, cleared his throat, and began.

"It goes back about a month ago. My birthday, actually. Gen gave me a really sweet present—this photo album of pictures of me and Pops I'd never seen before—and then, a few days later, she kissed me. I was so excited, because you both know how I feel about Imogen. But I was also surprised, because I knew that she wasn't allowed to do that. Not until she turned sixteen.

"But when you love someone, you wanna keep secrets for them. I didn't say anything to you, Mr. and Mrs. Parker, out of the love I have for your daughter," Zeke said. "And, if I'm being honest, because I wanted more kisses down the line."

My dad chuckled, though he still looked furious.

"I start planning Imogen's birthday party when, out of nowhere, this new kid Trevor shows up. I find out he's decent at playing ball, so I talk him up to Coach after introducing him to the squad. Well, the squad minus Manny since he was in detention, as usual. That *very same day*, Imogen is walking home with this guy, all up in each other's arms, making out on the sidewalk for the whole world to see. Had an eyewitness on that one too. Yelled at them to get a room as they drove by and everything."

"Imogen, is this true?" my mom asked.

"We . . . we weren't making out. We were just talking. It was— he was telling me—"

My dad held up his hand to stop me. "Continue, Zeke."

"So, this Trevor guy. He moves to town, goes after one of the most popular girls in school, and things get physical quick. Makes me think he's kind of pushy, if you ask me. Anyway, *then*, they're seeing each other for a while before her birthday. That night, when you two weren't here, she threw a huge party. Like, this whole living room was a dance floor. The kitchen was just loaded with booze," Zeke said.

"*You* threw the party!" I shouted.

"It was your idea," Zeke said. "But I did put it together because I wanted to do something a little selfish. I wanted to ask her out with this grand, romantic speech with spotlights, music, everything. I wanted to make her feel as special as she is. I was going to tell her how I felt, officially ask her out, after waiting like I was supposed to. So, I'm giving a whole big speech and at the end, when I ask her to be my girl, she kisses Trevor, right in front of me. In front of *everyone*. After that, everyone left the party, except Trevor. He cleaned up the house, then stayed the night with Imogen."

"He did *not*, he cleaned and then he left because he's a gentleman and a decent human being, unlike *you*, Zeke Ladoja. Ask Manny, he was there!"

I looked at my parents' faces. My mom was shaking her head as if to rid herself of a thought. My dad had stood and was pacing, rippling with fury.

"I hate to be the one to do this. I wish I was here asking you a different question. But this Trevor guy, he's suspicious. He's up to something. And he's got Imogen's head all spun around. I just couldn't stand by and let this happen to Imogen without letting you both know," Zeke said, folding his arms across his chest, barely concealing a smug smile on his face.

"Zeke," I said, my voice cracking as I sobbed. "Why are you doing this?"

"Because he's not right for you. He's no good and—" Zeke said, turning to face me. I don't know what he saw on my face, but when he looked at me, his smile vanished, his body went rigid with tension, and when he turned away, he did so with none of his earlier confidence. "A-and, uh, I am. Right for you, I mean," Zeke said, regaining his composure as he addressed my parents. "I love your daughter more than anything. She's my soul mate, beautiful in every way, and if she should be with anyone, it's me."

My mom coughed on the water she was drinking. My father stopped pacing and came to a standstill. He always got real still before he exploded, so when I noticed he wasn't moving, I closed my eyes and braced for the worst.

"You need to get the hell out of this house," he said.

"Dad, please—" I said, my eyes still closed.

"Not you," he said. I opened my eyes to see him pointing his finger at Zeke. "You, boy. How *dare* you treat my daughter this way? You think she owes you something? I don't know Trevor, but I can tell you, he's a nicer boy than you. Who do you think you are, coming over here, giving us a goddamn presentation on our own child?"

"And he a damn snitch, too," my mom said in a tone of voice I'd never heard her use.

"But she's been making out with this guy everywhere," Zeke said, though without that conviction he'd had before. "On the street, under your roof, in parking lots, and he's a complete mystery. What if he's lying about everything? But I've been here the whole time, always her shoulder to cry on, always helpful and supportive, always listening to her stupid problems, and—this is what you both wanted! You always wanted us together! Mr. Parker, you said I was the only man good enough for your daughter! And Mrs. Parker, you said you'd pay for the wedding and our honeymoon in Morocco!" Zeke shouted at my parents, tears in his eyes. "You said you couldn't wait for our grandkids, you told me every time I was alone with you. You even had baby names!"

"Ezekiel, I know it's been a hard year for you," my mom said. "Your father's illness, working instead of playing, missing the season—it's a tough time. I'm sorry for that." She got to her feet, her fists clenched, her nails digging into the meat of her hands. "But what you will *not* do is call my daughter's problems stupid. And do *not* tell my daughter to do anything she doesn't want to do. My daughter has told you no. Do you hear me? *No!*" she shouted.

I was too busy looking back and forth, perplexed about what was happening in front of me. Were my parents . . . defending me?

Zeke jumped to his feet, hands up as if to protect himself. "Fine, I don't care if we're together, but they need to break up! Aren't you mad she lied to you?" he said, desperate. "You need to break them up!"

"No, it doesn't mean that she and Trevor need to break up. No, no, no," my mom said.

Zeke's whole body was vibrating with anger. "You're both hypocrites! You're fucking liars!"

"The hell'd you call me?" Dad said, advancing on Zeke.

"Brian, don't," my mom said. She rushed to get in between the two of them. I got up from the couch too and pushed Zeke toward the door.

"What about Cara? Have you even thought about what this is going to do to her? This is *exactly* what I was worried about!" I shouted. And then a thought popped into my head. "And why'd you say me and Trevor were having sex? We haven't had—"

I saw Zeke's face go bright red. He seemed to notice too, as he put his hands to his face to cover it up.

I gasped. "Zeke, you *didn't*." His face went stone-stiff, and I knew everything I needed to know. "It was her first time. It was *your* first time. And then you turn around and do this? I never thought in a million years you'd be *this* despicable. I don't *ever* want to speak to you again, you hear me?"

I shoved him toward the door and, to my surprise, he didn't resist. He was lifeless, deadweight. I opened the door wide and threw his coat out into the slush. "Get the hell out of my house!" I screamed.

He turned, dead-eyed and emotionless, and walked outside. I slammed the door behind him and fell to the floor, bawling my eyes out.

"Come on now, baby girl," my dad said in an unfamiliarly soft voice as he got me to my feet and guided me to the couch. "It's gonna be okay."

"I'm calling Vanessa," my mom said.

"I'll stay here with Gen."

I was curled up in a little ball, my face pressed into the cushions, as my dad's hand rubbed circles on my back. I could hear my mom in the other room, talking with Zeke's mom.

A few minutes later, my mom returned, took a seat next to me, and kissed the back of my head. "It's okay, love. Imogen, turn around now, we need to talk."

"Do we have to?" I whined, my voice muffled by the cushions.

"We do. Now, turn around," my mom said.

I did as she asked. I uncurled myself and sat up on the couch. My dad's face was wet with tears that he was wiping away with his shirt. I'd never seen him cry real tears. Acting tears, sure, plenty of times, but never real ones. I was stunned.

"I'm—I'm sorry," I started to say.

"Us first," my mom said. She looked at my dad, who gave her a nod. "We're both really sorry for putting pressure on you to be with Zeke. We truly thought . . . well, it doesn't matter. Bottom line is, we didn't listen to you. We should've and we didn't. We're also really sorry about what just happened. That was awful. I can't even begin to describe how disappointed and shocked I am by what Zeke did and said."

I wrapped my arms around her as I started crying again. "It's been really bad, Mom. Everyone at school, they call me a bitch, a slut, a disloyal ho. The janitor, Mr. Randall, he keeps painting over the graffiti, but people keep doing it and—"

"Wait till I get my hands on that little fu—on him," my dad said. "I'm going to teach him a lesson he won't forget."

"Brian." My mom was glaring at him.

"I, uh, I mean," my dad stammered. "How do you want us to help?"

"What sh-should I do about Zeke?" I asked my parents, sniffling. "Am I just supposed to stop talking to him forever? I can't even talk to him now without feeling weird about everything."

"I don't know the answer, baby. But no one has the right to treat you like that, not ever," my mom said, pulling me in tight.

She ran her fingers through my hair, my dad still rubbing circles on my back, and we were like that for a minute. Peaceful, at ease with each other like we hadn't been in a while.

And then my dad ruined it.

"So . . . Trevor," he said.

I coughed, then made like I was going to get up, but my parents' hands kept me down.

"You thought we forgot?" my dad said.

"That we lost track of your secret boyfriend among all the drama?" my mom said.

"Jean, she thought we forgot, can you believe it?"

"Oh, we most certainly did not," my mom said. "His name's Trevor. Trevor what?"

"Trevor Cook," I said, straightening my posture and readying myself for the grilling that was about to begin.

"Where's he from?"

"Houston, Texas. He just moved here after his mom died. Ray's his dad."

"That poor boy," my mom said.

"Ray? Ray Brixton? Pappy's Ray?" my dad asked.

"Yeah. His mom never told Ray about Trevor."

"What's he into? We heard he plays baseball, too. He another rocks-for-brains athlete?" my dad said, then winced as my mom glared at him.

"He's more into comics and books and Star Wars and that sort of thing. He's really, really smart. Like, he can play really good, but his favorite part of baseball's all the stats," I said. "He's, yeah, he's a big nerd. Loves movies, too. This Aronofsky guy especially," I added.

My dad liked that, I could tell. He was quiet for a moment, then nodded approvingly. "I'm okay with it, as long as we get a proper meeting. What about you, Jean?"

"She's sixteen, rules are rules, so I'm fine with it. You're still grounded, though, until the end of the school year."

My life flashed before my eyes. "That's . . . three whole months!"

"You're absolutely correct," my mom said.

"And Trevor has to come over here for dinner next week and subject himself to our questions with no complaint or attitude from either of you," my dad said. "Are we understood?"

"Yes, I understand," I said, relieved. "Thank you. And I'm really sorry for hiding him from you."

"Well," my mom said with a loud exhale. "This has been an eventful night. Any more secrets or confessions people need to get off their chests?"

I thought about the hole in my closet.

"Actually," I said quietly, "there is . . . one more thing I've been hiding from you guys."

"Seriously, Gen?" my mom said. "What, you've been smoking weed, too?"

"No! What's with you and weed, jeez! It's nothing like that. It's . . ." I looked down at my feet, picked some lint from my pants, cleared my throat.

"Out with it," my dad said.

"Okay, but you guys have to promise to be chill about it, okay?"

"*Now*, Imogen."

I sighed. "Okay. No more secrets. Putting it all on the table, here goes."

I led them upstairs to my room, opened the closet, moved the shoeboxes aside, and removed the panel of drywall out of the wall.

"You cut a hole in the wall? Imogen!" my dad said.

"It was already there, I swear. That's not the secret. Um. These are," I said as I reached in and pulled out a stack of composition notebooks. I set them down on my bed and turned away from my parents. I couldn't bear to see their faces, or to let them see mine in all my vulnerability. I heard them leafing through the pages. I felt more exposed than I'd ever been, but beneath the fear, there was also an unexpected wellspring of pride in my bravery. It wasn't a lot, but it was enough for me to be assertive about my work. If I could stand up to Zeke, I could stand up to my parents.

"If I'm being honest, I didn't want to show these to you guys because . . . well, because sometimes you guys can be a lot," I said. "But I write. Like, I write a *lot*. There's a bunch of short stories in here, a whole novel, some poems. But you *have* to be chill, okay? I don't want your critiques, Mom. And Dad, if you steal any of this for a script or something, I'll never trust you ever again. You all have your art, and this is mine, and—"

My parents both let out deep, booming laughs that stopped me dead in my tracks. It wasn't the mean kind of laugh, but one of genuine delight. I looked at the two of them sitting on my bed, their heads almost touching, wide smiles on their faces as they read one of my stories.

"Oh no, he *didn't*," my mom said under her breath. It was like they'd forgotten I was in the room. "Valerie, *girl*."

My insides tumbled like a gymnast as my mom mentioned the name of *my* character. She was invested in *my* story, *my* art. And from the look on her face—on both their faces—they liked what they were seeing. I stood there, shifting awkwardly in the quiet, as they turned the pages.

"Are you still reading?" I asked. It wasn't that I was impatient or embarrassed. It was that I was, to my surprise, really eager to hear what they thought.

"Shh," my dad said as they turned the page.

I distracted myself by taking the time to text Cara. After the argument earlier, I wasn't sure she'd believe me, but I had to try. I wanted to tell her before Zeke did, because I didn't trust him to tell her what actually went down.

A few minutes later, my parents finished and set the notebook down.

"Imogen," my mom started to say.

"You wrote this?" my dad interrupted. "You, Imogen Eleanor Parker, wrote this? No plagiarizing or 'inspiration'? This isn't some fanfiction?"

"No, Dad." I rolled my eyes. "I know it's bad, but—"

"Bad? Imogen, this is good. It's *really* good," my dad said. "Better than most of the scripts I read. Better than some of the *books* I read."

"Have you shown this to anyone?" my mom asked.

I shrank away from them, surprised at their reaction. They were smiling, excited, happy. They were *proud* of me, even. "Um, n-no. Well, Trevor knows I write, but no one else. Not even Zeke."

"Doesn't your English teacher publish student writing?" Dad asked. "You should submit it. It was so easy to see, so clear. It could be a great short play, just three actors, a few sets. . . ."

"Brian. She literally *just* said—" my mom said.

"I wasn't gonna, I just . . . shoot, okay, I won't. I swear," he said. "Gen, it's your decision, but I think you should show the world your art. It's all we're really here to do. What's the point of all this living if not to create? To make beauty out of—"

My mom groaned, I rolled my eyes, and all three of us laughed, together, another first in a long, long time.

◆

Turns out, that was all the push I needed. It was their opinions—their judgment, really—I feared most, and with that out of the way, I couldn't stop thinking about what I would send to Ms. Granson.

After dinner, I holed up in my room and started poring over my notebooks. I had a handful of stories that I thought were decent, but they were all love stories, and after the day I'd had, that wasn't where my head was at. I was still furious at Zeke going behind my back, but more than that, I was just plain confused. I never would've expected something like that from him. Sitting there in the living room, watching him cursing out my parents, he seemed like a different person altogether. The Zeke I knew had been replaced by some cruel, vengeful facsimile, an alien imposter.

That's it! I thought. Right then, a story revealed itself to me, rising fully formed from the depths. I started typing like my life depended on it, sculpting a vessel that held everything that I'd felt—Zeke's betrayal of our friendship, the weight of my anxiety and discomfort, the pressure from my parents, Zeke's parents, and just about everyone else in my life—over the past few weeks. I had never written a story so quickly, and I had never loved a story so immediately. I knew, right away, that if I was going to show my work to the world, this was the story that I wanted the world to see. The message I wanted to send.

Hi, Ms. Granson,
I know it's almost eleven on a Monday, which is really, really, really late to be sending you an email but . . .

chapter thirty-three
THE PIER
BY IMOGEN PARKER

Every Saturday, at 8:32 p.m., I walk to the edge of the pier and hope I find my way home. I put away my disguise—a dress, heels, bangles and earrings, the made-up face that feels heavy on my skin—and wear only what I arrived in: a simple black bodysuit, the color of the space between the stars, the emptiness of the universe, home. I look out toward the sea for a light, a beacon, any sign whatsoever that I have not been forgotten. I wait for an hour, two hours, six. I wait until the world gets quiet—no rumbling engines, no music blaring from boom boxes and stereo systems, no loud laughter from people clustered around beachfront bonfires—before I give up and start the long walk home. I have come to the pier each and every week for three years. I have stood on the water-softened wood 156 times and have always left disappointed.

I come back to the house and take time to compose myself because I must keep up appearances. Because, on Sundays, I am expected elsewhere.

First, at church, where I sing along to songs I do not understand. Still, the melodies move me and the voices of the women, all as dark as I am, though none as dark as the void above from which I hail, make my skin crawl in delight. I listen to the words of a fancifully clothed man, words that are lost on me. He tells stories of great beings above, but the ones he references are not the ones I know. He speaks of beings who love and care about the world below, and given that I have been abandoned, that I have returned 156 times to the place where I found myself stranded and alone, I know that his beings and mine cannot be one and the same.

After the singing and the stories, I help set up the after-service for the congregation. There is food, there is conversation, and I eat and speak out of obligation, for I never hunger for either. And I know hunger, even though I do not eat, because I see it in the eyes of the people around me. Some hunger for the words of the fanciful man. Some hunger for the dishes spread out across the picnic tables. Some hunger for each other, even when they are not supposed to. And there is one man who hungers for me.

His name is Noah. I have not told anyone who I am, really, but if I were to tell someone, it would be Noah. I have told him *how* I am. I have told him of my sadness and of the emptiness I sometimes feel, but not the extent or the cause, because it was he who first found me just after midnight on a Saturday three years ago, wandering a world I didn't recognize. He smelled nice—something sweet and spicy, I remember—and his voice was as deep and calming as the sea.

He takes care of me. He has since that night. He is kind and good. He has not abandoned me like my kin, and I am grateful for that. But he does *want*. More and more, with each passing day. He thinks I am like the women who look at him with hunger in their faces, and who look at me as something to be devoured or discarded, and I cannot tell him the truth. I cannot tell him that I do not need breath and that, inside my body, instead of a smattering of soft organs, I am filled with small stars. I cannot tell him where I go on Saturdays and how I wait and long for something to pull at the lights in my chest and lift me back up to where I belong.

When the food is gone and the talking is done, when the tables are cleaned and put away, I am expected to join Noah and we are expected to leave together. Sometimes, he holds and squeezes my hand and it pains me but I let it happen. Human touch hurts, but I can't explain that to him without also telling him that I have no true body, that I am amorphous, and pressure on *any* part of me is pressure on *all* of me. When we reach my home, paid for by the church in exchange for my service, he walks me inside and lingers and his hunger fills the air like a bad smell.

"Valerie," he says, for that is what I am called here, a name I took from a pane of glass, a storefront near where he found me. "Can I . . . can we talk?"

I can hear his heart. I can hear his sweat. I can hear his eyes, restless in their sockets. I don't want his words, but I nod.

"It's been, what, three years since we met? It's crazy, because it only feels like yesterday to me. I think it's because, well, my life feels like it exists in two phases—pre-Valerie and post-Valerie. Who I was before I met you and who I am now, they don't feel like the same person. Different wants, different goals, different dreams. I can hardly remember what I wanted before I met you, if I'm being honest, only what I *know* I want now: You. Us. I want to travel the world with you. I want to grow old with you. I want to . . . I want to do *everything* with you."

I know this. I know it before he says it. I hear it in his footsteps, I hear it in his breaths, I hear it in the longing sighs he makes when he thinks I can't hear him, because he thinks that I am like him. He thinks I am curious about this world. He thinks I grow old. He thinks I have a heart, and I don't have the heart to tell him he is wrong, because I hear his sadness as loud as I do his desire. And I don't want to make him hurt, this kind human who has brought me into his life and keeps me safe and never asks too many questions.

"You don't have to say anything right now," Noah says. "Just . . . will you think about it? Will you think about me?"

I return to the church the next day to prepare for Monday night service. I like Mondays more, because there are more children, and they fascinate me. They remind me of meteors, tearing through space, colliding with whatever's in their path with hardly a care.

"So, did anything *happen*?" Leilani asks as we ready the church for the oncoming meteor shower. I have learned humor from Leilani, in the same way that I have learned desire from Noah. Both are subtle things, hard to pin down or describe in words, only in feelings. She tells me something and my body rocks with percussive force, as if the stars inside me are exploding, and I feel the closest I have ever felt to the idea of home, to comfort, to peace. I like her, most days. But not when she asks me about Noah, because then, she smells of hunger, too. It is a slightly different scent, like the smell of the ocean at night versus the scent of it when the sun hangs high overhead, but it is hunger nonetheless.

"What do you mean?"

"With Noah, I mean. Yesterday," she says, and playfully raises an eyebrow. "Girl, don't tell me you can't see it after this long. That man been in lurrrv with you for the longest. I don't know why you haven't gotten down and dirty with him, fine as he is. And Lord, is he *fine*. Word round the pews was that he was planning on making a move. You saying he didn't?"

I hesitate. Too long, it seems.

"Oh, he *did*, didn't he?! Thank goodness. You better love up on that man. And if you don't, girl, we'll come for you, 'cause I'm not the only one that's all kinds of jealous of you and him. So, you gonna spill or what?"

The first group of children arrive in that moment, and for the first time since learning of the god Noah and Leilani believe in, I wonder if he is, in fact, a real being looking out for me. I avoid Leilani the rest of the night and leave before she can question me further.

On Tuesday, I go to the grocery store. I buy food that I don't eat, drinks that I don't drink. Most of it, I give away. Too much of it, I throw away. In the aisles, I run into other church ladies and make small talk. It is an easy thing to do now. The questions are always the same.

When are you and Noah going to make it official?

When are you and Noah going to tie the knot?

When are you and Noah going to have some babies?

I am expected to smile and nod. I am expected to laugh and act bashful. I am expected to say, *Soon, girl, soon.* So I do. In my time here, I have learned that when you don't belong in a place, to a people, there is nothing more important than keeping up appearances, than meeting expectations.

Wednesday nights are Bible study. I make sure that chairs are set out, doors are unlocked, rooms are prepared. I am the only person, so to speak, that is present on Wednesdays, and in the emptiness, the building's acoustics make my every movement carry. I enjoy the sound of my footsteps in the empty church, echoing off the stained-glass windows, the polished wood of the pews. I find comfort in the paper-whisper when I flip through the thin, fragile pages of the Bibles.

Except that Wednesday, when I enter the church, I realize I am not alone. I smell him—Noah. Orange, cinnamon, the sweet and spicy I smelled the night we met. He is setting out chairs and Bibles, taking over my duties, and he grins as wide as he can when he spots me.

"Hey, Val," Noah says, and waves. "I had nothing going on tonight, figured I'd come help out. If that's okay with you?"

I don't know how to say no. I have no reason to. And when he asks me to accompany him to dinner, I agree to that, too. I don't like food, but I force it down to be good company. I laugh at his jokes. I smile at his stories. He is the only person I trust, truly, and I do not know how to do anything but make him happy in return. That seems to be what is expected of me, and in this strange place, expectation is all I have to go on.

At the end of the night, he walks me to my apartment, and again, he lingers on the doorstep as I look for my key. I find it, insert it into the lock, turn to tell him goodbye. That is when he steps forward and puts his hand on my cheek. It feels like a dozen needles prickling my skin, and then the feeling is worse when he presses his lips against mine. The moment is brief, painful like an electric shock, and when he steps away, he smiles and I, a slave to expectation, think of my conversation with Leilani and smile back. My lips hurt for hours after.

On Thursday, I am sick, the result of Noah's touch. He wants to come take care of me and I have to tell him no, several times, and he only relents after I tell him I am contagious. I make my apartment as dark as possible. I close the blinds, draw the curtains, turn off every light, every piece of technology I own. I even cover the small red light on the smoke detector overhead. I spend the day in the dark and try my hardest to imagine I am home, in the darkness between the stars.

Noah calls me four times on Friday. I do not answer.

He calls me twice more on Saturday, then knocks on my door. I see him, a bouquet of flowers in his hand, through the app on my phone for the doorbell camera he bought and installed for me. He is dressed up in a much nicer suit than the ones he wears to Sunday services. His hair is freshly cut, his beard newly trimmed, and he is wanting. But I am not there—it is 8:25 p.m. and I have somewhere else to be.

I walk to the pier. The moon is full, the night is bright. A man and a woman are sitting on the edge, their feet dangling over the waters beneath them. The man has his hand on the small of the woman's back. His thick braided hair rests on her shoulder. I hear her skin prickle up with goose bumps, with a sound like popcorn.

They are whispering to each other. They are saying sweet things, but there is pain beneath their words too. Something unsaid. Something hidden. A lie. Or, perhaps more accurately, a fantasy. A life they want to live but can't.

I am straining to listen, to understand, when I feel something in my chest. A fluttering feeling, like a shift in gravity, like a sudden fall. It is unsettling and frightening, almost, and then . . . familiar? I look to the stars above and I gasp: They are *moving*.

Dozens of pinpricks of light are twisting and turning in the sky, right in the center of my vision. They are growing larger, larger, larger. The man and woman do not seem to notice, and I can't tell if it's because they are caught up in their fantasy or if there's some other reason for their indifference. A moment later, I get my answer as time stops. My watch hangs on 8:32 p.m. and stays there for what seems like an eternity as the moving stars settle atop the waveless ocean and form, slowly, into a shape like mine. Human on the outside, in a black bodysuit. A masculine figure, a face seemingly chiseled out of black glass, with eyes like twin suns. He walks across the sea, then steps from the water onto the pier as if the two surfaces were the same height. This world's reality does not matter to him and with every step, I feel my body shiver in recognition. All at once, I understand desire, and for the last time, I think of Noah.

"I will not force you to return to the stars," the figure says. He doesn't speak—he *sings*. "But I have been searching for you, Carinae."

"Is . . . that my name?"

The figure laughs, a sound like ice crystals forming. "A name is a small thing. You are so much vaster than that. Carinae is what you are. Look."

The figure unzips his suit and what spills out is creation itself: a dozen stars, living, dying, and being reborn. Burning, blazing, erupting, re-forming.

"It's beautiful," I say.

"It's you. The true you. And you are beautiful too, Carinae."

"Who . . . what are you?"

"I am Argus. Look."

The stars change. They form new constellations, burn in brighter colors, dazzling and different. I reach out to touch them— to touch him. When we touch, there is no pain, only life. Only warmth. Only want.

"I have missed you," Argus says. He places a hand to my cheek and I blaze with starlight, brighter and brighter and brighter until the world disappears into its brilliance. When the light fades, we are gone, and I am where I belong. Time moves forward.

chapter thirty-four
ZEKE

I knew it was going to be bad when I walked in and saw my parents waiting at the kitchen table with *drinks*. Near-empty glasses, too; it was clear they had been sitting there a while. My only option was to act like I didn't see them. I came inside, kicked my shoes off, and made for my room without a word.

"Nuh-uh," my mom said. "Don't even think about it."

"Get back in here, Ezekiel. We're going to talk," my dad rasped.

"I can't now, I gotta—" I started to say.

"You have until the count of five," my mom said. "One . . . two . . . three . . ."

I sighed, stomped into the kitchen, and slumped down into a chair.

"Anything you wanna tell us?" she said.

"Uh, not really. Cara wants to go on a date this weekend, so I think we're—"

"Zeke," my father said. His voice was weak, but it still carried some of his old strength, commanding attention.

"Jean called us," my mom said, tapping her fingers on the table. "She told us what you did."

"What *I* did? I told them the truth, that's all," I said.

"Zeke, baby, you don't have to . . . I know this hurts. It's your first big heartbreak. It's tough, I know," my mom said.

I laughed. "What're you guys talking about?"

"Ezekiel," Pops said, placing a hand on mine. "Stop it."

I looked at him. He looked so tired, he knew I was lying, and he just wanted to get to the truth so he could rest, and *I* was the one holding him up. I started crying, and once I started, I couldn't stop.

"It's not fair," I wailed. "It's not fair. Pops has cancer, Ma's working too much, I left the team to work at Fro-Yo Jojo and we're still broke, and now Imogen's with someone else? It's just not fucking fair," I said. I banged my fist against the table.

"Wait, you left the team? You've been working? I specifically told you not to do that. Goddamn it, Zeke," my mom said. She was shaking her head, eyes closed, rubbing her temples. "I should've known something was up. I've just been so distracted, I can't believe I—"

My dad waved off her comment, his attention squarely on me. "So, let me get this straight, you're saying you mistreated this girl— who's supposed to be your best friend, mind you," my father said as the room went quiet, "because I got sick and now your life's hard?"

I felt like he had slapped me right across my face.

"Hey now, Samson," my mom said, her voice soft.

"Hey nothin'," Pops answered, more animated than he had been in months. "Zeke, son, is *that* what you're telling me? Because I'm sick, you told a girl's parents to break up her relationship and *make* her be with you instead. That's what you're telling me?"

"Samson! Ease up, he's just a boy," my mom said.

"I was here first, Dad! I've always been there, and I know all her favorite things, and what she's scared of and why she doesn't—They just met, like, a month ago, and we've known each other for almost a whole decade. She's just scared of being with someone who *really* loves her and who's *really* connected to her. Someone who knows her," I said. "So, of course she goes with the guy who's a stranger, because it's less threatening. It's safer. It's easier." I paused. Pops was looking at me like he didn't recognize who I was. I didn't like it. "Why are you looking at me like that?"

"Because I thought I raised you to be a man who respects the people he cares for, the women he's interested in. But now, you sound like some of those fools on the street corner yelling nonsense about Black queens and how a woman's supposed to behave. I'm just confused."

I couldn't believe what I was hearing—had everyone forgotten that they'd been telling me for my whole life that I should be with Gen? "You guys are such hypocrites, just like Jean and Brian! Pops, you've been teasing me about Gen since middle school. Mom, you always told me that we were gonna be together and made like we were soul mates. You always said, 'When you two get married' or 'The two of you'll understand when you're older' or 'You two are so perfect together.' But now, all of a sudden, no? Forget it? Give up? You're the one who told me to chase her! Remember what you told me the night of the party? Do you remember what you said, Dad? 'I didn't raise you to be a quitter.' Those were *your* words."

"Zeke, I . . . ," my dad started to say.

"We were wrong for that," my mom cut in. "It always felt so innocent and lighthearted, teasing you about her, talking about the two of you. As parents, I think we don't really recognize what that says and does until it's too late.

"At the same time, Zeke, we don't always know why we like the people we like . . . or why we don't. It's just something you feel in your gut. I know you feel it for Imogen, but she doesn't feel it for you, baby boy. Keep trying to push it now, all you'll do is push her even further and further away," my mom said.

"It hurts, but you have to accept it, son. It's time to move on," my dad said.

I stared at him in silence. "Okay, whatever. Can I go now?" I said, acid-tongued.

My dad sighed. "I don't want to fight with you, Zeke—"

"Who's fighting? We're good," I said. "Now, can I be excused?"

My dad threw his hands up and shrugged.

I glanced at my mom. "Can I?"

She shook her head in frustration and waved me along. I went to my room, slamming the door behind me. I couldn't stop crying, my mind racing between how awful things had gone at Imogen's house and my growing terror at how Cara was going to react. I had been on autopilot, driven by my anger at Imogen, and it was only just occurring to me that I had ruined everything with Cara. My clothes still smelled like her, like weed and citrus and patchouli and a hint of Febreze. I could still feel the warmth of her body pressed up against mine, the rise and fall of her chest as she breathed, the two of us nestled up together. I liked her, I realized. I really liked her. And it was over. I knew that, without a doubt. She was going to be furious, and Manny, he was going to be pissed at me too. He warned me. He said I was going to hurt her. And he was right. He was absolutely right. I had fucked everything up and all I could do was sob, late into the night, until I fell asleep.

I woke up the next morning exhausted, still in my clothes from yesterday, to my mom knocking on my door. When I didn't answer, she opened the door and stepped inside.

"Get up, we're going to the hospital. Your father's doctor called, told us to come in," she said.

"I already called the school and told them you went home sick after lunch yesterday, so you're excused for that and for today, too. I'm feeling generous, so I'm giving you a day to let things cool down a little. We'll discuss your punishment in the car, but know that, at the very least, you're grounded until we say you're not. Now, hurry up." My mom didn't bother to close the door as she walked away. She looked especially tired, and I could tell that she wasn't expecting good news. I would've felt deflated, were there any air left in my body to lose.

I was just glad I wasn't going to have to go to school and face Imogen or, worse, have to tell Cara what happened. I wasn't ready for that conversation, not yet. It wasn't much of a silver lining, but it was something, and I was grateful.

And then I checked my phone.

Cara: Fuck you Zeke

On the drive to the hospital, I typed, erased, and retyped a reply to her, trying and failing to find the right words to say to make everything okay.

I'm so sorry, Cara. I didn't mean for any of this to happen. I got so angry, I barely thought about what I was doing.

I'm so sorry, Cara. I know you must hate me. I'd hate me too.

Cara, please, please take me back. I really fucked up and I need you.

It was all wrong. It was all wrong and desperate and just not enough. Not enough to make up for the fact that I tried to break up Imogen and Trevor for my benefit. How could I explain that to Cara in a way that didn't make me look terrible? Who the hell would let that slide? Certainly not Cara. She'd cut folks out her life for a whole lot less.

As I tried to compose my message to Cara, I received a flurry of texts from the guys on the team with links to a story on the school's online literary journal. I was confused—most of the guys couldn't name a book to save their lives—until I followed the link and saw that the story was Imogen's. I read through it once and then again after I had gotten over the shock of realizing the story was clearly about me.

All the while, messages kept rolling in. I swiped away most of them without a glance, except for the texts from Manny and Jojo, which I couldn't ignore, even if I wanted to.

Manny: You stay the fuck away from my cousin
Jojo: I will not tolerate someone who has mistreated my niece this way as an employee. This week will be your last.

Everything was falling apart around me. I was losing everything—my friends, my team, even my job. I opened the browser on my phone as we sat in the hospital waiting room, scrolled to the top of the page, and read Gen's story for the third time.

We had been waiting for nearly an hour to meet with the oncologist. My mom was drumming her nails against the wooden armrests, quietly furious about the delay, while my dad was engrossed in an episode of *Family Feud* blaring from one of the TVs. All I could think about was the story. Gen felt like an alien. Like someone playing at being human. I didn't know if I should take it that literally—English class had never been my strong suit—but it was hard to take it any other kind of way, especially when I was so clearly the basis for Noah.

I had thought about showing the story to my parents, but I didn't want to get into any more trouble. They'd spelled out my punishment on the way here. I was grounded for an undetermined length of time. They had taken my keys and put me on a heavy-duty chores rotation for the next few months.

But, more than anything, I was embarrassed. I had let my parents down when they needed me most, when they needed me to be strong so they could focus on doing what they needed to do to fight my dad's illness. In my selfish fixation on Imogen and what *I* wanted, I'd caused an enormous mess that only added more stress and more complication to the difficulties they were already facing. I felt like the worst son on the planet.

"Ladoja, Samson!" a nurse called out.

"About damn time," my mom said as she helped my dad to his

feet. I started to stand up, but my mom shook her head no. "I want you to stay out here."

"But—"

"Ezekiel, don't back-talk me. You're in enough trouble as it is, so you're gonna park your butt in that seat and you're not gonna say another word. Am I clear?"

I sighed and nodded. "Yes, Ma. I'll stay right here."

"Good," she said. She didn't need to explain why. If the news was bad, she wanted to be the one to tell me, not the doctor. And, if I had to guess, she didn't want me to see her or my dad cry. She wanted to protect me from that and make the situation feel less horrible, even if it was only just by a little bit.

So I waited. I flipped through a few old magazines. I tried to zone out and watch *Family Feud*, but that just reminded me of Cara. She referred to Steve Harvey as Mr. Sweet Potato Head, and until that moment, it'd never failed to send me into a laughing fit. A *Maury* rerun was on another TV, but the segment was about a man who'd cheated on his wife with her best friend, and that struck a little too close to home, so I read Imogen's story again.

I don't know why I kept reading it. Maybe I thought that if I read it enough, I could find the right things to say to make all of this go away. That somewhere in the lines, or between them, was a way to put all the pieces of my broken life back together so that everything went back to how it had been. Something that'd convince Imogen that she belonged here, on this planet, and that I wouldn't dare hurt her with a touch or a kiss like Noah. But maybe that was impossible. Maybe I already had.

I was halfway through the story when my parents reentered

the waiting room, their faces wet with tears. I was ready for the worst when I realized my mom was smiling. For the first time since the diagnosis, she was *really* smiling. Her shoulders weren't sagging with the weight of her worry, and she had a spring in her step.

I jumped to my feet and hurried over to the two of them. "Mom? What's going on? What'd she say?"

"It's gone," she said. "It's all gone. They didn't find anything. Not a trace. He's got more tests coming up, but the oncologist, she—"

She didn't have a chance to finish her sentence, not before I threw my arms around the two of them and hugged them so tight, I heard my mom's back crack. In that moment, for the first time in a long time, it felt like everything was going to be okay.

chapter thirty-five
IMOGEN

My phone had been blowing up all morning, buzzing like a bee in my pocket before I silenced it altogether, trying my hardest to ignore it. Ms. Granson hadn't wasted a single second—an hour after I emailed her my story, she emailed me back to let me know that it was going up on the school's online journal and that she'd have printed copies by morning waiting in her classroom. And since it was more fuel for the gossip fire that was me and Zeke's situation, it had made the rounds on social media quick as lightning.

"I didn't think it would happen so fast," I told Trevor, who squeezed my hand—a small comfort—as we walked to school. "Like, I thought she'd edit it and maybe it'd be another week or, I dunno, something. Yesterday, no one knew I wrote stories, and now all of a sudden everyone knows and I—what if everyone thinks it's stupid and makes fun of me?"

Trevor wrapped his arm around me and pulled me into his body. "Well, if it helps any, I loved it. Your voice felt like the stars themselves, distant and beautiful. I sent it to Dink, too. He said it was one of the best things he's ever read. Plus, Ms. Granson thought it was good enough to publish right away, so I can't imagine people are gonna think it's stupid. Definitely can't get any worse than the past few weeks."

I laughed. "Trust me, you don't know the kids around here like I do. It can *always* get worse."

"Fair enough. But at least you did the damn thing, right? You put your voice out there, put your foot down, and no one can take that away from you. You came right out and said that no matter what people tell you, no matter what folks want of you, you choose who you love. You choose how you live. You choose who you are. People are gonna take it how they're gonna take it, but that's the thing—they're *gonna* take it, 'cause of you."

My heart fluttered in my chest at him saying "love"—that alone was almost enough to chase all my fear away—and I snuggled into him closer as we walked. I took a deep breath as we rounded the corner and Hampton High came into view, steeling myself for what was to come. It was early—I'd escorted Trevor to his morning workout—and it was quiet as we approached. Inside, I didn't see any other students, but I did see Mr. Randall, push broom in hand. He wheeled his big trash can over to me with a wide grin on his face.

"Well, well, if it ain't Richardina Wright!" he said with a big laugh. "And here I thought you was just one of the nicest, smartest kids in this school. Didn't know you had that kinda talent in you, girl!"

Trevor was doubled over laughing at "Richardina" while I could only stand there, blushing, embarrassed. "Th-thanks, Mr. Randall, but it wasn't *that* good."

"Nonsense and poppycock, little lady. I won't hear it, not a damn word," he said, tapping his broom loud against the linoleum.

"That's what *I'm* saying," Trevor chimed in, his laughter subsiding. "It was good as hell."

"This the boy you *do* like, huh?" Mr. Randall asked. "You that new kid. Texas." He narrowed his eyes and looked Trevor up and down.

"Yes, sir. Gen told me you painted over the graffiti about her. I appreciate you doing that." Trevor smiled and extended a hand.

Mr. Randall gave Trevor a firm handshake and held his gaze. "Don't need no thanks for that. Just doin what's good and right. Speaking of, I painted over the mess about your mama, too. Damn shame, some of these kids ain't got no home training. I'm really sorry about her, Tex. My own sister, she took one too many needles into her arm and fell out about a decade back. Sad thing, but it's hard to help folks who ain't wanna be helped. You ever see any more nonsense like that, you tell me, I'll take care of it right away."

"Y-yes, sir. Thank you, sir," Trevor said. His body stiffened up in surprise and I saw him working his jaw, trying hard to keep his tears in, moved by the unexpected kindness.

"Well, they don't pay me to stand around jawing, so let me get my old ass back to work," Mr. Randall said. "You two take care of each other now, okay?"

Trevor and I nodded and watched Mr. Randall walk off, whistling as he went.

"Mr. Randall is a real one," Trevor said softly.

I nodded in agreement.

"All right, girl, I gotta get before Coach's got something to say. But, hey, so far so good, right? I'll see you at lunch, if not sooner."

Trevor kissed me on the forehead, which I felt from the crown of my head to the soles of my feet, and took off toward the gym.

I decided to head down to Ms. Granson's classroom. I wanted to thank her in person, and more than anything, I wanted a physical copy of my story. I was nervous about how it was being received—though Mr. Randall's reaction helped—but nothing could tamp down the excitement I felt to have my very first publication printed and in my own hands.

She was laying the story out in neat stacks on her desk when I walked in. As soon as she saw my face, she started beaming. She rushed toward me and wrapped me up in a hug.

"I'm so, so, *so* proud of you, Imogen. I *knew* you had talent. And have you seen the reaction? It's blowing up!" Ms. Granson said, speaking a mile a minute.

Her praise and excitement washed over me the way a wave does. It felt good at first, like I was being carried with it, by it, weightless, floating without a care. But then, the churn. I felt like I was being sucked down, pulled into the depths by the current and the force of the water.

"Imogen? You okay?"

Ms. Granson's voice sounded muffled, distant.

"Oh no, was I too much? Did I freak you out?"

I swam up toward the surface, hungry for air, and shook my head. "Can . . . can I see it?"

She nodded and handed me a copy. It wasn't fancy, but it was well laid out in elegant columns on nice, heavy paper. It felt professional and substantial and—I brought the paper to my face and inhaled—it smelled like writing, like paper and ink, and with that,

I rose up above the waves, air in my lungs, and the panic passed. Right there, on the page, was my story, my name: "The Pier" by Imogen Parker.

"It's not too much. Thank you. Thank you so much for doing this," I said, choked up.

"All I did was print it. *You* did this, Gen. And I've got a feeling that this is only the beginning."

I heard activity from beyond her classroom door. Kids yelling up and down the halls. The pounding of footsteps. Lockers opening, slamming. School was starting soon, which meant that I was about to find out exactly what the rest of the school thought of me and my work. I thought I'd be more nervous, but holding a copy in my hands, I had a hard time feeling anything but accomplished. The fear was gone, replaced by something closer to freedom.

"Now that's the smile I was hoping to see," Ms. Granson said as she squeezed my shoulder. "But don't for a second think that this means you can skate on through the rest of my class this semester. I'll be expecting a lot from you, Ms. Parker." Ms. Granson smiled and winked, then waved for me to go on and get.

Braejon was the first person I saw when I stepped out of Ms. Granson's. He seemed to be heading toward her classroom, and when I saw him, I quickly spun around and started walking the other way. I heard him calling me from behind, asking me to slow down. I pretended I didn't hear him for the longest, and when that no longer worked and he was standing in front of me, right in my path, I braced for the worst.

"Damn, girl, you walk quick! Been tryna catch up and holla at you a second," he said.

I always forgot how big he was until I was right next to him. He was closer to seven feet than he was to six. Absurdly tall.

"Sorry," I said.

"Look, I wanna say I'm sorry. For real."

I hadn't expected that, and he must have seen my confusion, because he explained.

"We—the whole team, I mean—fucked up. Like, we messed with Tex and all, and that was wrong. We had to haze the brother a little, sure, but the mess about his ma was crossing a line. Yeah, Zeke's our boy, but that don't mean everything he does is right, and he sure wasn't right here. Won't lie, I was all for him saying something at your birthday. And, honestly, I thought it was mad fucked how you reacted. Still do, really."

This was not what I needed right now. "Thanks, I guess?" I said. "Look, I gotta—"

"I read your story," he interrupted. "You're Carinae. Zeke's Noah, right?"

"I mean, it's up to the reader's interpretation. . . ."

Braejon gave me a look.

I sighed. *No more hiding.* "Yeah. That's right."

"Thought so. I don't know, it got me feeling some kind of way. Like, I didn't think you felt like that. So . . . different, you know? Like it was painful to you for him to feel that way about you. Like it made you wanna just run and hide and disappear. Always thought you was just playing hard to get and that's why he had to keep at you, but nah."

I was taken aback. I hadn't expected Braejon, of all people, not only to read my story but also to understand and internalize it. He

277

was looking at me with soft, sad eyes, his shoulders hunched with guilt, and I found myself deeply moved and at a loss for words.

"So, yeah," Braejon said, after a beat. "I'm sorry for my part in makin the last few weeks for you as bad as they've been. You don't deserve that shit. You're good people. Always have been. That's what I wanted to say. I'm late for morning workouts, so I gotta bust outta here. I'll catch you later, Parker." He didn't wait for a response, didn't expect anything. He just said what he needed to say to apologize and took off down the hallway.

I was still processing what he'd said as I headed for my locker, when I saw Raquel Damaris and Niecy Adams waiting for me, leaning up against Cara's locker, right next to mine. I tensed up, remembering what they'd said about me after the party, and was about ready to turn and run when they spoke up.

"Hey, girl," Niecy said, uncharacteristically demure. "Can we talk?"

"Just right quick," Raquel said. "We . . . we wanna say we're sorry."

I let out a sigh of relief and nodded.

"Yeah girl, been there," Niecy said. "With Yovani and Axel both. Just 'cause I think they funnier than fuck, they think I wanna get with them. They stay hollerin at me so much I had to block them *both* on Insta."

"There's this college boy at my church who's always trying to talk me up," Raquel said, her voice suddenly heavy with old anger. "My mama thinks he's just the sweetest and most handsomest brother around. She keeps trying to get us together even though he's, like, six years older than me. I keep telling her how that's weird as hell, but she don't listen. He sent me a nasty Snap once of him with no shirt on too. Gross. But my ma thinks I'm just . . . I don't even know what she thinks."

"And I'm sorry I called your pops an Uncle Tom," Niecy added. "That's a fucked-up thing to say. Also, I love your mom's art. Makes me cry sometimes. But if you tell *anyone* I said that, I'll make *you* cry. Got it?"

I laughed and nodded. "I appreciate the apology. And, trust, your secret's safe with me."

"So . . . it true Z came by your place to blow up your spot? I can't believe Z turned out to be just like all those other dusty-ass low-bottom niggas tryna bring us down on they level 'cause otherwise we too high up for they ass," Raquel said.

Part of me wanted to nod along and tell her to talk that talk, and part of me wanted to defend Zeke, who was, despite everything, still my friend. I opted for the middle ground.

"Where'd you hear that?"

"Girl, where you been this morning? Ramirez *been* going off on Insta. Shit, everybody knows."

As if on cue, I saw Cara round the corner. People whispered and glanced as she passed by, hands in her pockets, her face hidden in a hoodie. She was heading my way and when she saw me, she looked as if she was about to turn and walk away, so I texted her real quick.

Me: Can we talk?

I watched Cara pull her phone out of her sweatshirt pocket, glance at the screen and then at me, and nod.

"Y'all mind if me and Cara . . . ?" I asked Raquel and Niecy.

"Nah, girl. Do your thang," Niecy said. "And . . . yeah, sorry again."

Raquel dapped me up, then the two of them took off down the hallway.

Cara waited for Raquel and Niecy to leave before she came over to me. From afar, she looked like she'd either been crying for a long time or was very, very stoned. Once she was up close, with her puffy eyes and her hair smelling of herb, it was clear that it was, in fact, very much both.

"Hey, Cara," I said. "You okay?"

"Fuck no," she said with a dry laugh. "I'm fucking *terrible*, Gen. The guy I like tried to break up my best girlfriend and her boyfriend so that he could get with her. The whole school has somehow figured out that I lost my virginity to that asshole. Plus, I just got my period, and it's a bad one. And it's only *Tuesday morning*. But, hey, it's Zeke's fault, not yours."

"No, some of this is *definitely* my fault. And besides, I really haven't been a good friend to you," I said. "I've known about your crush on Zeke since the beginning of freshman year, but I didn't do anything about it. I didn't do anything to support you, to open the way for you. *I'm* the one that's sorry. Nothing I've gone through's as bad as what you're going through right now, so let's not pretend any different, okay?"

"You're . . . you're not mad, are you? That I told people about what Zeke did? After you told me, I couldn't keep it to myself, else I was gonna explode."

I shook my head and stepped toward Cara, arms open for a

hug, waiting for her consent. She nodded eagerly and pressed herself into my arms. The both of us tried to keep from crying and when we pulled apart, our wet faces proved our failure.

"Thank goodness, I'm glad we're cool," Cara said, wiping her eyes. "'Cause I'm pretty sure Ray and my mom are, like, *really* into each other. I even caught my mom looking at wedding dresses the other day. Trevor might be my brother soon, and it'd really suck if I wasn't getting along with my new brother's girlfriend."

I laughed. "Trust me, I know about Ray and your mom. There've been times I've been at Trevor's, and I've . . ." I shuddered. "I've *heard* things."

"Oh god, girl, me too. It's the worst. It is the motherfucking worst, pun intended," she said.

We both laughed, and for a second, it was like nothing had ever happened.

"So . . . has he tried to talk to you?" I asked Cara.

"Doesn't matter. I know my worth. I'm not gonna stick around with some man that's gonna disrespect me. I saw my mom date all kinds of disrespectful, mean, name-calling men before she started gettin busy with Ray. No thanks, not for me."

"So you think that's just how Zeke is? Like, it's not the pressure? What if he still feels—"

"Does it matter? He said what he said. I'll never be able to look at this guy I was *so* in love with and not see him pleading with your parents to force the two of you together, like we weren't even a thing. Like me and Zeke hadn't *just* had sex. He had me feeling like . . . like I was more than just a stop on the highway of his life, but a destination. An exit with a lot of restaurants and six different gas stations, at the very least. But really, I guess I was just . . ." Cara paused, lost in her metaphor.

"A lowly little state line welcome center?" I said.

Cara doubled over, she laughed so hard. "Thanks, girl. I needed that," she said, grinning her way through her hurt.

"For whatever it's worth," I said, once the laughter had died down, "I think he liked you, Cara. He had real feelings for you. It wasn't fake."

"Yeah, well, luckily, I'm not like you. I don't believe in the whole grand romance and blah blah blah. If I did, this'd be catastrophic. I'm a simple girl, I just want a boy, a girl, or a person who's sexy, kind, and funny—but most importantly, someone who's good to me. And Zeke ain't that."

"You think you'd ever want to be friends with him?" I asked just as the bell started to ring.

"Doubt it. I won't be all *Waiting to Exhale* on his ass and burn his shit down, either. Far as I'm concerned, Zeke don't exist."

"Fair," I said.

"Most of all, though, I'm glad I still got you, sis," Cara said, and gave me a hug.

I couldn't fault her for wanting to be done. If I were her, I think I would feel the same. It was just hard to accept the fact that our little squad would never be the same again. It was over. *We* were over. And that hurt.

chapter thirty-six
IMOGEN

When we heard about Samson's clean bill of health a few days later, we decided it was time to drop the surprise on Mrs. Ladoja. Manny, Cara, and I made our way over to Zeke's house. Manny had it on authority that Zeke was returning his uniform and picking up his last check at the store, so we had a window where we knew he wouldn't be home.

"Hey, Mrs. L, is it true they took out his butthole?" Manny asked as soon as we were inside. I hadn't even taken my shoes off yet. "Does he still have a crack, or did they, like, seal it up or something?"

"Jesus, Manny," Cara said. "What is wrong with you? How are we even related?"

"What? *She* thought it was funny," Manny said, gesturing toward Vanessa, who was clutching her belly, laughing so hard tears were squeezing out the corners of her eyes.

"We have to be quiet—Samson's napping," Vanessa said, once

the giggle fit subsided. "But no, Manny, they did not take out his butthole. Which is good, too, 'cause otherwise, he'd be full of shit." Vanessa laughed again while I sat shocked that she had cursed in front of us.

"I'm so happy to see you in such a good mood," I said.

"Girl, same. But, more importantly, how are you, Gen?" She took my hand in hers. "I owe you an apology. Samson, too. We're so sorry about everything that's happened. We put so much pressure on you, and we didn't even realize we were doing it. It's so easy to make mistakes. To miss things. We messed up."

I nodded. "It's been tough, but I've got Cara. And Manny, I guess. For whatever that's worth," I said.

"Hey!" Manny whined. We all laughed, even Cara.

"So, Samson's treatment worked?" I asked.

Vanessa nodded. "No more cancer, far as anyone can tell. Finally done with his chemo. Forever, hopefully," she said. "Honestly, I'm exhausted. I'll be able to ease up, a little. I mean, I'm gonna be pulling doubles for a few more months still, but—"

Cara cleared her throat.

"Well, Mrs. L," Manny said. "That's kinda what we wanted to talk to you about. Can I see your iPad?"

Vanessa handed it to him, confused. I watched as he tapped his way to GoFundMe. He pulled up the page we'd created. At the top, there was a picture of Samson and Vanessa with a five-year-old Zeke. It was winter in the photo. The snow was still more white than gray and came up to Samson's and Vanessa's knees. They were holding Zeke, the two of them, Samson by his hands, Vanessa by his legs, and you could tell they were about to launch him into the air. The ground was pocked with large holes left by previous landings. The photo was perfect, taken just at the moment before they let go, when Zeke's glee was at its peak. He had a bit of snow on his nose that almost looked like icing. It was hard to see much else, as his hood was drawn tight, but you could see his brown eyes, bright and joyful, and the warmth of the smiles on Samson's and Vanessa's faces.

As soon as Vanessa saw the page for Samson—and the $100,000 we had raised—she started crying. She looked like she was about to collapse, so I raced to hold her up as she sobbed and heaved in my arms, her body loose and heavy with relief, for what must've been minutes.

"I can't—how did you—"

"It wasn't easy," Manny said.

"I was against it at first," Cara said. "Zeke said he didn't want to do one, and I know Mr. L wouldn't want that either. But we figured, men and their stupid pride. So we made this and kept it a secret."

"You know, this is one of my favorite pictures of us," Vanessa said, looking at the iPad again, quiet, a thought she hadn't realized she'd spoken out loud.

"Yeah, I know. Zeke told me when we were . . . I mean, it was one of the ones in, uh, the present Imogen gave him," Cara said, her face turning red, which everyone but Vanessa noticed.

"*Any*way, we didn't send it around school. Didn't want Zeke to know. We got my mom, Ray, tío y tía, Coach, and the Parkers to pass it around with the people they knew. Adults and whatnot," Cara said. "Ray may be a broke-ass, but he got some rich friends. Between him and Brian's actor friends, it was easy peasy, bada boom bada bing."

"A hundred thousand dollars is easy peasy?" Vanessa asked with a laugh. "Samson needs to see this . . . wait here." She got up and went to their bedroom, returning a few moments later with a very sleepy Samson, still in his pajamas.

"What you wake me up for all early on a Saturday, Nessa?" Samson asked, yawning. I was happy to see the color was returning to his face, the energy to his eyes. "Oh, hey, kids. What's going on?"

Vanessa handed the iPad to Samson. "Look. Look what they did."

He glanced at the screen and his eyes went wide. He looked up at us, all of us smiling wide, and then he started to wobble. Cara and I rushed to his side before he lost his balance and held him up, one of his arms draped across each of our shoulders.

"Girls, Manny, you . . . did Zeke know? Help me to my chair," he murmured, dazed. We guided him over to his armchair and eased him down into it. It wasn't until he was sitting down that I realized he was crying.

"Nah, Zeke didn't know," Manny said. "He thought you wouldn't like it, so we did it all secret-like, because not taking help when it's offered is dumb as hell, Mr. Ladoja, no offense. Especially when everyone likes you. And *especially* when your kid's an up-and-coming athlete and this might derail his career. *All* these woulda-been football players that Ray knows about, they come out the wallet with a vengeance, trying to relive their glory days. Hell, we only stopped at 100K 'cause we figured more than that attracts too much attention."

"We hope you're not mad. But we had to do something," I said. "You guys are family to me." My eyes welled with tears. "Mr. Ladoja, you've been there for me more than my own dad. I mean, you're the one who taught me how to ride a bike. And Mrs. L, you helped me through my first period." I swatted at Manny when he made a face. "I was miserable and terrified and you came through with hot water bottles on deck, all the ibuprofen a girl could ask for, and kept me distracted by telling me *all* the gossip around the hospital."

Vanessa laughed, wiping tears from her face. "Oh, girl, I forgot, musta been a dozen affairs going on all at once that year. What a mess. I just, I can't believe you kids did all this, for us."

Samson didn't say anything. He was still looking at the iPad, still crying, and I couldn't read the expression on his face. He wasn't angry, exactly, but I could tell something was weighing on him.

"So, yeah, we'll go ahead and get it all transferred over," I told Vanessa. "There's some stuff we just need to do and that'll—"

I was interrupted by the sound of the front door opening. I looked up and saw Zeke in the doorway. He looked as he had at school the past couple days—stiff, hood up, head down—and when he saw us, he froze. No one said anything. Vanessa was the one to break the silence.

"Zeke, baby, look! Look what your friends did," she said, and handed Zeke the iPad.

He took one look at the screen and went statue-still. A slow drip of tears worked its way out of his eyes and down onto the tile between his feet. "I can't—I don't even know what to say."

Zeke looked up at Manny. He looked as if he wanted to say thank you but couldn't figure out how to make his lips move or his tongue work. Zeke just held his gaze on Manny, neither boy moving nor reacting, until he shifted to look at Cara, who kept her gaze focused on his parents.

"We're just glad we could help," she said. "We all care a lot about you and Samson. It's the least we could do." She then turned to me and Manny. "I'm gonna go outside and wait for y'all." She walked out of the house, and I watched Zeke's eyes follow her every step.

I wasn't sure if it was the GoFundMe, Cara's cold shoulder, or the fact that for the first time in weeks we'd all been together, but something broke Zeke open, and his silent tears transformed into an all-encompassing wail of grief so loud, I jumped in alarm. Before anyone could react, Zeke ran up the stairs to his bedroom and rushed inside. Even from the first floor, I could hear him crying his throat raw. Every ragged sob I heard come out of Zeke pulled at my heart. I wanted to hug him, even still, even after everything.

Vanessa sighed and looked up toward Zeke's bedroom door, then gave us a sad smile. "Why don't you all go on home? We should go talk to Zeke."

Manny nodded and gave Samson and Vanessa a big hug before following after Cara. I did the same, wrapping my arms around Vanessa real tight.

"Can you just tell Zeke . . . ," I started to say, struggling to finish the sentence. "Tell him I'm still here?"

chapter thirty-seven
ZEKE

"Zeke," my mom called from downstairs. "Everyone's gone. You can come back down now."

I didn't respond. I was sitting on the floor, my back pressed up against my bedroom door, my face in my hands. I couldn't make sense of what I was feeling, because I was feeling too many things. I was angry they'd done the fundraiser behind my back, against my wishes, but I was so incredibly grateful at the same time. It hurt to see all of them together, without me, but it had felt so nice to be in the same room, too. They cared so much about me and my family, despite everything I'd done. I didn't deserve their kindness. I didn't deserve them.

"Hey, kiddo," my dad said in a tight, choked voice. "Get on down here." It wasn't a request.

I sighed, got to my feet, wiped my face with my sleeve, and met them in the living room. My dad was in his chair, looking at the ground between his feet, leaning his head against my mom's side as she rubbed his back.

"What's going on, Zeke?" she asked. "Why'd you run upstairs? Is this about what happened at Imogen's?"

I was struck by just how little I'd told them. They didn't know about Imogen's story. They didn't know about Cara. They didn't know that I hadn't talked to Manny in days.

"No, I . . . Cara and I, we, we started dating. After Imogen's birthday," I said. "But then, uh, the thing at Imogen's happened and, um, by then me and Cara . . . we'd had sex. And now, um, she's not talking to me, and neither is Manny. And Jojo fired me."

"Oh, Zeke," my mom said, shaking her head.

I walked over to my backpack and dug around in it. "And Imogen published this in the school journal," I said, handing each of them a copy of "The Pier" I'd grabbed from Ms. Granson. I bounced my leg as they read the story, waiting for the two of them to finish.

"See?" I said when they looked up from the paper. "It's basically about me, and I didn't realize how much pressure I was putting on her and how bad it made her feel, like it actually *hurt* her, and now they all hate me. They all hate me and they don't wanna talk to me ever again. And I deserve it, 'cause this is all my fault," I said.

My dad banged his fist on the arm of his chair, startling me and my mom.

"If someone's at fault for this whole thing, it's me. It wasn't just your friends who wanted to raise money to help us out. Folks wanted to do this when I was first diagnosed last year, and I said no. Your mom asked, I said no. Pappy asked. Jojo asked. That really old woman in the front office of your school, even she asked. Everyone wanted to know if they could donate or help and I said no, to every one of them, because I was proud. Because I am proud. If I had just taken the help, things'd be better.

"Zeke, son, I'm sorry. I'm in this story too. Me and your mother and Jean and Brian, all of us, the people telling Valerie to get with Noah, asking when and where and how it's gonna happen, over and over.

"And if I'd been out of bed, if I hadn't been dealing with this stupid damn body, I might've seen how wrong I was and helped you off this path, but I didn't. I didn't. I didn't do a damn thing, this whole time. I haven't—" he growled, his breaths coming quick and shallow.

"Dad, hey, relax," I said, and looked him in the eyes. "Just relax. Deep breaths."

I looked at my mom and saw that she was smiling. Beaming, almost.

"What's . . . up, Mom?" I said, peering at her.

"He hasn't ranted and raved in months. Hasn't had the strength to. It feels so good to hear him talk with some oomph behind it again," she said, kissing my dad on the forehead. He smiled at her and continued to take deep breaths. "Now, you said and did some pretty messed-up stuff, to Imogen, to Cara. And we'll get to that. But most of all, Zeke, from the bottom of my heart, I'm sorry. We're sorry. We . . . we let you down," she said.

I shot up straight in my chair. "What?"

"You know, we've both been gone. I've been working, your dad has been sick, and that just left you on your own. More nights than not, you got home and the house was either empty 'cause your father was at the hospital or might as well've been empty 'cause he was so in and out of consciousness," my mom said.

"And even when I was awake, it's not like I was the sharpest around," Pops said. "Cancer brain, and all that. It's been hard, I know it has, not just on us, but you too. Hell, we didn't even realize you'd quit the team. That's how out of the loop we've been."

"We're so sorry that we haven't been there for you," my mom said. "You felt like you had to try to become an adult faster than you needed to for our sakes, and it's not supposed to work like that. That's not what a parent's supposed to do. That's not the kind of burden you should have to carry."

I ran toward my parents and buried myself in their arms, my shoulders heaving as I sobbed so hard it made my chest hurt. We were like that for a while, tangled up in each other, until I was able to calm myself and pull away.

"So . . . now what?" I said.

"Now you have to figure out how to apologize to your friends and really mean it," my mom said, taking my hands in hers. "You have to take responsibility for this, Zeke. You need to understand what you did and why you did it. Not just for the here and now, but for the rest of your life, too."

I looked up at my mom, at the warmth in her eyes and the love in her smile, then at my dad, who had nothing but patience and care for me on his face, and nodded. If my dad could fight off cancer, I could fight for my friends. I thought about the nights that my mom spent crying over bills at the kitchen table. I thought about the days when my dad couldn't move, couldn't think, couldn't speak, worn down from the cancer and the chemo. But they didn't give up. They didn't lose hope. And I couldn't either. I owed my friends that much. I owed them an apology—a real one. And that meant coming clean, clean as my dad's scans, about everything to everyone.

"I'll be better. I swear," I said.

"But lest you forget, don't think just 'cause we're all crying and boo-hooing that you're not still *all* kinds of grounded," Pops laughed.

chapter thirty-eight
ZEKE

It took me a week to gather up the courage to start my apology tour. Manny was the first stop. I took a deep breath, gathering my thoughts, and knocked on the door. I heard the pitter-patter of Almanita's footsteps as she let out a loud screech of excitement.

"Zeke! What's the password!" she cried out.

"Get away from the door, you little dingus," Manny shouted. He peered out through the peephole, then called out, loud enough for me to hear through the door, "What do you want, Zeke?"

"I want to apologize," I said. "Can we talk?"

There was a pause, long enough that I was about to turn around and walk home, and then the door opened.

"You can't come inside," Manny said. "Pops's rules. He's still mad about Cara. You know he did the dance with her for her quince? You hurt his little girl."

"I know." I looked down. "I can go and come again a different day . . . ?"

"Nah," Manny said. "Ma, I'll be back in a bit! Nita, go bother Mamí, okay?"

Almanita gave an excited nod and rocketed deep into the house as Manny stepped outside.

"Walk and talk?" I asked. Manny nodded, and we moved off his stoop and onto the sidewalk. "I miss you, man," I told Manny after a long pause. "I really do. And I know I screwed up, big-time. I should've listened to you from the very beginning. I should *always* listen to you, 'cause you're almost always right."

"Finally, you admit it," Manny said. "Yeah, you should've listened to me. Yeah, you really fucked up. I'm mad as hell about what you did to Cara. I hope she doesn't somehow see us talking, 'cause I think if she even caught us looking the same direction, she'd never let me hear the end of it."

"Has . . . has she said anything about me?" I said.

"Nope. And I don't think she will. You're pretty much dead to her, and I don't blame her."

We walked for a few blocks, not a word between us. I knew what I wanted to say, but I couldn't get it out. It felt like, no matter what, it was going to sound like bullshit, so wildly insufficient next to all the mistakes I'd made and the damage I'd done. But I had to try.

"I've imagined this conversation a hundred times. I've thought about all the ways it could go, replaying it over and over, like I'm watching tape before a game, trying to come up with the right play, the best strategy, the perfect plan. That's what I want in life, Manny, more than anything. To be the best. To win. Until recently, that included winning Imogen. She was the top prize in my mind.

I say that now and it makes me feel a little sick to my stomach. Thinking of her like a prize, I mean, 'cause she wasn't that. She wasn't something to be won and possessed and lifted up over my head after the big game, but that's how I was acting. Not just like she was a prize, but like she was *my* prize and was always gonna be my prize, if that makes sense. I treated her just like state finals: like it was inevitable, in the bag, mine for the taking."

"And now?"

I kicked what I thought was a clump of slush and hurt my foot when I discovered it was a hefty chunk of ice early in its thaw. "And now—damn, that hurt!—now I don't care about winning or losing. I just want my friends back. I just want to stop hurting the people I care about most in the whole world. I'd quit baseball, right here, right now. I'd never play another game again if I knew it'd make up for everything that's happened. I'd do it and never look back. I swear, Manny. And . . ." I reached into my backpack and pulled out Clemente's ball, still in its protective case. "I want you to give this back to Jojo."

"Shit, man, that was a gift. I can't—"

"Manny, just take the damn thing," I said, pushing it into his chest. "I don't deserve it. I dishonor his memory. Tell Jojo—and I know it's not worth much coming from me right now—that I'm really sorry."

Manny looked at the ball, at its yellowed cowhide exterior and the faded autograph, and nodded. "I got you. And if it weren't for that, I'd just straight tell you that all of this ain't shit to me. But I miss my friend. And just because that friend's fucked up big-time— and you have, Zeke, like worse than anybody I know—but, thing is, boys is boys for life. Pops, he said he'd still take a knife for the guys he used to play ball with. Even though they ain't spoke in a *minute*. They grew up together. That's unbreakable, homie.

"But you hurt family, man. You hurt her bad. And coming back from that? It's gonna be a slow road, bro. I'm the easiest one, of course. I just wanna make moves, have a good time, play music. Nobody I know gets down like that except you. You my partner in crime. And we can still kick it and everything. But you're on thin ice, man. And it's gonna take a whole lotta work for you to thicken that up and not fall in, you get me?

"For everyone else, I don't know. I bet you and Gen'll talk it out at some point. And if you start playing again, you and Trevor can probably make it work. But Cara . . . she was soul over sneakers in love with you man. And you crushed her."

I sighed. "Yeah. Cara. The worst part is, man, I liked her. I did. She got all my jokes. She knew what got me to laugh. She made every day feel so easy and effortless, 'cause it was just . . . it just felt good to be around her. When we kissed, shit was electric, man. Made my spine tingle. And I just royally messed it up," I said.

"Sure did," Manny said.

"What if . . . what if she was the one?"

"Maybe she was. You would've been great together, and I really mean that. Power-couple vibes and everything," Manny said.

"Gee, thanks for your support and sympathy."

"For what? Something that didn't happen and won't happen? That's the thing, Zeke. You got all these notions in your head of how life's supposed to go. A path, a soul mate, a marriage, a family, a career. You have this plan in your head for just about everything. I know you, I know how you think, and you're like a train, dude.

You got one direction and one direction only, and no matter what, you're gonna get there," Manny said.

I looked at him and shook my head. "Nah, I don't think so."

"Yo, didn't we start this conversation with you telling me I was always right?"

"*Almost* always."

"Well, I'm *almost* done, so slow your roll and listen," Manny said. He was looking right at me now. "It's like you got this plan. The more you try to hold on to it, the more fucked you are when—not *if* but *when*—the plan changes. Your dad's cancer wasn't part of the plan. Not being with Imogen, that wasn't part of the plan either. No one owes you anything. You can't expect shit, either. All we are is what we do, Zeke. Pops tells me that all the goddamn time, so much that I swear, I say it in my sleep.

"And, most of all, no one else is just a part of your grand plan. I think, sometimes, you're so handsome and athletic and well-liked that you forget that you're not the main character of everyone's story, just your own. You aren't the chocolatey center of the world around which everything and everyone else revolves. You're just Zeke. Imogen has her own world, her own life, her own feelings. Cara, too. I think, somewhere in there, you forgot all that. You got all woe-is-me, and all of a sudden, only Zeke's needs mattered because you felt like you were at the heart of everything."

"Yo, this nigga *smart*," a man said. Manny and I looked over and saw that a man in a tailored black suit that had seen better days was leaning up against a wall nearby, smoking a cigarette. "Little man, what's up with you? You a little *Smart Guy* type? Like Tia and Tamera's little brother? You like that?"

I looked at Manny. He shrugged.

"We don't know what that is," I said.

"Y'all too young to know about them Mowry family, huh," the man said. *"Sister, Sister, something something somethin missed her,"* he sang.

I looked at Manny again. He made the eyes for *let's get outta here* and that's exactly what we did. We decided to loop around to end up back at Manny's house. Cara was less likely to see us that way. We had been walking, making up for lost time and roasting each other like our lives depended on it, when there was a lull in the conversation.

"Do you think she'd ever—" I said.

"Nope," Manny said, without the slightest hesitation. "Absolutely not."

"Yeah, didn't think so."

"But, hey, you and me? We're okay. I'm mad at you, but you still my guy. We won't be kicking it for a minute, but let me know if you wanna get your ass beat in *The Show.* Again," Manny said, laughing.

"Aight, that's how it's gonna be? Then I'll see you on them sticks, bet," I said, laughing with my best friend for the first time in what felt like—and may have been—weeks. "And, uh, thanks, Manny. I, um, love you, dude."

While Manny wasn't a hugger under normal circumstances, this was not "normal circumstances." He stepped forward and wrapped his arms around me. "Love you too, my guy."

chapter thirty-nine
IMOGEN

The abandoned baseball field was beautiful in the early spring. At least, that was what Trevor said as he tried to convince me to wade into the tall grasses.

"You gotta come see these—"

"I most certainly do not. I'm not about to get chronic Lyme disease for the rest of my life from some tick bite, no thank you. I've heard horror stories from all the White ladies who buy my mom's art. They won't stop talking about it."

Trevor started laughing. "I know a fight I can't win when I see one," he said. "How about I just throw a blanket down in the bed, then?"

I nodded. We had been doing that a lot over spring break, driving out in the mornings to watch the clouds, the leaves, the birds, whatever happened to be moving most that day. Sometimes, I read and Trevor just stared up at the sky or napped. Sometimes, we made out. And sometimes, we just talked. That day, I had something I wanted to talk about.

Trevor took a thick blanket out of the back seat, spread it out across the bed, then climbed up into the bed of the truck and lay down on his back, patting the spot next to him. I joined him, snuggling against his body. It was quiet for a long time. I lost myself in thoughts, lulled by the rhythm of his heartbeat, the rise-fall of his chest, and I was startled when he spoke.

"So, uh, I'm not sure if Cara told you, but me and Ray and Cara and Lisette, we're going to Houston for Mother's Day. I'm gonna show them the city but, uh, we're also gonna go to my mom's grave," Trevor said. "Well, me and Ray are. He says he wants closure. Cara said she's gonna try and have herself a spring fling. Anyway, I'd, uh, I'd really like it if you could come. Tickets aren't cheap, but—"

"My dad still feels guilty; he'll cover it. Plus, he likes you," I said.

"And your mom would be cool with it? Missing Mother's Day and all?"

"Yeah, my family doesn't really do holidays. Except for Christmas. So, if you want me there, I'm there."

We were quiet for a while, watching the clouds drift across the sky, until I broke the silence. "So, on the subject of closure . . . I think I'm ready to talk to Zeke."

"Oh yeah? You been thinking about that message he sent you a week ago?"

I nodded. On the same day I heard that he and Manny made amends, I'd gotten an email from Zeke.

Gen,

I've been thinking about the very first time I saw you have a panic attack. We were in my living room. I think we were ten? My parents were out working, so it was just the two of us. I don't remember how it started. I hope it wasn't something I did. Given the way things've been going lately, I can't be sure that it wasn't, but I hope not.

What I *do* remember was watching you grabbing at your chest and your throat as your face turned bright red.

I remember calling our parents and feeling terrified because all four calls went to voicemail.

I remember you squeezing my hand so tight, I thought you were gonna break my fingers, and I didn't even care. If you needed to break every bone in my body to be okay, that was fine by me.

For a second there, I thought you weren't going to make it. I thought I was going to lose my best friend. I didn't know what to do, I didn't know how to help. I got close to calling the police, I was so scared, right up until you started breathing normal again. I don't think I'd ever been so scared in my life. Until now.

I've spent the last month and a half making your life miserable, making one wrong choice after another, and I'm scared again, Gen. I'm scared that I've ruined us. I'm scared that this time, I *will* lose you and I'll have no one to blame but myself. I didn't want to admit that—that this is my fault. I blamed everyone else. You, Trevor, Manny, my parents, your parents. Hell, at one point, I was talking shit about Mr. Randall in my head. *Mr. Randall*, of all people, who's one of the nicest folks for miles around.

'Cause the truth is, this is on me. It's always been on

me. I can point a finger at society's expectations, at gender norms or whatever. I can point a finger at our parents talking about us nonstop. But, at the end of the day, I was the one who wouldn't let it go. I was the one who, instead of *ever* asking you how you felt, built up this complex fantasy in my head about our lives together. I was the one who made sure the other guys at school stayed away from you, like you belonged to me. I mean, Braejon threatened folks on my behalf to make sure they didn't step to you. It seemed right and normal then, but it sounds so crazy now. I didn't realize how much it hurt you—how much *I* hurt you—until I read your story. How many of those panic attacks were partly (or entirely) my fault. How often I made you feel like you were trapped and like you wanted to disappear.

I wanted you to be mine. Writing that sentence now makes me wanna puke a little bit. Mine. Like you're not your own person. Not only did I want you to be mine, I thought I *deserved* you. Like, I put in the time and the effort with you the same way I put in the energy and practice on the mound. I deserved to be starting pitcher, we deserved to make it to finals last year, and I deserved to have you as my girlfriend. Never in a million years would I consciously equate you to some kind of trophy or prize, some reward I earned, but, unconsciously, that's exactly what I did. You were a prize I put on a pedestal, mine for the taking. I turned you into a *thing*. Treated you like an object, not a person, and took away your free agency. I did everything

I could to lock you into a contract you didn't want or ask
for. Then I had the nerve to get pissed off when you were
forced to make it clear—because I wasn't listening—that
it wasn't at all what you wanted. I know it's a baseball
reference but, well, you know me. I treated you—I've *been*
treating you—the way the League treated Curt Flood back
in the seventies. I'm sorry it took me so long to see it.

I'm just so sorry, for everything. For how I hurt you,
for how I hurt our group. I'm not expecting a response. I'm
not expecting anything at all. I just, I dunno, I needed to
tell you this. This isn't me trying to make excuses or justify
my behavior. There's no excuse for what I did, no way to
justify my actions that isn't bullshit. It just . . . it doesn't feel
like it's enough to just say that I'm sorry. I feel like I have to
explain how I felt or what I was thinking to show you that I
understand, in some small way, how I fucked up.

Hope you have a good spring break,

Zeke

"You wanna talk about it?" Trevor asked.

I nodded. I felt emotional, but I knew I wasn't going to cry. I
was done shedding tears over Zeke Ladoja. "I decided that I don't
want to lose him. I don't want him out of my life. Cara told me
she never wants to talk to him again, but I'm not like that. There
was this one Fourth of July—Mr. Ladoja always went hard on the
Fourth—not for America 'cause, yeah right—but for the explosions, the dazzling spectacle of it all, and that made me and Zeke
love it too. We chased each other in the street, sparklers in our

hands, and wrote our names in the air with sizzling light. It's one of my favorite memories. Dancing in the sprinklers, trips to the pool, barbecues, karaoke, long car rides. Running errands around town with his pops, waiting in line at the bank, the dry cleaners. He's a part of my life, a big part, and I'm not ready to lose that."

Trevor wrapped me up in a big hug. I was proud of myself; I wasn't crying.

"Anything you need from me? Anything I can do to help?"

"Just keep holding me like this," I whispered. "And we'll go from there."

chapter forty
ZEKE

With the snow all but melted, Quail Park was practically empty. Its most notable feature was a steep hill that flattened out into a narrow, bumpy field, which made it perfect for sledding and terrible for just about everything else. Calling it a park, most everyone agreed, was a little strong.

I sat on a bench, hands in my pockets, headphones on, waiting for Imogen. I was trying not to look too nervous as I practiced in my head what I was going to say. I had been so relieved when I got her text the day before that she wanted to talk, but I hadn't felt a moment's calm since. I hoped she wanted to be friends still, but I didn't know if that was what she wanted to say. Maybe she was coming to light me up. Maybe she wanted to tell me I was dead to her, like I was to Cara. Maybe—

"Hey, Zeke," Imogen said from behind me. I flinched and whirled around to see her standing there, a nervous look on her face. "Sorry if I scared you."

"Uh, it's okay. Do you wanna . . ." I scooted to one side of the bench. "Or we can walk and talk. Whatever—up to you, just let me know—"

Imogen held up a hand to stop my stammering and sat cross-legged on the other end of the bench so she could face me. I struggled to look at her and kept my eyes focused on the ground.

"So, I hear you're gonna be back on the team soon," Imogen said after a long, quiet minute.

"Uh, yeah. Coach's excited. Has . . . Trevor said anything?" I asked. "I sent him a couple messages."

Imogen shook her head. "I kinda think he's waiting to find out how I feel."

"After this, you mean."

Imogen gave me a small nod.

"Guess I'll just give him space, unless he says something," I said. I took a deep breath as I readied myself to get into the real reason we were there, but Imogen held up a hand and cut me off.

"Me first, okay?"

I nodded.

"When we were little, you were the brother I always wanted. As you know, my mom was one and done, and my dad, he can barely be there for one kid, let alone two. It was lonely, Z. It's part of why I write and a lot of why I love books. The worlds I made and the stories I read kept me company when my mom was locked up in her studio and my dad was away on a shoot.

"And then you came along and, god, I can't tell you how thankful I am that I didn't have to go through those years without you. My parents didn't want me having friends over. The house was too nice for all of that. But your parents *loved* having me over, and treated me like their kid. I've been to the pool more times in a year with your parents than I have with mine in my whole life.

"You always looked out for me. When my dad first started blowing up as an actor and people started making fun of me, you made it a part of the whole anti-bullying campaign. Everyone was on me after he had that kissing scene, folks saying all kinds of things about him and my mom, and you weren't having *any* of it. You stood up for me, the same way you'd been standing up for Dink and all the other kids having a rough time, because that's who you are. You try to protect people. You try to do the right thing. Unlike my parents, who are so caught up in themselves that thinking of other people's a real struggle.

"That's why being with y'all always felt so nice. Like being in a *real* home and a *real* family. I felt so comfortable, accepted, and, most of all, *safe* with you and your parents. I felt accepted, unconditionally, and isn't that what love is?"

She paused, and I could tell she was trying to find her next words.

"But the way people talked about us, cheered us on, pushed us together . . . They all made it so hard to believe that a boy and a girl could just be friends, you know?"

I shrugged and looked away, embarrassed, because I didn't think I'd ever believed that was all we were.

"That's why I had that stupid idea to kiss you. Everyone was telling me that we were perfect for each other, and I don't know, I started to doubt my own judgment. I thought if I kissed you, I'd know for sure, but that wasn't fair to you, and I wish I could take it all back," Imogen said.

"But we can't go back," I mumbled. It took me a second to realize I'd said that out loud. "Sorry. For interrupting," I said, glancing up at Imogen.

"It's okay. I'm done."

We sat there, quiet, me trying to process what Gen had just said, her waiting for my response. "I just don't get why you never said anything," I said at last. "I mean, you knew I liked you, right?"

"I did . . . but I don't know," she said. "I guess I was scared? I didn't want to risk losing my best friend, my favorite person in the world. It's not the easiest thing to say to someone you care about, like, 'Oh, by the way, I don't like you like that.' And honestly, until recently, I wasn't sure how I felt about you. All I knew was that you were the easiest person to be around. At any given moment, if I had to spend time with another person, I wanted it to be you.

"You said something to my parents that day," she said, and I winced at the memory. "You called them out for all the times they talked like we were already a couple. Which made me realize that you've been feeling the same pressure as me. Like, everyone's been telling you, too, that we belong together. But where you didn't mind the pressure, for me, it's felt like moving through a confusing, convoluted maze while everyone shouts at me to take this turn, go down that corridor."

I looked up at Imogen. Her cheeks were flushed, her eyes wet. She was so frustrated, her body wound so tight. I glanced up toward the sky, trying to find my words, and a cold, whistling wind blew through the park's bare-branched trees.

"You know, my parents actually apologized to me for always teasing me about you," I said.

"Really?" Gen asked.

"Yeah. But you're right—I liked that the whole world was rooting for us. And not to say I didn't really like you, but with all that talk about us being perfect for each other, I didn't even consider anybody else." I didn't have to say Cara's name for Gen to understand who I meant.

"I just . . . you know, I've had this dream, ever since you kissed me the first time, where I was standing at an altar in Millennium Park. The Bean was officiating. Manny, Ray, and my dad were my groomsmen. I didn't know your bridesmaids. They weren't from our school or our neighborhood, but they were so happy for you. Your parents were there. Brian was crying, like a faucet. Jean couldn't've been more excited.

"When you appeared in the aisle, the Bean told everyone to rise. It had the same voice as that Allstate guy, deep as all hell. You came down the aisle in this beautiful white dress, but your veil was all beads of gold and, your favorite, seafoam green. Everyone got to their feet as you walked down, even Pappy and Jojo, and you know how hard it is to get either of them to stand when they ain't working.

"We never got through the whole wedding, though. The dream always ended once you were up at the altar. We never said the vows, did the rings, kissed. None of that. I had that dream more times than I can count, Imogen, and it never changed. So, yeah, maybe there was some doubt. But everyone wanted us together. Everyone at school. Everyone around the neighborhood. Your parents, my parents, *everyone*. It was hard not to fall into that, I guess?

"So, yeah, it made things feel simple—destined, almost—but

it wasn't *easy*. I had doubts. I never understood why we never got through the wedding. I never understood why I felt so unsettled every time I woke up from that dream. But then your mom'd ask me what I thought our wedding song'd be. Or my dad'd make faces at me when he knew I was talking to you on the phone. I'm not trying to say it was harder for me, or even *as* hard, but, like, if you were given all the gear to play baseball, if everyone wanted you to play baseball, if baseball was all you knew, why would you ever think to play any other sport?"

After a beat, Imogen burst out laughing.

"What the hell, Imogen? I'm trying to be honest," I said, my cheeks hot.

"Sorry! The baseball metaphor really got me. It works really well, and it's so on brand for you," she said, giggling. "Okay, okay, serious. Like I said, they did the exact same thing to me. No, not even the exact same thing, because no one was telling you to stay in shape because an athlete's wife's gotta look her best. No one—"

"Who said that?"

"Coach."

"The hell? Why didn't you tell me?"

"'Cause he wasn't the only one! Your dad told me, over and over, never to let any girls step to you and to make sure I kept my eye on you too. Your mom was sending me pictures of rings on the regular, claiming she wanted my opinion on how they'd look on her. My parents were just as bad. Guys on the street were even worse. No one was telling you that kind of stuff, I bet, right? You wouldn't believe the things people have said to me over the years about your Louisville Slugger."

"You never—you should've told me," I said. "I would've done something!"

"I know you would have. Maybe I should've. But I didn't want to make a big deal out of it. It would've just made everything worse."

My legs were bouncing. They always did when I was stressed. "Well, I don't know what to say, Gen. I don't know—tell me what I should do." I just wanted everything to go back to how it was. I wanted everything to be okay.

Gen looked up at the sky and then at me. "I just want you to be a normal best friend. Throw me a party without some weird declaration of love. Quit giving me puppy-dog eyes. Move on. I want you back in my life too. But only if you can do that. And if you don't think you can—and I need you to be real honest about that—then you need to tell me right now."

I was quiet for a long while. The wind rustled the bare trees, not yet recovered from the winter. Someone laid on their horn for what felt like forever. Birds chirped away, eager for the spring. All that noise, and I was quiet.

"I wanna say yes, but—if you want me to be completely honest? I don't know," I said, after a minute.

"Let me ask you another way. We're watching *X-Files*. You, Manny, me, and Trevor. Trevor and I are holding hands," Imogen said.

I tried not to react, but despite myself, I felt my nose crinkle, my jaw clench.

"So, when you can imagine it without freaking out, then we can talk. But I'm not going to tiptoe around the fact of my boyfriend to make you feel better. I'm never putting myself—or Trevor—in that position again."

I took a long, deep breath. "Okay. I understand."

"Maybe other people hate you, but I don't. If I hated you, we wouldn't be having this conversation. Have I been on the fence about talking to you because of what you did to me and to Cara? Yeah. Hell yeah. But I don't wanna lose you, and I don't wanna hate you. I just need you to be better. *Do* better. That's it."

I looked Imogen in the eyes and, for the first time, held her gaze. "That's it?"

"You say that like you think it'll be easy. Believe me, it won't. But, yeah, that's it," Gen said. "No grand gestures, no repeat apologies, no special treatment. Just actually be better, okay?"

"Sorry. I know it won't be easy. I just—I didn't think . . ." I shook my head, then gave her a firm nod. "You know what, it doesn't matter. I'll be better, I will. I swear."

two years later

chapter forty-one
ZEKE

My parents pulled out all the stops for our graduation party. Vincent's catered. Pappy's baked up all sorts of pastries. Jojo had their rolling yo-mobile, the Fro-Yo-to-Gogo, parked at the curb, with two machines swirling out cups of cold treats. But Pops invited the whole neighborhood, so on top of what he got from Vincent's, he was out back on the grill doing his thing. Ray was on plating and distribution, slinging burgers and brats and grilled corn left and right. The street out front was blocked off and a dozen kids were running through the sprinklers with abandon. Everyone was enjoying themselves. Everyone except Pappy.

"When I was comin up, you get out of high school, you didn't get nothin for it except a job. What, we supposed to celebrate you doin what you're supposed to do, gettin your schoolin? You kids. So soft," Pappy said.

He was sitting in my dad's favorite armchair. Trevor, Gen, and Manny shared the couch while I sat cross-legged on the floor.

"I mean, you raised the kids that raised us, so doesn't that mean it's your fault?" Manny said.

"Jojo, if I weren't achin all over just sittin here, I'd beat your behind," Pappy said. "Always been such a disrespectful little boy."

A soft quiet settled over us. Trevor said we weren't supposed to correct Pappy in those moments where the dementia took over, so we weren't sure how to respond. Eventually, Manny broke the silence. "Sorry, sir, for my behavior," he said.

"Well, now! An apology from little Jojo Léon, I'll be. By the grace of our Almighty God, boy's found himself some manners!" Pappy said.

"Okay, okay, Granddad," Trevor said. He got up from the couch and took Pappy by the hand. "Let's get you something to drink, okay?"

"Granddad? Where'd you come from? Ray made *you*?"

"He sure did, Granddad," Trevor said, helping Pappy to his feet. "But he didn't know that until two years ago and that's when we met. Remember?"

"Oh yeah. The boy from Texas. That's you?"

"Darn tootin," Trevor said, playing up his accent.

"Oh, *now* I remember," Pappy said, nodding his head as Trevor guided him toward the kitchen.

We were quiet, watching him leave.

"I still can't believe Trev's giving up baseball," I said. "He's *so* good. Like, he's not crazy, right?"

"He's not crazy. He just doesn't want that life," Gen said. "He wants to be a nurse and help people. He was on the phone with your mom for, like, two hours the other day."

"I know. I had to finish making dinner that night. Turned out better that way too, but don't tell her I said so."

Imogen smiled. "Your secret's safe with me. Plus, since he's going to Loyola, he can help out at the donut shop, now that Pappy's not doing great, Deedee's on her way too, and Ray's leg's hurting more and more."

"His third leg workin, though! Can you believe he and Lisette just had a baby?"

"Right?!" Imogen said with a laugh. "Did you hear that Trev and Cara are gonna take care of little Reese so that Ray and Lisette can take a proper honeymoon? It's all so romantic with those two. Both of them losing a partner, in very different circumstances, but still. It's a beautiful story."

"Speaking of," I said. "I saw you published another one, congrats. That's three stories now?"

Imogen smiled and nodded. "They're not, like, huge publications or whatever. But they're something. I'm doing it."

"They've all been great so far," I said.

"Even the first one?" She smirked.

"Ha ha, yes, even the first one. Brown's lucky to have you."

"Thanks. I can't believe you're going to Rice."

I nodded. "Funny, right? That I end up in Trevor's old neck of the woods. He's been going on and on and on about coming down and tearing the city up. Plus—"

"Plus, ya boy's gonna be down there too," Manny jumped in. "The Dastardly Duo, tag team, back again. I'll go to class and shit, but I'm going to be hustling, making beats, getting into the music scene. I'm only trying to do music here on out, and I got interest already."

"And Alma and Jojo are fine with this?" Imogen asked.

"They're not gonna find out, not until I'm balling so out of control they can't fight me on it," Manny said.

"Heyooo!" Cara shouted as she and Rinky-Dink appeared in the doorway. "Sorry we're late! We were at Dink's and his dad kept going on about how great Stanford's gonna be for us."

Trevor and I waved to Dink, while Imogen jumped up from her chair, rushed over, and hugged Cara tight. "No sweat! Girl, we did it, we are *outta* here."

Imogen, Cara, and Dink came over and sat with the rest of us in the living room. Cara gave Manny and Trevor a hug. She nodded to me. Things between me and Cara were still a little awkward. Less so, thankfully, after Cara and Dink got together at the start of junior year. Cara had been eavesdropping on the Dungeons & Dragons campaign Dink ran for Trevor and a few other people. She fell for the game first and Dink second, which was when they both knew they were meant for each other.

"Pops says you beat his ass in chess the other day," I said as I nodded back at Cara.

"Shit, that's an understatement. I swear, he was better when he had the cancer," she said. We both laughed, then Cara turned from me and started talking with Imogen. That was how most of our interactions went, and I was fine with that. Trying to be, anyway.

I took a moment to look around the room to see who else was there. Almanita, the Perez brothers, and Braejon, home from college for the summer, were deep in a very tense *Mario Kart: Double Dash!!* tournament. Almanita was in the lead, but not by much. Yovani was about fifteen seconds from unplugging Axel's controller.

Braejon was quiet, focused, concentrated. Nearby, Brian and Jean were talking to Coach about the arts. He desperately wanted out of the conversation but couldn't find an opening.

It was nice. Comfortable, for the most part. There was a time, not that long ago, when I thought having all of us in the same room was going to be impossible and that we'd never laugh with each other ever again. I was glad to see that I'd been wrong, even if it wasn't perfect. Not everything had to be perfect, and besides, perfect was an illusion. My reality was good—great, even, and that worked for me.

"All right," Cara said, a couple hours later. "We've gotta get outta here. Dink's folks wanna do a fancy dinner or whatever. Gen, we still on for Wednesday?"

"Girl, of course, we gotta work on these college *lewks*." Imogen laughed.

"And I'll see you Sunday for the game, Trev?" Dink asked.

"Bruh, wouldn't miss it. I got fresh dice and everything."

"We're almost at the end. It'd be a perfect time for a certain Bard to make a surprise appearance . . . ," Dink said, and looked at Imogen.

She let out a loud belly laugh. "No, no way, not for me. Gave it a shot, no thanks. I'll stick to reading my books instead. Y'all go ahead and roll your little dice."

"Manny, as usual, fuck off," Cara said, waving goodbye.

"You too, cousin!" he said, quite chipper.

"And Zeke? Congratulations," Cara said.

"I'll cheers to that," Trevor said. "Go us." He raised his cup.

321

"Go us!" we shouted as we toasted each other.

"And go Panthers!" Dink said.

"Hah, you dweeb." Cara laughed and kissed him on the cheek. "Let's go, dork. Bye, y'all!"

I watched Cara and Dink leave. I must've had a look on my face, because a few moments later, Manny slid up next to me.

"Yo! E-Zeke Bake Oven! You good?" Manny was standing there, posturing like he was about to make fun of me, but his eyes were all care and warmth.

"Yeah," I said. And I was, I realized. I felt light, ready to go, unburdened. I shook myself, loosened up my neck and my shoulders. "I'm good, actually. For real." I stood up and gave Manny a hug. "Man, I love you, you know that? You're my best friend. It's official, I'll give you a badge and everything."

"It's about time I get the respect I deserve," Manny said. "Same, bruh, same. And when we make it to Houston?"

"Shit, Ladoja and Léon on those streets? The L&L Boys down South? They won't know what hit 'em."

acknowledgments

To my agent, Jess Regel: you brought all of this together, and I couldn't be more grateful.

To my editor, Christian Trimmer: thank you for your energy, passion, and belief in this book. I'm fortunate to have had your insight and expertise as we worked it into shape. An additional thanks to the rest of the Simon & Schuster and MTV Books teams and to Jenna Stempel-Lobell for the beautiful cover.

Big thanks to Charles Baxter: you changed the way I saw my words and got me back into writing fiction something fierce.

Endless thanks to V. V. Ganeshananthan: I don't know what I would've done if you hadn't come to Minnesota. I can't thank you enough for everything you've done and do.

To the teachers who got me here: Karen Downing, my high school English teacher who first lit the fire; Linda Bolton (rest in peace); Jenny Zhang; Tim Denevi; Ryan Van Meter; and Andre Perry. You convinced me to keep going when I was ready to turn away from writing altogether. To Kiese Laymon and David Mura, who showed me how to write with, not against, fear.

So much love to my MacDowell crew. Y'all are some of the most brilliant artists and wonderful human beings I've ever met. To Kemi Alabi, Brittany K. Allen, Clare Beams, Rachel Breen, Alice Elliott Dark, Chelsea Garunay, Ted Hearne, Janine Kovac, James Leng, Jodie Mack, Suzanne Mathew, Ryan McKenna, Nell Irvin Painter, Cecily Parks, Alison Pebworth, Chana Porter, Lance Richardson, Jeff Sharlet, Julie Tolentino, and the entire MacDowell staff—thank you.

Acknowledgments

To the friends who have held me up: Emily Maloney, my staunch-est supporter; Veronica Kavass, the older sister I always wanted; Nick, who takes great headshots and gives even better advice; Matt and Elisah, I don't know what I'd do without y'all, seriously; Willy and Julia, the best brother and sister-in-law I could've asked for; Matt and Jenna, thank you for your humor, care, and all the D&D; Ben and Sara, no one cheers me up like y'all do; John and Anna, no one makes me laugh as hard as y'all do; Sun Yung Shin, I'll never forget how you were there for me on one of my hardest days; Hiba, you've always had my back, and I've always got yours; Jill, Amrita, Chloe, and Megan K., thank you for all the encouragement when I needed it most; Rita and Peter, our Writopia students are brilliant, so thank you for the opportunity to do that work; and Skyler, Brandon, and Travis, my D&D crew, I'm so, so grateful for y'all, may we never stop rolling dice together.

To my mom, who first taught me to love books and to never leave the house without one, *this* book isn't about you, so you can rest easy. To my siblings, y'all mean everything to me. All my love, truly.

To my son, Cameron. You didn't exist when I started writing this book, and now you do. Absolutely wild.

Most of all, to my love, my partner, my coparent, my wife, and my favorite person in the whole world: Catherine. None of this would be possible without your hard work, your belief in me and my words, your keen eye for typos, or the way you make me feel when I'm with you. There aren't enough words. You are my heart. Thank you for never letting me give up, for making me take back the unkind things I say to myself, for giving me the time and the room to focus on writing. Thank you for wanting to dream my dream with me.

about the author

JORDAN K. CASOMAR is a Black writer from West Des Moines, Iowa. He holds an MFA in Creative Nonfiction from the University of Minnesota. He has been awarded a MacDowell Fellowship, was a runner-up for a *Pinch* Literary Award in Creative Nonfiction, received a Minnesota State Arts Board Artist Initiative grant, and is an alum of the Voices of Our Nations Arts Foundation workshop for BIPOC writers. He lives in Washington, DC, with his wife, their son, and their two cats. He works as a professional Dungeon Master and creative writing instructor for teens. *How to Lose a Best Friend* is his debut novel. Visit JordanKCasomar.com.